ALL ABOUT MIA

www.davidficklingbooks.com

Also by Lisa Williamson:

The Art of Being Normal

ALL ABOUT MIA

LISA WILLIAMSON

David Fickling Books

31 Beaumont Street
Oxford OX1 2NP, UK

All About Mia
is a
DAVID FICKLING BOOK

First published in Great Britain by
David Fickling Books,
31 Beaumont Street,
Oxford, OX1 2NP

www.davidficklingbooks.com

Hardback edition published 2017
This edition published 2018

Text © Lisa Williamson

978-1-910989-11-1

1 3 5 7 9 10 8 6 4 2

Papers used by David Fickling Books are from well-managed
forests and other responsible sources.

DAVID FICKLING BOOKS Reg. No. 8340307

A CIP catalogue record for this book is available from the British Library.

Typeset in Sabon by Falcon Oast Graphic Art Ltd.
Printed and bound in Clays Ltd, Bungay, Suffolk.

For Jake

Everyone in Rushton knows the Campbell-Richardson sisters.

Grace is the oldest and destined for a first from Cambridge. Signature scent: grapefruit shampoo, second-hand books and perfection.

Audrey is the youngest and destined for the Olympics. Signature scent: chlorine, Lucozade Sport and discipline.

Then there's me, Mia. I'm in the middle. I have no idea what my destiny is. Signature scent: coconut oil, Haribo and TROUBLE.

1

'I feel like getting wasted tonight,' I announce.

It's a Friday evening in early June. Me and my three best friends – Stella Fielding, Mikey Twist and Kimmie Chu – are packed into Stella's messy bedroom, the air thick with perfume and hairspray.

Mikey rolls his eyes at the others. 'No offence, Mia,' he says, 'but when do you *not* feel like getting wasted?'

He makes a valid point. My fondness for getting drunk is one of my trademarks.

'Yeah, but tonight I feel like getting *especially* wasted,' I say, sloshing at least three fingers' worth of vodka into a plastic beaker before topping it up with a splash of Diet Coke. I stir it with my straw, watching as the liquid turns the colour of dirty paint water.

'Why? What's the occasion?' Kimmie asks, blowing on her newly painted fingernails.

'Does there have to be one?'

'I suppose not.'

The truth is, I've had a crappy week. The evidence so far:

On Monday, I dropped my iPhone on the patio when I was out on the roof having a late-night cigarette, and now the screen is all cracked and Mum and Dad are refusing to replace it again.

On Wednesday, the English essay I worked really hard on for once came back with a big fat 'D' on it and the words 'a poor effort' scrawled on the top in red pen.

On Thursday, I was hauled into Mr Joshi, the head of sixth form's, office for 'flouting' the sixth-form dress code for the third time this term. Apparently my ripped jeans were 'inappropriate for an academic environment'. I argued back for a bit, telling him that whether you could see my kneecaps or not had no reflection on my ability to discuss the symbolism in *A Streetcar Named Desire*, but he was having none of it, confiscating my hooped earrings while he was at it for good measure.

The real nail in the coffin though, the cherry on top of the big fat cake, happened earlier today. I was in the sixth-form social area scrolling through Instagram when a selfie of my ex-boyfriend Jordan, kissing some blonde girl I've never seen before, popped up on my feed. Straightaway I got that horrible sick feeling in my stomach, the sort that makes your insides slosh about like unset jelly.

I down my drink and pour another.

'Someone's phone,' Stella says, turning down the iPod speakers.

It's mine. I pluck it off the bed and peer at the shattered

screen. 'MUM' flashes back at me. I consider not answering, but I know she'll only go and leave me a really long voice-mail message if I don't.

'I'll be back,' I say, putting down my beaker and heading out onto the landing, shutting Stella's bedroom door behind me.

I swipe my finger across the screen.

'Hey, Mum, what's up?' I ask, dangling my spare arm over the banister.

'Hi, sweetheart, change of plan, I'm going to need you at home tomorrow,' Mum says.

'But I've got plans with Stella.'

'You see Stella every day at school.'

'That's not the same. This is chill time,' I say, my voice venturing dangerously close into whining territory, some-thing I know Mum *hates*.

'Well, I'm sorry, Mia,' she says, 'but you're going to have to *chill* another day.'

'Why? What's going on?'

'Grace is coming home.'

What? But Grace isn't due back for another six weeks. Since last September my older sister has been in Greece volunteering on an archaeological dig. Which I just don't get. I mean, Greece is nice for a holiday and everything, but why would you willingly spend your entire gap year digging for bits of broken pottery when you could be somewhere cool and exotic like Thailand, sunbathing and tubing and going to full-moon parties? But then most of what Grace does bewilders me. Grace and I may have the same blood

3

and DNA and stuff, but that's kind of it; we are chalk and cheese to the extreme.

'When?' I ask, swapping my phone to the other ear, as if that's going to make a difference to the news Mum is delivering.

'Tomorrow,' she answers.

'But how come?'

'She just said that she'd done all she wanted to do, and it felt like time to come home. Between you and me, I think she might be feeling a bit homesick.'

I scrunch up my face. Who suddenly gets homesick after nearly nine whole months away?

'Anyway,' Mum continues, 'they're due to arrive home about one o'clock tomorrow, so I'll pick you up from Stella's in the morning after I've got Audrey from training.'

'Hang on a second, who's "they"?'

'Grace and Sam.'

'Sam? As in Grace's lame-arse boyfriend?'

'Mia . . .' Mum says in a warning voice.

Even though she's yet to meet him face-to-face, Mum won't hear a word said against Grace's new boyfriend. Apparently he and Grace bonded on their dig because he's also going to Cambridge this autumn, to study medicine. Mum almost wet herself when she heard that. I keep hearing her refer to Sam as Grace's 'doctor boyfriend' on the phone. Audrey's chatted to him on Skype and reckons he's really nice, which everyone knows is just the polite code word for 'lame'. If anyone ever called me nice I'd probably chuck myself off the nearest bridge.

4

'Anyway,' Mum says again, 'we should be with you around ten thirty tomorrow.'

'Ten thirty?' I splutter. 'As in ten thirty a.m.?'

'Of course. It's not going to be in the evening, is it?'

'But why so early? You know Saturday is my only chance for a lie-in.'

'I'd hardly call ten thirty early. Besides, we've got a lot to do.'

'Like what?'

'Well, you need to sort Grace's room out for a start. It's a complete tip.'

'It's not my fault she gave us zero notice she was coming back so soon,' I huff.

But Mum ignores this. Just like she ignores anything negative I ever say about Grace. Because Grace is perfect, and I am not.

'And then I need you and Audrey to get started on lunch while I do a cake delivery,' Mum adds.

'Can't Dad do the delivery?' I ask, picking at a loose thread on the pyjama shorts I'd put on to wear while I was getting ready.

'No,' Mum says. 'He's been on nights all week and he *does* need a proper lie-in. When I spoke to him earlier he was so shattered he could hardly string a sentence together.'

'It's not fair,' I say.

Mum tuts. 'Oh, come on, Mia, I'm only asking you to tidy up a bit and maybe chop some salad for lunch, not go down a bloody coal mine.'

'Fine,' I mutter. 'Look, is that all you wanted? I kind of

need to start getting ready. The party starts at seven and I haven't even had a shower yet.'

'Where is this party again?'

'Andrew Stark's house, remember? And before you ask, yes, of course his parents are going to be there.'

The second part is a lie. Obviously. Not that I'm going to let Mum know that.

'Stella's mum is going to pick us up at midnight,' I add.

Another lie. Stella's mum, a flight attendant for Virgin Atlantic, is currently en route to Shanghai, leaving Stella's older brother Stu in charge. Stu doesn't care what we do, providing we don't burn the place down and keep our hands off his beer stash.

'Can I go now?' I ask.

'Fine, fine, I'll leave you to it,' Mum says, sighing.

There's a pause. I know what's coming.

'Now have fun tonight, Mia.'

I wait for the inevitable 'but'. She doesn't let me down.

'But just try not to go too crazy.'

'Mum,' I groan. 'Please don't do this.'

'It needs to be said,' she says, talking over me. 'I don't want a repeat of New Year's Eve.'

'You promised not to keep banging on about that,' I said, closing my eyes, my hand curling round the banister, fingernails digging into the soft wood.

'I'm not "banging on",' Mum says. 'I'm just reminding you of what happens when you get carried away.'

'Look, I've really got to go now, Mum. Stella needs me. I'll see you tomorrow, OK?'

She sighs again. 'OK. Ten thirty a.m. Make sure you're ready, I don't want to be hanging around waiting for you.'

'OK, OK.'

Back in the bedroom, Stella is sitting at her dressing table, frowning at her reflection.

'What's up?' I ask, tossing my phone on the bed.

'Hair dramas,' Mikey says.

'I can't believe I didn't notice how disgusting my split ends were until now,' Stella moans, holding her hair out in front of her as far as it will stretch.

'I could have told you that,' I say.

'I'm serious!' she cries. 'I can barely look at them without wanting to throw up in my mouth.'

'They're not that bad,' Kimmie offers, her eyes round and hopeful. Of the four of us, she's the closest we have to a peacekeeper.

'Yes they are,' Stella snaps. 'I should have gone to the hairdressers, I knew it.'

'Well, you didn't,' I say, flopping onto the bed next to Mikey. 'So quit whining.'

Stella turns round in her chair to face us. 'Trim them for me, Mia? Please?'

'Why me?'

'Because you're good at hair.'

This is true. Sixteen years of taming my own hair – a big fat curly Afro – has forced me to develop some pretty advanced hairdressing skills. Stella and Kimmie are always begging me for 'fishtail plaits', or 'beachy waves', like I'm their on-demand personal hair stylist.

'Fine,' I say. 'Have you got any scissors?'

A prolonged search produces a pair of craft scissors from an ancient pencil case, the inside blackened with ink and pencil shavings. I run the blade against my finger. I secretly long for blood, but they're as blunt as can be.

'These will barely cut through a piece of paper,' I say.

'I don't care,' Stella replies. 'At least try.'

'Well, on your head be it.'

'Literally!' Mikey chimes in, high-fiving Kimmie.

'You guys are so lame,' I mutter, brushing Stella's hair so it falls in a single straight sheet down her back. 'So how much do you want taking off?' I ask, snipping in mid-air.

'Just the very ends,' Stella says. 'I don't want to lose the length. A couple of centimetres at the very most.'

Thanks to the fine texture, the scissors cut through Stella's hair more easily than I'd anticipated.

'Done,' I say, taking a step backwards.

Stella inspects my work. 'Maybe a tiny bit more?' she says. 'The ends are still kind of raggedy-looking.'

'Fine,' I say, rolling my eyes at the others as I resume cutting. I work faster this time, taking big swishy slices out of her hair.

I'm beginning to quite enjoy myself when Stella lets out a scream.

'What the actual fuck, Mia!' she shrieks as she falls to her knees to retrieve the chunk of hair I've just hacked off.

It's five centimetres long at the most but she's wailing like I've just scalped her or something.

'You were the one who bugged me to cut it,' I say, putting the scissors back down on the dressing table. 'I told you I didn't want to do it.'

In the mirror, I can see Mikey and Kimmie gaping at Stella, wearing a mixture of horror and delight on their faces. Meanwhile Stella continues to kneel on the carpet and scream over the piece of hair like it's a dead baby.

Calmly, I sit down on the chair she's just vacated.

'Jeez, relax, Stells. It's only hair.'

But that just makes her scream even more.

I know for a fact I should feel guilty, but the truth is, I don't feel anything at all.

2

You have got to be kidding. I swear I only set my alarm about three minutes ago. How the hell can it be 10 a.m. already?

I open my eyes a crack, praying to see darkness, despite the fact the birds were already singing when the four of us stumbled off the night bus. Instead, I'm greeted with full-on blinding sunshine blasting through Stella's white organza curtains and threatening to burn my poor hungover retinas to dust. I squeeze my eyes shut again and pull the duvet over my head.

The alarm is getting louder. Where the hell is my phone? Beside me, Stella doesn't even stir. She sleeps like a corpse, flat on her back and eerily still, her mouth slack and shimmering with drool. The piece of hair I cut yesterday sticks out from her skull at a right angle. She finally stopped going on about it last night, around the time we located the exotic booze stash at Andrew's party.

Over the other side of the room, Mikey and Kimmie are totally out of it on the inflatable mattress; Mikey is star-fished on his front, the soles of his skinny pink feet poking out from under the duvet, Kimmie nestled at his side, curled up in foetal position.

I hang over the edge of the bed, figuring I must have plugged my phone in to charge when we got in, my hand almost upsetting a plastic washing-up bowl on the floor. I peer in. A couple of centimetres of congealed vomit clings to the bottom. The stench of regurgitated banana tequila hits my nostrils at the exact same time the flashback of sitting on the edge on the bed, head between my knees, whooshes before my eyes. Bile gushes up into my throat and before I know it I'm puking all over again. A curl falls loose from my ponytail and dangles in the vomit. I pluck a tissue from the box on Stella's bedside table and attempt to wipe my hair and chin clean. With the other hand, I locate my phone in the tangle of wires under Stella's bed and manage to turn off the alarm. I expect the silence to make me feel better but it does the opposite, drawing all my attention to the ringing in my ears instead. I flop back on the bed, my head hitting the pillow like a ton of bricks.

This is all Grace's fault. If it wasn't for her stupid welcome-home lunch, I could sleep in until one or two, then spend the rest of the afternoon lying in Stella's massive bed watching Netflix and guzzling full-fat Coke and Domino's pizza, and by 4 p.m. I'd be more or less back to normal. As it is, I'm destined to feel crap until tomorrow morning at the very earliest.

11

It's worth it, though; last night was a right laugh. Once we got bored of Andrew's, I suggested we get the bus into town, sparking a mass exodus from the party. As I headed up the group on our way to the bus stop, I couldn't help but picture that experiment Mr Crowley did in Year 7 science, the one where he held a magnet above a pile of iron filings and they all leaped up in the air to cling on. It's always been like this. When I was younger Mum used to call me the 'Pied Piper' because wherever I went, other kids would follow, no questions asked.

When we got into town, we almost didn't get into the Cuckoo Club because the bouncer didn't believe Kimmie was over eighteen. Poor Kimmie, she's so dinky that when we went to Pizza Express for Mikey's birthday last year, the waitress gave her the kids' menu and a packet of crayons (we nearly *died* laughing). Anyway, I had to flirt like mad to get the bouncer to let us in, fluttering my false eyelashes for all they were worth until he groaned and unclipped the tatty velvet rope.

Once we were inside, loads of boys came up to me. I didn't really fancy any of them, but who cares, especially when they're buying the drinks and telling you how gorgeous you are.

The next thing I know, my alarm is going off again, this time right next to my head. Only it isn't my alarm, it's a call. I must have drifted back off to sleep. I jab at the screen with my index finger.

'Hello?' My voice sounds like gravel.

Stella rolls away from me, yanking the pillow from under my head and pulling it over her face.

'It's me. We're outside,' a female voice crackles down the line.

It's Audrey. I check the time. 10.30 a.m. bang-on.

'Coming,' I say, struggling to sit up, my head still pounding. I can hear Mum tutting away in the background, bitching about how much we have to do before Grace arrives.

Grace, Grace, Grace.

Groaning, I hang up and start the search for my clothes.

'I thought I asked you to get rid of those shorts,' Mum says as I climb in the back seat of the car five minutes later.

Audrey is in the passenger seat directly in front of me, eating a protein bar, a damp semicircle on the back of her T-shirt from her wet hair.

'Why, what's wrong with them?' I ask, even though Mum's issue with my shorts is well established.

'Well, for starters, I can see your bum cheeks,' she says.

'You're supposed to,' I mutter, pulling on my seatbelt and gazing mournfully up at Stella's bedroom window.

The shorts in question are my very favourite pair of denim hot pants. Mum hates them with a passion. But then she hates most of my clothes. Which is totally unfair. It's not my fault I have a naturally hot body and everything I put on looks automatically sexy whether I intend it to or not. In fact, if it's anyone's fault, it's Mum's, considering the fact her DNA is fifty per cent responsible. Sometimes I think she'd be happier if I just went full-on Amish and started wearing a bonnet and woolly tights with dresses down to my ankles.

13

It's going to be a hot day, a proper scorcher according to the weather report on the radio, which of course means the entire country will fall apart temporarily. I can already feel sweat patches forming under my armpits. The sweat smells of booze, I swear. I peel my T-shirt away from my skin and try to waft some non-existent air with the loose material, making a mental note not to let Mum get too close.

Mum and Audrey are talking about Audrey's new training schedule, their voices low and serious. Ever since she won a string of medals at the British Junior Swimming Championships last year, people have been throwing the 'O' word around, like it isn't totally outlandish to imagine Audrey up on the podium one day in the not-so-distant future, a shiny Olympic medal dangling round her neck and the British national anthem blaring out over the tannoy.

I fiddle with the hem of my T-shirt, curling it round my index finger until the skin goes bright white. I let go, watching as the blood rushes back, turning my finger pink again. I can smell Audrey's protein bar. It reminds me of the stuff she feeds her guinea pig, and makes me feel a bit sick. I look down at my legs. They're covered in bruises and inspire another flashback to last night – me and Mikey on Andrew's trampoline, competing to see who could jump the highest. From the state of my black and blue legs it didn't end well. I catch Mum's eye in the rear-view mirror. She frowns. I pretend not to notice, rifling in my bag for my sunglasses. I slip them on and try to ignore the churning in my stomach as Mum and Audrey talk about 'land training' and 'kick boards' and 'county times' and a ton of other swimming stuff that has nothing to do with me.

Not that I'm surprised. I know perfectly well where I come in the family pecking order – right at the very bottom.

3

Ten minutes later, Mum pulls into our weed-infested driveway, parking up next to her treasured motorbike. I open the passenger door of the car before Mum has even turned off the engine, and make a beeline for the kitchen.

After downing a cup of black coffee and sneaking a couple of Nurofen from the stash behind the tea bags, I'm despatched straight to Grace's room with strict instructions to return it to its *former glory*. And fast.

Despite Mum's instructions, I hesitate at the bottom of the stairs. Ordinarily I charge up them without paying much attention to the framed photographs and memorabilia that hang on the wall, but today I take my time, actually looking at them for the first time in ages.

The jumble of photos and certificates and press clippings are in no particular order. I'm convinced Mum and Dad have done this in an attempt to disguise the fact that, unlike my sisters, I'm not award-worthy in any shape or form. As it is, it would probably take a moment or two for the untrained eye to notice that evidence of *my* personal achievements on the Campbell-Richardson 'Wall of Fame' is woefully lacking.

About halfway up the stairs, nestled between the press cutting from last August's *Rushton Recorder* article celebrating Grace's record-breaking A-level results, and a photograph of Audrey diving into the water at a recent swimming competition, her body long, lean and powerful, is a picture of all three of us. It was taken when Grace was still at Queen Mary's, and Mum paid the visiting school photographer extra to take a photo of the three of us together.

It's super-cheesy. Shot from the waist up, it shows the three of us sitting astride an unseen wooden PE bench in age order, our heads turned to face the camera, arms looped around each other's waists. I remember the photographer – a tall skinny guy wearing a shiny waistcoat – repeatedly urging us to 'move in closer', so in the end my boobs were all squished up against Grace's ramrod-straight back and, behind me, Audrey was stuck with a mouthful of hair. But even without the awkward pose, I would have still looked the odd one out.

Grace and Audrey got Dad's height and Mum's slim boyish build and although I'm an above-average 5'5", Grace (5'10") and Audrey (5'8" and still growing) make me feel like a midget in comparison. Figure-wise, I have the sort of curves that get grown men flustered – something that isn't lost on either of my parents and perhaps accounts for their disapproval of ninety per cent of my wardrobe. Although all three of us inherited the same chocolate-brown eyes, while

Grace and Audrey got our Irish mum's smooth, wavy hair, I landed the massive Afro, courtesy of our Jamaican dad. When I was little I used to hate my hair and cry every time Mum combed it, begging her to let me have it relaxed so it would look like Grace's and Audrey's. These days, I love it. It's still a pain to look after sometimes, and I could do without the creepy blokes in bars who sidle up to me and try to guess *where I'm from*, like there's a prize going for the correct answer, and then get all shirty when I tell them I'm from Rushton. But despite all that, the payoff is worth it every time I strut onto the dance floor, or walk down the high street or corridor at school, heads turning like falling dominos as I pass. Because there's no one else in Rushton who looks quite like Mia Campbell-Richardson.

The day Grace left for Greece, I moved out of the bedroom I share with Audrey and took over Grace's. As I look around, I have to admit Mum wasn't exaggerating about the state it's in. Whatever way you try to spin it, it's a complete tip. It's been hard though, putting my stamp on a room that's still full of all of Grace's stuff – the piles of books, the billions of awards and certificates proclaiming just *how* brilliant she is, the stacks of old diaries filled with her perfect handwriting, the framed photographs of her collecting her Duke of Edinburgh award or posing triumphantly with the school netball team. It doesn't help that Grace's room is barely bigger than your average cupboard.

I wonder where Grace's spoddy boyfriend is going to sleep, whether Mum and Dad will make him go downstairs on the sofa or if he'll be allowed to join Grace in her single bed. When Jordan and I were still going out and I asked if he could sleep over one time, Mum and Dad reacted like I'd just requested to take over the house for a mass orgy or something.

I strip the sheets off Grace's bed, bundling everything up and chucking it onto the landing, before sinking down on the carpet for a rest, my head still pounding. I'm unsure where to start. There are clothes and magazines all over the floor, makeup and toiletries littering every other available surface. The other day I knocked over an entire can of Diet Coke and there's a brown stain the size of a dinner plate on the pale blue carpet.

I can't cope with any hardcore cleaning so I start with the cosmetic stuff, peeling my posters off the walls. I crawl onto the bed and reluctantly pull down a topless Zac Efron, revealing the vintage map of Cambridge that Grace has had hanging over her bed since she was about eight years old.

Time for a fag break. I crawl out of the window and onto the kitchen roof. Both Grace's bedroom and mine and Audrey's look out over the back garden. When we moved here nine years ago, the three of us were expressively forbidden from ever coming out here. It's a rule I've broken pretty much every day since.

I peek to check Mum and Dad are safely inside before lighting up, dangling my legs over the edge, climbing ivy tickling my calves.

Before she went away, Grace used to stick her head out of her window and beg me to stop, reeling off facts about lung cancer and blood circulation and premature aging. My response was always the same – just because I like to unwind with the *occasional* cigarette, it does *not* mean I'm addicted.

I take out my phone and, before I can stop myself, bring up the photo of Jordan and his new girlfriend again. The photo is pretty gross. Jordan's practically chewing on the girl's lip, like it's a piece of grisly steak or something, his arm outstretched to capture the moment for prosperity on his phone. Since yesterday I've discovered the girl's name – Hattie Trevellion – and from poring over her Instagram feed, it's quickly become clear she's the polar opposite of me in pretty much every single way – tall, blonde, skinny, no tits, posh. I know she's posh because in one of her posts she's wearing the Toft Park uniform, and everyone knows it costs an arm and a leg to go there. I sometimes see Toft Park girls in Rushton town centre after school, wearing the stupid straw boater hats that even the sixth formers have to wear, and carrying their school books around in Marc Jacobs handbags, their noses in the air. I bet Hattie is a right stuck-up cow; she certainly looks it from her photos.

It takes over an hour to remove all evidence of my occupation from Grace's room, shoving everything into bin bags and transferring them back to my old room where Audrey is lying on the carpet in low plank position, her face red with determination. As I pile the bags onto my bed, she lowers her chest to the floor for a few seconds before transitioning into cobra position.

'I'm glad you're back,' she says.

I pull a face. 'Seriously?'

'Yes. I get lonely without you.'

20

'You need to get out more, Auds.'

Of the three of us, Audrey is the biggest homebody. Even though she's popular at school and swimming club and has plenty of friends, given the choice I reckon Audrey would always choose home over anywhere else.

I go back to Grace's room and do one final sweep. The room looks sort of sad and empty without my fairy lights and postcards, lava lamp and hot-pink duvet cover brightening up the place. I push the bed so it's under the window. It means Grace won't be able to open her wardrobe door all the way, but at least the Coke stain will be hidden from immediate view. I sigh, shut the door, and head downstairs.

In the kitchen, Mum and Dad are snogging up against the fridge.

Ew.

They've always been pretty hot on PDAs, but ever since they set a date for the wedding they're all over each other any moment they get.

People are always surprised when they find out my mum and dad aren't married. They met when they were teenagers, in a dodgy Rushton nightclub called Rumours that no longer exists. Within six months Mum was pregnant with Grace. Dad proposed the day Mum found out (in the loo at Grandma Jules's house apparently), but they've never actually got round to saying 'I do'. Then on Christmas Day last year, with Grace on Skype in Greece, Dad got down on one knee amongst the discarded wrapping paper and re-proposed to

Mum with a brand-new diamond ring to replace her crappy twenty-year-old Argos one.

They're getting married at the end of July with Grace, Audrey and me as bridesmaids. There are only two real downsides to any of this:

1) The wedding preparations are making Mum and Dad super-frisky, and;

2) They're being even tighter than usual, because even though they're apparently on 'a strict budget', Dad is determined to give Mum 'the wedding of her dreams', which is all very cute and everything, but means I haven't had a new pair of going-out shoes in ages and keep having to borrow Stella's like a total pleb (not to the mention the fact she's a full size bigger than me).

'Get a room, guys,' I say, squeezing past my parents to fill up the kettle.

They separate reluctantly, grinning, Dad holding a tea towel over his crotch. Double ew.

I turn away, grabbing a teaspoon from the cutlery drawer and heaping coffee granules into an oversized mug. If I'm going to make it through a full-on family lunch, I *definitely* need more caffeine.

'I thought you were supposed to be in bed,' I say over my shoulder.

'I couldn't sleep,' Dad replies. 'Too excited about having all my girls back under the same roof.'

I roll my eyes. Dad can be a proper sap sometimes.

He gives Mum a kiss on the cheek and scampers out of the kitchen to sort himself out.

'Another coffee?' Mum says, eyeing the jar of Nescafe in my hand. 'All that caffeine isn't good for you, you know, Mia.'

'Well, if I hadn't had to get out of bed at the crack of dawn this morning, I probably wouldn't need it,' I say, adding hot water to my mug and watching the liquid turn inky black as I stir.

'Oh, don't be such a drama queen,' Mum says, fiddling with the temperature on the oven.

I take a slurp of coffee. It burns the back of my tongue.

'Ooh,' she says, turning round. 'I forgot to ask, how'd you do on that English essay?'

'Oh. OK. I got a B.'

I don't even know where my lie comes from. Only that I'm too hungover to deal with Mum's disappointed face today. I'm unprepared for how thrilled she is, smiling and hugging me tightly.

'See, I told you you'd start to see results if you put the effort in.'

I look at my feet. There's a dirty tidemark across my toes from the pair of shoes I wore last night.

Mum lets me go and opens the cutlery drawer. 'Here you go,' she says, thrusting a bunch of knives and forks at me.

I frown. As usual the kitchen table is covered with bits of newspaper, unopened post and change from Dad's pockets.

'Not there, we're going to eat outside,' Mum explains. 'Oh, and remember to set an extra place for Sam.'

'About Sam,' I say. 'How long exactly is he staying for?'

'I don't know,' Mum admits. 'The weekend at least, I imagine, maybe longer. Why?'

'No reason,' I say, sighing and slumping against the fridge.

'Come on, chop chop,' Mum says, clapping her hands together and motioning towards the patio doors. 'The table isn't going to set itself.'

I groan and head outside. The garden is a proper suntrap, the hot paving slabs beneath my bare feet forcing me onto my tiptoes.

'And once you've done that,' Mum calls after me, 'you can go upstairs and change out of those bloody shorts.'

I make my way round the table, chucking the knives and forks down haphazardly. I'm not overly thrilled at the prospect of Sam gate-crashing for the weekend or however long he plans on sticking around for. It means I'm going to have to act all polite and civil. I expect he's a total dullard too, just like Grace's ex, Dougie. Grace's taste in men is boring with a capital 'B'. They're always total suck-ups with neat haircuts and good table manners, the sort of boys who offer you their jacket when it's cold and point out the constellations and *ask* if they can kiss you. Snoooooooooze.

Dad ends up doing the cake delivery for Mum so I manage to sneak upstairs for a quick nap while Audrey helps with lunch. I must be totally out of it when Dad gets back because the next thing I know the doorbell is chiming and Mum's bellowing, 'They're here!' up the stairs.

I peel myself off the mattress, blood rushing to my head as I slowly become vertical. My nap has had the reverse effect it was supposed to, and somehow I feel even worse than I did before I lay down. I go over to the mirror to survey the damage. I look like shit, my eyes bloodshot, a massive lightning-shaped crease down the left-hand side of my face and a brand-new spot the size of Mount Vesuvius slap bang in the middle of my chin.

I know they're probably expecting me to go straight down and join the welcoming committee, to be all fake and huggy and say, 'Oh, Grace, I've missed you soooooo much!' but I can't bring myself to do it. Instead, I creep out onto the landing, ducking into the bathroom quickly and turning on the radio at maximum volume before Mum or Dad have the chance to summon me downstairs.

I take my time in the shower, letting the water pummel against my back and shower cap while I sing along to the radio. By the time I get out, my skin is wrinkly and tender and there are puddles all over the tiles. I chuck a towel down and push it around with my foot, soaking up the excess water, then wrap another round my body and pad over to the mirror. The remnants of last night's smoky-eye makeup are smeared down my cheeks. It's actually kind of a cool look, although I doubt Mum would agree. Reluctantly, I wipe my face clean with a cleansing wipe, quickly turning it a muddy grey before helping myself to a big dollop of Mum's nice moisturizer, smoothing it on all over.

Clean and creamed, I turn off the radio and step out onto the landing. It's eerily quiet. Which is weird. Our house is many things but quiet is rarely one of them, and from the way Mum and Dad have been acting about Grace's premature return, I'd been expecting a carnival atmosphere.

I'm distracted by my stomach rumbling. The last thing I ate was a McDonald's Happy Meal at about 4 p.m. yesterday. I wonder what's for lunch. I bet Mum has made a proper effort. Anything for her darling Grace.

Back in my room, I get changed quickly, pulling on a clean pair of shorts and my favourite T-shirt – grey marl with the words 'It's All About Mia' splashed across the front in hot-pink lettering. I consider attempting to cover up the volcano on my chin before remembering there's no one important here – just my parents, Audrey, Grace and her stupid boyfriend. I abandon my makeup bag and head downstairs. About halfway down, I encounter Audrey huddled on one of the steps, her bony knees drawn up under her chin. Again, weird. Why isn't she in the kitchen with everyone else?

'What's going on?' I ask, peering over the banister and noting the closed door. 'Why are you out here?'

'Mum and Dad are talking to Grace and Sam,' Audrey replies.

'But what about lunch? I'm starvacious.'

'I don't know.'

I pause and listen. I can hear raised voices, though not quite loud enough for me to make out actual words. They don't sound happy, which is even weirder still. Mum and Dad are *always* happy with Grace. It's usually me they reserve their shouting for.

I frown and continue past Audrey down the stairs.

'I don't think we're meant to go in there,' she calls after me.

I throw her a look over my shoulder (so?) and open the door.

Out in the garden, lunch is laid out on the patio table, untouched and attracting flies. Everyone is inside, sitting at the kitchen table. Dad's mouth is set in a straight line, while Mum's eyes are glossy with tears. On the other side of the table with their backs to me are Grace and Sam. They're holding hands.

'Mia,' Dad says, noticing me in the doorway. His voice is flat and he looks like he's aged about five years since I saw him this morning.

In unison, Grace and Sam twist round in their seats. It's strange seeing Grace's face after so many months. She's cut her hair into a bob and her skin is noticeably darker.

'Hey, Mia,' she says.

'Hey,' I reply, shrugging.

She removes Sam's hand from hers and uses the table to push herself up, before turning to face me head-on.

I blink.

OK, I'm seeing things. I *have* to be seeing things.

Because Grace, my perfect sister, has either got a beach ball shoved up her top or is 100 per cent pregnant.

I look over at Mum and Dad. Mum is staring at the ceiling. Dad is staring into the depths of his mug.

Back to Grace. Her hands are resting on her swollen tummy. She does this little nod, as if to say 'yes, it's true', her eyes wide and doe-like.

That's when I start to laugh.

4

I can't believe I'm being thrown out of my own house.

Mum denies this of course. She says I'm being 'melodramatic'. At least Audrey is being shipped off too, to her friend Lara's place, which at least hints at *some* effort to be fair. We're both practically shooed down the path as we're given strict instructions to stay away until further notice.

My laughter probably didn't help our cause. Not that I could have stopped even if I'd wanted to. It was like that time I got the giggles during the two-minute silence for Remembrance Day back in Year 9, only about ten times worse. Anyway, Mum and Dad weren't terribly impressed, which is totally unfair because Grace is the one they should be angry with, not me.

At Stella's, Stu answers the door. He's wearing a ratty dressing gown and holding a massive bowl of Coco Pops and a soup spoon.

'Didn't you just leave?' he asks.

'Change of plan.'

'How's Grace?'

Stu and Grace were in the same year at Queen Mary's. I reckon he has a bit of a thing for her because he's always asking how she is.

'Pregnant,' I say.

Stu's eyes almost pop out of his head. 'What?'

'Exactly.'

I push past him and bound upstairs to Stella's room, throwing open her door. The three of them are sitting on Stella's bed, surrounded by pizza boxes and watching *Orange Is the New Black* on her laptop.

'What are you doing back?' Stella asks, pressing pause and scooting over to make space for me on the mattress. 'I thought you had family shit to do.'

I climb on the bed and start opening the pizza boxes, searching for leftovers. I score on the final box, folding the last slice of Hawaiian in half and taking a massive bite.

'You're never going to guess in a trillion years,' I say once I've swallowed it, licking grease off my fingers.

'In that case, you may as well just hurry up and tell us,' Stella says.

I leave a suitably dramatic pause.

'Grace is pregnant.'

They gasp in satisfying unison.

'But how? Grace has always been so good,' Kimmie cries.

'Not any more,' I singsong, tracing my finger along the seam of Stella's duvet cover.

Because Grace the great and powerful has *finally* messed

up. Not only that, she's messed up in the most spectacular way imaginable.

'Is she keeping it?' Stella asks.

'She must be. She's massive.'

'Who's the father?'

'This bloke she met in Greece.'

'Is he Greek?' Kimmie asks, her eyes wide.

'I don't think so, he's ginger.'

'What's his name again?'

'Sam. He's in our kitchen right this second.'

'What's he look like?' Mikey asks. 'Is he fit?'

I try and fail to get a picture of Sam in my mind. I seem to remember him being tall and having reddish hair but that's about it.

'He's OK,' I say. 'Like I said, gingery.'

'OMG, ginger babies!' Stella shrieks.

'Hang on, Ed Sheeran ginger or Eddie Redmayne ginger?' Mikey demands. 'You need to be way more specific with the hue, Mia.'

'I dunno. I was too busy gaping at Grace's massive pregnant belly to pay all that much attention.'

'Prince Harry ginger?' Kimmie suggests, her eyes shining hopefully (Kimmie is *obsessed* with the royal family).

'Are they gonna get married?' Stella asks.

'God, I don't know.'

'I bet he asks her,' Kimmie pipes up.

'Yeah, shotgun wedding,' Stella chimes in. 'Old school.'

If that happens before the year is out, Grace will be nineteen and married with a baby. An actual baby.

I don't like them one bit. Babies, I mean. I once helped look after my cousin Poppy while Auntie Ali had her hair done. It was only for an hour, but it was enough. Pops screamed literally the entire time, and for the few minutes she wasn't screaming she kept trying to use my fingers as a teething ring, which was beyond disgusting. God, is Grace going to expect me to babysit? I bet she is. And probably for free too.

'How far gone is she, do you reckon?' Stella asks.

'Far,' I say. 'Like out here.'

I hold my hands out about ten centimetres in front of me, cupping them around an imaginary baby bump.

'Wow,' Stella says. 'That's far then. How many months, do you know?'

I shake my head. Just thinking about it creeps me out. I mean, my sister is growing a baby inside her – an actual human being, with fingers and toes and stuff.

'I bet she looks well nice pregnant,' Kimmie says. 'I bet her bump is really cute.'

God, Kimmie is soppy sometimes. I roll my eyes at the others.

'Yeah, not like my mum's,' Mikey says, his voice dripping with disgust. 'When she was preggers with The Accident, she was massive. Even her fingers got fat.'

The Accident is Connor, Mikey's five-year-old brother.

'Are your parents totally flipping out?' he asks.

'God, mine would be,' Stella says.

'Mine too,' Kimmie agrees, nodding solemnly. 'They'd probably lock me up until I was twenty-seven or something.'

31

I picture Mum and Dad's faces when I barged into the kitchen earlier. 'They looked so upset they could hardly speak,' I say.

'Poor Grace,' Kimmie murmurs. 'Your mum and dad can be proper scary when they want to be, especially your mum.'

Mum doesn't lose it often, but when she does it's terrifying. I've never seen her lose it with Grace though.

'They've told me not to come home until they say so, so she must be getting a proper bollocking,' I say.

'Shit, do you think your dad might beat him up?' Kimmie asks, her eyes bulging. 'Her boyfriend, I mean.'

'I don't think so.'

Dad is a big guy but a complete softie. His nickname down at the ambulance station is the 'Gentle Giant'. No, he wouldn't hurt a fly.

Would he?

A vision of Sam pinned up against the kitchen wall, Dad's hands around his throat, pops into my head.

'Hang on a second, are you smiling?' Stella asks.

'No.'

She gasps. 'Oh my God, you totally are! Look, guys, she's smiling!'

'No, I'm not!' I say, desperately trying to stop my lips from curling upwards. It's impossible though, my grin is inevitable.

'You shady bitch!' Mikey says, laughing.

'Oh, give me a break,' I reply, swatting him away. 'It's about time Grace got in some trouble for once.'

Because it is. It so, so is.

5

The following morning, I leave a dozing Stella in bed and walk to work.

The Rushton farmers' market takes place every Sunday morning in the playground of my old primary school. I work on the 'Brilliant Bangers' stall, flogging packs of fancy sausages at four pounds a pop to people who have more money than sense.

When I arrive, my co-worker Jeremy is already there. He's a politics student at the local uni and totally up himself.

'Afternoon, Mia,' he says, wearing this trademark smirk. 'Nice of you to join me.'

'Oh, shove off, Jezza,' I mutter, tying on my apron. 'I'm only a few minutes late.' I turn my back on him and pounce on a middle-aged couple hovering by the stall. 'They're four pounds a pack,' I say. 'A bargain.'

'Oh, we're just browsing,' the woman says, taking a step away.

'No probs. Browse away, absolutely no pressure to buy. It's just probably worth mentioning you're not going to get this kind of quality at such a low price anywhere else.' I turn to the bloke. 'Here's a guessing game for you, sir. How much meat do you think is in our sausages? Say, as a percentage.'

He glances at his wife.

'Tell you what,' I continue. 'If you get it right, I'll give you a pack on the house, any flavour you like.'

Another glance at his wife. She shrugs as if to say 'why not'.

'Er, ninety per cent?' he suggests.

'Commiserations! Close, but not close enough. It's one hundred per cent, sir, one hundred per cent pure meat in all our sausages. I don't blame you for not guessing correctly though, sir, not one bit. You're not alone. Very few sausages can live up to the quality and taste of Brilliant Bangers – brilliant by name and by nature. Now, you may not have won a free pack, but what I can offer instead is an exclusive deal – three packs for a tenner. That's a massive saving of over two pounds.'

Behind me I hear Jeremy snort.

'We don't really eat all that many sausages,' the woman says apologetically.

'Not to worry, just stick them in the freezer. They freeze brilliantly.'

She fingers the clumsily painted pasta necklace hanging round her neck.

'Let me guess. Grandkids?' I ask.

'Yes. Five.'

'They'd love our chipolatas,' I say. 'Seriously, they go down a storm, even with the pickiest of eaters.'

'Really?'

'Yep. Clean plates all round every time. So, what do you say to a couple of packs of those and some classic Cumberland for yourselves? Or perhaps you'd like be a bit more daring and try my personal favourite, the sweet-chilli variety? Anything you fancy.'

By the time I've finished with them, I know the names of all five of their grandchildren and they've bought twelve packs of sausages.

'I can't believe that spiel actually works on people,' Jeremy says as I shut the cashbox and flash him a triumphant smile.

'What spiel? I was just chatting.'

'Whatever. It's like watching an episode of *The Apprentice*. And I *don't* mean that as a compliment. All that exclusive-deal nonsense. It's three packs for a tenner as standard.'

'So? They don't need to know that, do they? It's simple business, Jezza.'

'It's Jeremy,' he growls.

'Do you want a bonus today or not?'

That shuts him up. Our boss, Steve, often slips us an extra twenty if he arrives at the end of our shift to discover we've sold all the stock. If that happens today, I'll be able to pay off Newquay before the end of the month.

At the beginning of August, me, Stella, Mikey and Kimmie are going to Newquay in Cornwall for a week. Apart from school trips it's the first time the four of us have been away together with no parents or anything. Not that it was easy to persuade them. It took a full week of pestering and promises to get my mum and dad to agree to it; and another two for Kimmie's parents to get on board. Stella's mum offered to book the accommodation and flights on her credit card, providing we paid her back in instalments. We're going to be staying in a caravan right near the beach and I can hardly wait. No parents, no school, no overachieving sisters making me look bad – just me and my three best mates and an entire week of sweet, sweet freedom. Best of all, though, I'll turn seventeen while we're there.

It's almost two thirty by the time I get home. I unlock the front door and drop my backpack on the hallway floor. The house is calm and still. I can see through to the kitchen and garden where yesterday's lunch has been cleared away. Voices drift from the living room on my left. I follow them, discovering Mum and Grace sitting on the sofa, their backs to me, looking at something on Mum's laptop.

'Oh, hi, Mia,' Mum says, glancing over her shoulder. 'Did you have fun with Stella?'

I don't answer. I'm too busy staring at Grace's baby bump. She's ditched the hippy-dippy tunic she was wearing yesterday in favour of a stretchy navy and white striped jersey dress. As Kimmie predicted, her bump is *OK* magazine spread-worthy – so perfectly round it looks almost fake.

'How about that one?' Mum says, pointing at the screen. 'The reviews say it's very lightweight.'

Grace clicks to zoom in.

I take a step closer.

They're on the Mamas and Papas website, happily browsing rows and rows of identical-looking pushchairs, all of which cost at least five hundred quid.

What the—???

My brain spinning, I back out of the living room and straight into Sam, my forehead bashing into his chin.

'Shit, sorry,' he says as I stagger backwards, banging into the radiator. 'You OK?'

'Fine,' I murmur, rubbing my head with my palm.

'We didn't meet properly yesterday, did we?' he says.

That's one way of putting it, I suppose.

'I'm Sam.'

'Mia,' I reply reluctantly.

He's posh. Like 'Prince William' posh. No wonder Grace is all over him. She's always had a thing for posh blokes. Dougie was posh too and went to this fancy private school (the brother school to Toft Park) right over the other side of Rushton even though he only lives two streets away from Queen Mary's.

Sam sticks out his hand for me to shake, which only cements his poshness. His handshake is firm and confident; he's clearly had practice.

There's an awkward pause.

'I really like your top,' he says eventually.

'Oh, right. Thanks,' I say, rolling my eyes slightly. I'm still in my 'It's All About Mia' T-shirt from yesterday. It smells of sleep and sausages and the body spray Stella douses herself in.

Another pause, equally awkward.

'So, is it?' he asks.

'Is it what?'

'All about Mia?' he says, gesturing at the words on my chest.

'Oh, right. No. I wish.'

I fold my arms, not enjoying the fact we're having a conversation about what's written across my tits, even though Sam's eye line is at an entirely respectable level.

'It's *supposed* to be ironic,' I add.

'Ironic how?'

'Er, because it's *never* about me.'

He tilts his head to one side. 'It's not?'

'Have you met my sisters?'

He smiles. He has good teeth. I bet he had braces when he was younger. They're those kind of teeth – artificially straight. Up close his hair is more auburn than full-on ginger and his arms and face are covered with a fine sprinkling of light brown freckles that almost look like they've been drawn on individually with an extra-fine felt-tip pen. He's wearing a pair of black-rimmed glasses, the sort that celebrities stick on to make themselves look more intelligent, only in Sam's case I suspect he probably has a prescription. His outfit is standard posh-boy summer uniform – polo shirt, chino shorts and Havaianas.

I hear the toilet flush and a few seconds later Dad emerges from the downstairs loo.

'Hi, sweetheart,' he says, dropping a kiss on the top of my head. 'Good time at Stella's?'

Why is everyone pretending stuff is normal?

Dad turns to Sam. 'Ready to go?'

Go where?

'Yep,' Sam replies. 'Let me just say goodbye to Grace. Excuse me, Mia.'

He smiles and squeezes past me to go into the living room. God, he even *smells* clean-cut (signature scent: fresh laundry, peppermint and privilege).

'Where are you going?' I ask Dad.

'Just down to The Bell to watch the match. Don't worry, we'll be back in time for Soprano's.'

'Soprano's?'

Soprano's is a cheap and cheerful Italian restaurant on the high street. It's where we go for family celebrations – birthdays and anniversaries and exam results.

Before Dad can answer me, Sam returns from the living room. There's a sticky pink lip-balm stain on his left cheek.

Dad unlocks the door. 'Bye, sweetheart,' he says, heading out into the front garden.

'See you later, Mia,' Sam adds, following him.

The door falls shut behind them. I can hear Mum and Grace still murmuring together in the living room. I lean against the radiator. What the hell is going on?

I find Audrey in our bedroom, lying on her yoga mat with her eyes closed. I'm about to ask her what's going on when something fluffy with claws runs over my foot.

I scream and leap onto my bed.

'Shush!' Audrey says, opening her eyes. 'You'll scare her.'

She rolls onto her stomach. 'Beyoncé,' she calls under her bed. 'It's OK, baby, come on out. It's only Mia.'

'I wish you wouldn't bring that animal up here,' I say, climbing down off the bed. 'She stinks the place out.'

'No she doesn't,' Audrey said, wriggling out from under her bed with her guinea pig in her arms. 'She smells lovely, don't you, baby?' She buries her head in Beyoncé's fur and makes a load of kissy noises.

I pull a face and plonk myself in the desk chair, wheeling it with my feet into the centre of the room. 'Never mind Beyoncé,' I say. 'What the flip is going on, Audrey?'

'How do you mean?' Audrey asks as she reaches for a cotton bud from my open makeup bag on our shared desk/dressing table and proceeds to clean the goop from Beyoncé's permanently gluey right eye.

'How do you think I mean?' I ask. 'Everyone's going around acting like Grace being up the duff is no big deal. Do you know what Mum and Grace are doing right now? They're downstairs cooing over pushchairs, Auds. Pushchairs! And Dad just took Sam down the pub and was acting all matey with him. What happened to them being angry?'

'I don't know. They must have just got over it.'

'Got over it? *Got over it?* Audrey, you don't just "get over" the fact your teenage daughter has a big fat bun in the oven. That's not how it works. I mean, Grace has totally ruined her life!'

'What makes you say that?' Audrey asks, looking up from Beyoncé's gammy eye. She looks genuinely interested in my answer.

40

'Duh. Of course she's ruined her life. Babies wreck every-thing, everybody knows that.'

'Having Grace at seventeen didn't ruin Mum's life,' Audrey points out.

'That's different. Mum was at catering college when she got pregnant. Grace is meant to be going to like the most famous university in the world!'

I wonder what's going to happen with that. As far as I know, people don't take babies to uni with them. Which means Grace is going to have to stay here. At least maybe now Mum and Dad will get their fingers out and build that extension. After all, the baby is going to have to go some-where. Oh God, what if they really can't afford it and make me and Audrey swap rooms with Grace and the baby? I wouldn't put it past them. We'll have to sleep in bunk beds if we share Grace's old room, and put all our stuff in stor-age. I shudder and push myself out of the chair into standing position.

'Where are you going?' Audrey asks.

'To get to the bottom of this,' I reply.

I march downstairs. Mum is in the kitchen, making tea.

'Want one?' she asks, waggling the box of tea bags at me.

'No thanks,' I reply, sitting down at one of the breakfast-bar stools.

She takes out two mugs, setting them down on the counter. I reach for the biscuit tin.

'Don't ruin your appetite,' she says. 'We've got an early dinner reservation.'

Her voice is calm and bright. It's like yesterday didn't even happen.

I take a chocolate bourbon from the tin anyway, prising apart the two pieces of biscuit and biting off the chocolate cream with my teeth.

'About dinner,' I say. 'Since when did an unplanned pregnancy become something you celebrate over spaghetti carbonara and a tiramisu?'

Mum sighs. 'Not now, Mia.'

'It's just that if *I* came home one day and announced *I* was pregnant, you'd go mental. You'd probably never let me leave the house again. You certainly wouldn't be booking a table at Soprano's.'

'It would be a totally different situation, Mia. You're sixteen.'

'Nearly seventeen. And is it totally different?' I ask, leaning forward. 'I mean, is it, Mum? Really?'

Mum folds her arms. 'I think we both know the answer to that, don't you?'

'Whatever,' I say, prodding at the fruit in the fruit bowl. The bananas have black speckles all over them and feel mushy to the touch.

'The fact is,' Mum says, 'Grace is a nineteen-year-old woman. And no, perhaps it's not ideal timing, but she and Sam have thought all of this through very carefully, and as loving parents, your dad and I are going to support them one hundred per cent.'

'Of course you are,' I mutter. 'Anything for Amazing Grace.'

Mum pours hot water from the kettle into the assembled mugs. Some of it splashes on her hand, making her swear under her breath.

'What do you want from me, Mia?' she asks, running her hand under the cold-water tap. 'Do you want me to ground Grace? Send her to her room? Take away her pocket money? She's an adult now, remember. And guess what, you're not.'

'Gosh, really?' I say, with a mock-gasp. 'Oh my God, I had no idea. I guess that explains why you treat me like a five-year-old half the time.'

Mum turns off the tap and glares at me. In addition to whining, she also hates sarcasm, *especially* when it's coming out of my mouth. She appears to hesitate for a moment before falling back on her most common refrain (at least it is where I'm concerned):

'Grow up, Mia.'

6

I spend the rest of the afternoon at the bottom of the garden sunbathing in my bikini. For a bit, I chat over the fence to our next-door neighbour, Paul, while he waters his lawn.

As Paul makes small talk about the weather and Mum and Dad's wedding, it's blatantly obvious he's trying really hard not to look at my tits, staring into my eyes so intently it's almost like he's trying to hypnotize me.

'You still OK to babysit next month?' he asks.

'Sure. The fifteenth, right?'

I don't normally like kids, but Duncan is nine and super-easy to look after. He lives with his mum most of the time, staying with Paul every other weekend. The moment I arrive to babysit he locks himself in his room with his Xbox and stays there all night. Plus, Paul has a really good Sky TV package (unlike at home where we're total peasants and only have Freeview) and always lets me help myself to anything I want from the fridge.

Eventually Paul's landline starts ringing and he has to go inside to answer it. He looks a bit gutted to have to cut our conversation short and I can't help but smile as he slopes back towards the house, stealing an extra look at me over his shoulder before disappearing inside.

I'm getting comfortable on my towel when I notice Grace heading across the grass towards me.

Great.

I pick up my phone and pretend to be engrossed in a message.

'Hey,' Grace says, coming to a stop at my feet. There's a sheen of sweat on her forehead.

'Hey,' I reply flatly, keeping my eyes on the screen.

'How are you?'

'Fine.'

'What were you and Paul chatting about?'

'None of your business.'

'I see . . . How are things going with Jordan?'

'We broke up.'

'Oh. I'm sorry.'

'Don't be. He's a prick. Anyway, it was me that broke up with him. Look, did you want anything in particular? It's just that you're kind of blocking my sun.'

She takes a side step to the right. 'I was just wondering if you fancied a drive out to Waterside,' she says.

'What for?'

'We're going to have a look at some baby stuff. You know, pushchairs and things. You don't have to stay with us though, I mean, if you don't want to. You can go off and do your own thing if you like and meet us later. Audrey's coming.'

Part of me is tempted. I love going shopping at Waterside. But I know if I accept the invitation, Grace will interpret it as me being excited about this baby, which I am most definitely not.

'No, thanks,' I say. 'I'm not in the mood.'

Her face falls and I'm pleased.

Another pause.

Grace swats at a fly. 'Mia, have I done something to upset you?'

I sit up and push my sunglasses up onto my head. 'Yes. You've come up smelling of roses yet again.'

'What are you talking about?'

'Like you don't know.'

'I don't!'

'In that case I'll spell it out. If I got pregnant, Mum and Dad would go ballistic and probably lock me up until the kid turns eighteen. You get pregnant and they're practically leading a round of applause.'

'No, they're not. You're totally exaggerating.'

'Barely.'

'I don't know what you expect me to do, Mia. Force them to be madder with me?'

'You could at least acknowledge the fact you've totally gotten away with this.'

'Look, you weren't there yesterday. You have no idea how hard it was to convince Mum and Dad we're capable of having this baby.'

'It doesn't matter, Grace. All I know is that twenty-four hours later, they're fine and dandy with it.'

She has the nerve to look confused. God, it's irritating.

'I just don't get why it makes any difference to you,' she says.

'Because! It's not fair!'

'Oh, don't be such a child, Mia. Why can't you just be happy for me? For us?'

I roll my eyes.

'All this added stress isn't good for the baby,' Grace adds.

I laugh. 'Seriously? You're using your unborn child to try and make me feel guilty now?'

'I just don't want to spend my pregnancy arguing about something I have no control over. If you have a problem with Mum and Dad's reaction, take it up with them, not me.'

'Fine. Forget I said anything.' I flop back on my towel and pick up my phone.

'You know,' Grace says, tilting her head to one side. 'I stupidly assumed you might have grown up in my absence.'

I ignore her and roll onto my front, inserting my earbuds and whacking up the volume on my phone to maximum. I wait a couple of beats before peeking over my shoulder. Grace is already halfway back to the house, her back as straight as a ruler, her head held high.

A few minutes later I hear the car reversing out of the driveway.

Good.

*

47

I wait a solid ten minutes before heading inside. I find a box of ice lollies jammed at the very back of the freezer. I pick a pineapple-flavour one and peel off the plastic wrapper.

I wander with it through the empty house, opening drawers at random, sifting through the unsorted post on the kitchen table (nothing for me, as per usual), checking my reflection in three different mirrors. My fingers are sticky from the ice lolly. On my way to the bathroom to wash my hands, I stop outside Grace's room. The door is ajar. I hesitate before going inside.

It already smells of Grace again, her natural scent cancelling out mine. Plus something else. Or more accurately, someone else. Sam. His suitcase, a battered gunmetal grey Samsonite, is standing upright in the corner. It dawns on me he might be staying for longer than a weekend. Which is all I need. Our house is crowded enough as it is without an extra body in it.

The bed has been moved back to its original position. The Coke stain on the carpet is paler than it was yesterday but still visible. My eyes fall on Grace's bedside table. Next to a glass of stale tap water is a glossy book entitled *Pregnancy: Your Week-by-Week Guide*. I pick it up and sit down on the bed. The cover is super-cheesy – an airbrushed photograph of a woman gazing lovingly down at her baby bump. I open it up to the page Grace has marked with a train ticket. The chapter heading is 'Twenty-eight Weeks'.

Twenty-eight weeks. Is that how pregnant she is? I count on my fingers to convert the weeks into months. About six and a bit. That means she must have known she was pregnant before Christmas. I think of all those Skype calls home where she must have carefully hidden her belly from view while she talked to Mum and Dad. Liar, liar, pants on fire.

I start to read.

Congratulations, you're two-thirds of the way there!

Yep, six months.

Your baby is about the size of a large aubergine.

A large aubergine? Wtf?

The opposite page is taken up by a really bad drawing of a baby in the womb, its head way out of proportion with the rest of its body, like an alien's. It isn't even vaguely cute.

Your baby has eyelashes and can blink his eyes . . .

So far, so creepy.

. . . and as his eyesight develops, he may even be able to see the light that filters in through your womb.

Really? How does that even work?

Your baby is regularly passing urine into the amniotic fluid.

I have no clue what amniotic fluid is, only that it sounds *disgusting*.

His heartbeat is getting stronger and can be picked up with a standard doctor's stethoscope. If they're lucky, your partner may be able to hear it by pressing their ear against your abdomen!

OK, I guess that's sort of cool.

I turn the page. The next section is all about indigestion and heartburn and water retention. Gross.

I shut the book with a snap. The sun catches the sticky fingerprints I've left all over the cover.

I glance up. A photograph of a smiling Grace at her sixth form Leavers Ball looks down at me. In it she's wearing an emerald-green one-shoulder dress that makes her skin gleam, her hair (then shoulder-length) piled on top of her head in the intricate up-do she begged me to do for her (if there's one thing Grace isn't good at, it's hair – she can barely manage a ponytail). As I slide the book back onto the bedside table, I can feel her watching me from behind the glass, judging my skimpy bikini and sticky fingers.

I stand up straight, so my face is level with hers and we're eyeballing each other, and try to pinpoint exactly where it all went wrong between me and my big sister.

7

'Are you nearly ready?' Audrey asks, hovering in the doorway of our room.

I'm sitting at the desk/dressing table we share, applying a coat of coral-pink lipstick.

'Nearly,' I say, pouting at my reflection in the mirror.

Audrey sits down on her bed, mesmerized as I apply a second layer. I'd forgotten how much she likes watching me doing my makeup.

'Want some?' I ask.

Her face lights up. 'Really?'

'Sure. Why not.'

I join her on the bed, holding her chin steady with one hand as I apply the lipstick to her plump mouth with the other.

'Now rub them together like this,' I say, demonstrating.

She copies me, then stands up and peers cautiously in the mirror. 'Is it OK?' she asks. 'Do I look silly?'

'Of course you don't. That colour looks gorgeous on you.'

'Girls!' Dad hollers up the stairs. 'We're waiting.'

I check my appearance once more and follow Audrey out of the room.

Mum doesn't like my outfit – I can tell by the way she looks me up and down as I clatter down the stairs, her disapproving eyes taking in the chunky heels, skintight jeans, cropped vest top and hint of leopard-print bra. If we weren't already running late she'd send me straight back up to change, I bet.

Grace has swapped the stripy dress she was wearing earlier for a raspberry pink one in the same stretchy jersey material. Next to her, Sam is wearing jeans, a blue shirt, grey blazer and navy Converse trainers. He looks like an off-duty MP trying to be trendy and 'down with the kids' to attract young voters. Either that or a member of the world's most boring boy band.

'About time,' Dad says as I reach the bottom of the stairs. 'We were supposed to be out the door ten minutes ago.'

'Sorry.'

Not sorry.

I'm about to step out the front door when Mum pulls on my arm, forcing me back into the hall.

'Play nice tonight, OK?' she says in a low voice.

'But I'm always nice,' I reply, tossing my hair over my shoulder and fixing her with a sugary sweet smile.

'You know what I mean, Mia,' she says, sighing.

*

There are too many of us to travel together so Mum goes ahead on her motorbike.

In the car, Grace gets the front seat. In the back, Sam volunteers to sit in the middle, apologizing profusely for accidentally touching my thigh while putting on his seatbelt. He's wearing aftershave. It smells clean and expensive.

Even though it's still relatively early, Soprano's is teeming with customers. In all the years we've been coming here, it hasn't changed one bit. It's dark and cosy with exposed brick walls and bunches of dusty plastic grapes hanging from the ceiling, interwoven with twinkling fairy lights. Italian accordion music is piped through massive speakers, the same few songs on loop – 'That's Amore' and 'Volare' and 'Quando, Quando, Quando'.

The owner, Mr Soprano Senior, bats away Dad's apologies for being late and guides us to a round table in the centre of the restaurant. He congratulates Grace and pulls out a chair for her. Rolling my eyes, I sit down between Audrey and Sam.

Oversized leather-bound menus are distributed and drinks orders placed. Mum asks for a bottle of prosecco. When the waiter attempts to pour some for Grace, she puts her hand over the glass like a shield.

'Not for me, thank you,' she says.

'Oh, go on,' Mum says. 'You can have a little one.'

'Yeah, go on,' Sam adds, rubbing the small of Grace's back.

But my sister is resolute. 'I know the guidelines say the

odd glass is OK, but I don't want to take any chances,' she says.

I've only ever seen Grace drunk once and even then it was legal, on her eighteenth birthday. We had a party at the house and she drank too much white wine and puked in the rose bushes. She begged me not to tell Mum and Dad, desperate not to tarnish her perfect record of behaviour, despite the fact everyone knows it's obligatory to get wasted on your eighteenth.

As the waiter makes his way round to me, I angle my glass towards him.

'Just a small one for the two younger girls, please,' Mum says.

'But, Mum,' I moan, 'we've got the whole bottle to get through. It's not like you and Dad can have any more; you're both driving.'

'I suspect that's plenty for now,' Mum says, smiling tightly at the waiter.

I lift up my glass to the candlelight. 'But it's barely a thimble's worth,' I say. 'Two sips at the most. I'd have to be a Borrower to get pissed on this piddly amount.'

'Mia,' Dad says sharply. 'Language.'

'What? Pissed? Seriously? Since when is "pissed" not allowed? You say "piss" and "pissed" all the time!'

A second waiter appears with a notepad and pen. 'Are we ready to order?'

Dad lies and says yes, forcing us all to scour our menus at record speed. I order the pumpkin and sage gnocchi and down my prosecco, leaving a coral-pink lipstick mark on the rim.

'You know what,' Sam says. 'I was going to have the calzone, but what Mia's having sounds really good.' He snaps his menu shut. 'I'll have the gnocchi too, please.' He grins at me.

What a suck-up.

Dad proposes a toast, angling his body towards Grace and Sam who are holding hands over the top of the table.

'I'm not going to lie,' he says. 'Yesterday was one of the hardest days of my life. But it was also one of the proudest. Grace, if anyone can make this work, it's you, my darling.'

Grace's mouth turns down at the corners, the way it always does when she's about to cry. Sam leans in and kisses her on her cheek.

'And not forgetting Sam,' Dad continues. 'Twenty years ago I was in your exact same shoes. My girlfriend –' a quick glance at Mum '– was pregnant and, I have to admit it, I was terrified. But with hard work and communication, Nikki and I have turned something that was unplanned into one of the best things that's ever happened to us. Sam, I know sincerity when I see it, and I believe you when you say you're going to do everything in your power to take care of Grace and my future grandchild. Welcome to the family, son.'

'Thank you, sir,' Sam says, standing up and shaking Dad's hand.

Son? Sir? Give me strength.

'So if you'd all like to raise your glasses . . .' Dad continues.

'Hang on a second,' I interrupt, waggling my empty glass in the air. 'I need something to toast with. It's bad luck otherwise.'

'Mia, don't push your luck,' Mum says through gritted teeth.

'But it is!' I insist. 'I read it on the internet. Tell them, Dad.'

Dad responds by sloshing tap water into my glass. 'There,' he says, 'you can toast with that. Happy now?'

I slump back in my seat. 'Just don't say I didn't warn you if it all goes tits up.'

Everyone acts like they can't hear me.

Dad raises his glass. Reluctantly I copy him, lifting mine a few centimetres off the tablecloth.

'To Grace and Sam,' he says.

'To Grace and Sam,' we echo with varying degrees of enthusiasm.

When the food arrives, Sam makes lots of over-the-top yummy noises, declaring his gnocchi as good as the stuff he had in Rome last summer. He's clearly trying to impress my parents in any way he can. To be fair, he's doing a pretty good job, the two of them almost melting into a puddle as he describes his career plans.

'Any idea yet as to what you'd like to specialize in?' Dad asks.

'I'm not sure,' Sam says. 'Maybe surgery.'

'Grace considered medicine briefly,' Mum says.

'For about five minutes,' Grace says. 'Classics is definitely a lot more me.'

I don't even know what the classics are.

'You're still going then?' I say. 'To Cambridge, I mean.'

'Of course,' Grace replies, blinking as if surprised by my question.

'But who's going to take care of the baby when you're at lectures and stuff?'

'We'll take it in turns.'

'And if there's a clash, my mum will help out,' Sam says.

'Sam's mum lives a few miles outside Cambridge,' Grace adds.

How convenient. Trust Grace to land on her feet and score a boyfriend with a free babysitter on tap.

'She must know then,' I say.

'Who?' Grace asks, her eyes flicking towards Sam.

'Sam's mum. You must have already told her about the baby if she's already agreed to babysit.'

Mum sits up a little straighter. Grace and Sam exchange mildly panicked looks.

Busted.

'Grace?' Mum says. 'Is this true?'

'Well, yes,' Grace says quickly. 'But only because we wanted to have the childcare issue sorted before we came home.'

'My dad doesn't know yet,' Sam adds. 'No else one does.'

Mum is still upset though; I can tell by the way she takes an extra-long sip of her water, her eyes lowered.

'Wait, are you seriously telling me none of your mates know?' I ask, tracing my finger round the top of my empty champagne flute.

'That's right,' Grace says.

'Not even Elise?'

Elise is Grace's best friend.

'Not even Elise,' Grace repeats. 'It was important to us that we told Mum and Dad before anyone else.'

'Well, apart from Sam's mum,' I say, biting the top off a breadstick.

Grace widens her eyes at me as if to say 'shut up'. I smile serenely back.

Sam quickly changes the subject by asking Mum and Dad about the wedding, otherwise known as their favourite topic of conversation. It's a smart trick, Mum and Dad immediately launching into an enthusiastic blow-by-blow account of the latest wedding-related drama. The entire time, Sam sits with his chin propped on his hands, expressing what seems to be a genuine interest in table plans and florists who never email back and the astronomical price of profiteroles.

Bored, I prod Audrey on the arm with my fork. She looks up from her chicken salad (no dressing), blinking as if I've just woken her up from a deep sleep. Poor Audrey, she isn't allowed to eat anything fun. Ever since scary Steph took over as her coach, the fridge door is covered with laminated lists of all the things Audrey can and can't eat.

'All right, Nemo?'

Nemo is my nickname for her. I haven't used it for ages though.

Audrey nods and smiles with her mouth closed, hiding the fixed braces she wears on both sets of teeth. She must have wiped off the lipstick when she popped to the loo earlier, because only a hint of pink remains. At thirteen, her face is still in that awkward phase, teetering on the verge of beauty as her features race to catch up with each other. It's at odds with her powerful upper body; her racer-back vest revealing the tight network of muscles in her shoulders and back, physical evidence of all those hours spent in the pool.

'So, Audrey,' Sam says, as the waiter collects our plates. 'Grace was telling me all about your swimming. It sounds incredible! When are you next competing? I'd love to see you in action.'

God, he's an arse-licker.

Audrey takes a sip of water and tucks a loose strand of hair behind her ear. 'I'm in the British Junior Championships in Newcastle the weekend after next,' she offers.

'There are going to be Olympic scouts there,' Dad adds.

'And because Audrey already swims for her county, she'll get to wear a special green cap,' Mum says, 'which gives her a good chance of getting noticed by the Olympic scouts. Right, Audrey?'

'In theory,' Audrey says.

Audrey is disgustingly modest. If I was her I'd wear my medals all the time, strutting around the place like Mr T.

'Cool!' Sam says. 'Can we come along? Wave a banner?'

I roll my eyes. Is this guy for real? It's almost like Grace paid a visit to the perfect-boyfriend factory, programmed in her specifications, and out popped Sam.

Audrey just pushes a piece of lettuce around her plate with a fork and blushes. I'd forgotten how shy my little sister gets around new people and for a second I wonder if she might have a crush on Sam. No matter how hard I quiz her about the cute boys in her year, she hardly ever reveals anything so it's kind of hard to know.

'Audrey won five silver and two bronze medals last year,' Mum says. 'But she's going for gold this time round, aren't you, sweetheart?'

Audrey gives up on the piece of runaway lettuce and plucks a forbidden breadstick from the basket in the centre of the table, breaking it in half. It crumbles between her fingers.

'Hopefully,' she says, smiling another closed-mouth smile and brushing the breadstick crumbs into a little mound on the tablecloth.

Mum reaches across and squeezes Audrey's shoulder. 'My modest baby,' she says. 'We don't know where she gets it from,' she continues. 'I'm terrified of water, and Jason's an appalling swimmer.'

'Now, hang on a second,' Dad says. 'I may be no Michael Phelps, but I'm not that bad.'

'Oh, really?' Grace says. She turns to Sam. 'On holiday last year, Dad got "rescued" twice because the lifeguard on duty was so convinced he must be drowning.'

Everyone laughs, even me. Dad's doggy paddle is infamous.

'Oi, watch it, you,' Dad says, wagging his finger at Grace. 'Or I might have to take back all those nice things I said about you just now.'

Grace smiles, knowing he'll do no such thing. Even though she's the oldest, Grace is the biggest Daddy's girl of us all.

I can feel something vibrating on the floor near my feet.

'Sam, could you pass me my handbag, please?' Grace asks.

Obediently he dives under the table, emerging a few seconds later with a triumphant smile on his face, like a deep-sea diver who's just found a treasure chest at the bottom of the ocean.

'Thanks, baby,' Grace says, pulling the handbag onto her lap and rooting around for her phone. 'Sorry,' she says, switching off the beeping. 'Folic-acid time. If I don't set an alarm, I forget to take it.'

She makes a proper performance out of opening the box and pushing out the pill from its foil casing.

'What's it for?' Audrey asks.

'It's important for the development of a healthy foetus,' Grace replies importantly.

Oh God. Is this what every mealtime is going to be like from now on? Grace acting like she's the first pregnant woman to ever walk the earth?

'Hey,' she adds. 'If you're *really* lucky you might be able to feel the baby kick tonight.'

Audrey's eyes light up and I have to resist the urge to pinch her.

'Yeah,' Sam says. 'Bean's a bit of a night owl.'

'Bean?' I say. 'You're going to call your baby "Bean"?'

'Of course not,' Grace says, laughing. 'It's just a nickname. We felt bad using "it" all the time.'

'Although Bean Castle has a bit of a ring to it, don't you think?' Sam says.

'Hang on a second,' I say. 'Rewind. Bean *Castle*?'

'Yes,' Sam says.

'Your surname is Castle?'

'Yes.'

I almost choke on my gnocchi. 'Sam Castle?' I splutter.

'Yes.'

'Were your parents taking the piss?'

'Mia, don't be so rude,' Mum says.

'I'm not. I'm asking a question.'

'Yes, a very rude question.'

'It's fine, honestly.' Sam says. 'Mia has a point; it *is* a pretty silly name. To be fair to my parents though, they always called me Samuel, so it wasn't until I got a bit older and went to a nursery where everyone called me Sam, that the penny finally dropped.'

'Well, *I* think it's a very cute name,' Grace says, nuzzling Sam's neck like a needy cat.

'The baby's taking Castle as its surname then?' I ask.

'Yes,' Grace says. 'Why?'

'I'm just surprised, that's all. Aren't you always banging on about being a feminist?'

'I just think Bean Campbell-Richardson-Castle is a bit of a mouthful. It's nothing to do with feminism.'

'If that's the case, why don't you drop Castle and take Campbell-Richardson?' I ask. 'Why automatically take the bloke's name?'

Mum is glaring at me. I get the feeling this isn't quite what she meant by 'playing nice'.

'Sam,' she says, her voice artificially bright. 'Do you have any brothers or sisters? I can't believe we haven't asked yet!'

'Nope. Just me,' Sam says.

This surprises me. I thought posh people usually churned out three or four kids at least. Probably because they can afford to have nannies to do all the icky stuff like change nappies and mop up puke.

'I've always wanted sisters though,' Sam adds, smiling at Audrey and me in turn.

Cue beams from Grace and nausea from me. I mean, how cheesy can you actually get?

The waiter arrives to collect our plates, asking us all if we enjoyed our food. Sam starts harping on again about the gnocchi he had in Rome, before trying to talk to the waiter in Italian. Mum and Dad elbow each other, clearly impressed, while Grace beams at him adoringly. Meanwhile I try to resist the urge to vomit all over the white tablecloth.

Mum leans across and whispers something in Dad's ear.

'I'll be back in a mo,' she says, standing up. 'Don't order dessert without me.'

Sam asks Audrey more questions about her swimming, quizzing her on personal bests and favourite strokes. I zone out, taking my mobile out of my handbag and resting it on my lap. I've got another seventeen 'likes' for my latest Instagram post. It's one of the shots from Friday night – me on Andrew's trampoline, jumping in mid-air. Already six girls have begged me to tell them where my little black dress is from.

Sorry, it's vintage, I type. The last thing I want is half of

63

Queen Mary's rushing out to buy the same dress. Not that they'll be able to wear it quite like me. A dress like that isn't just about having a good body; it's about attitude. Which is why I can make a twenty-quid-in-the-sales ASOS dress look one-of-a-kind.

'Earth to Mia,' Grace is saying.

I glance up. Everyone's looking in my direction, expectant expressions on their faces.

'Sam just asked you a question,' Grace says. She has her arms draped round his neck.

'What?' I asked, slipping my phone back into my handbag.

'I was just curious about you, Mia,' Sam says. 'And about what *your* thing is.' He smiles. His eyes are husky-dog blue, clear and uncomplicated.

'My thing?' I repeat slowly.

'Yeah, your thing.'

I hesitate. The rest of the table is looking at me like they're genuinely curious to hear my response.

'I don't have a thing,' I say eventually.

'Oh, come on, you must,' Sam says. 'Everyone does.'

'Well, *I* don't,' I reply.

There's an awkward pause.

'What about your drawing?' Grace suggests.

Sam's face lights up. 'You're an artist, Mia?'

'No,' I say, making a face. 'Not even remotely.'

'What are you talking about? You used to draw all the time,' Grace says. She turns to Sam. 'She used to draw these amazing comic strips.'

'Exactly. *Used* to. I haven't picked up a pencil crayon since I was about nine.'

'Well, maybe you should get back into it.' Again to Sam, 'She's really good.'

'No, I'm not,' I snap. 'I didn't even do Art for GCSE.'

My sister sighs. 'I wish you wouldn't do yourself down, Mia.'

'How can I do myself down over something I don't even do any more? Look, just drop it, Grace.'

She shrinks back in her seat, blinking her big old Bambi eyes.

'Now steady on, Mia,' Dad says. 'Your sister's only trying to be nice.'

'Well, I wish she wouldn't bother,' I mutter.

I grab for the bottle of prosecco, but Dad whips it out of reach.

'Wow!' Audrey gasps, distracting us all.

She's looking over my shoulder. I turn around. Mr Soprano is making his way towards the table holding a ricotta cheesecake (Grace's favourite) with a lit sparkler stuck in the top, Mum scampering along beside him looking *very* pleased with herself.

Mr Soprano slides the cake in front of Grace. '*Congratulations Grace and Sam*' is piped round the edge of the plate in blood-red coulis. I half expect the waiting staff to gather round the table with tambourines the way they do when it's a customer's birthday.

'Oh my God, Mum!' Grace cries. 'This is amazing! Thank you!'

Once she's ascertained that the cheesecake is baked, and the cheese pasteurised and therefore safe to eat, she beams away as Dad snaps pictures of her and Sam slicing into it together like it's their wedding cake or something. People at the surrounding tables smile and applaud.

And I am invisible once more.

8

I'm woken up by Audrey's 5.15 a.m. alarm call.

'Sorry,' she whispers, switching it off and climbing out of bed.

In the dim light I watch as she scoops up her kit bag and slips out of the room, closing the door softly behind her. The floorboards creak as she crosses the landing and ducks into the bathroom, where she'll change into her swimming costume, dinosaur onesie over the top, before heading downstairs to eat a bowl of porridge while Mum whizzes her up a rank-looking smoothie in the blender to drink in the car on the way to the pool. By 6 a.m. she's in the water. She does this four mornings per week, plus sessions after school and at the weekends. On Wednesdays she rests. Providing she doesn't have a competition or meet, she used to rest on Saturdays too, but over the past few months Steph has been calling her in for extra one-to-one work in the run-up to the British Junior Championships.

I don't know how she does it. If I had to get up at 5.15 a.m., I'd be a permanent zombie. Not to mention how bloody boring it must be spending all that time with your head under water, the same thoughts swirling round your brain. I'd go mad, I swear. Sometimes, though, I wonder how it must feel to love something that much. Mum keeps saying I'll get my 'calling' one day, but I'm not so sure. If I had a calling, wouldn't I know what it was by now?

Unable to get back to sleep, I roll onto my back. I'm aware of Grace and Sam on the other side of the wall, sleeping literally inches away from me. I picture them spooning in Grace's single bed, Sam's body wrapped around hers, his chin nestling on her shoulder, his hands cupping her swollen belly, the two of them smiling in their sleep, not quite believing their luck.

Last night, as Audrey and I got ready for bed, their giggles floated out of Grace's open window and in through ours. It made my annoyance flare up all over again; the fact they were being congratulated for something I'd be punished for. Audrey didn't seem to get why I was so fed up, which irritated me even more.

'Would you rather lots of yelling and fighting?' she asked as she peeled back her duvet and climbed into bed.

'At least it would be appropriate to the situation,' I grumbled.

Audrey just smiled this sad sort of smile and turned out the light. She hates conflict, regardless of who started it in the first place, which is weird because when she's swimming she's *so* insanely fierce. Yep, if Grace and I are

68

two warring nations, then Audrey is most definitely Switzerland.

'I can't believe she got a cake with a sparkler in it,' Stella says later that morning as we walk arm-in-arm to English. 'That is just so effing weird.'

'Thank you!' I cry. 'Finally! Someone who gets it!'

I should have known I could rely on my best friend to back me up on this one.

'What happened to your parents being really mad?' she asks.

'God knows. It's like they've been brainwashed. All I know is, if it was me who'd gone out and got herself pregnant, it would be like Armageddon in our house right now. Instead they're treating Grace like she's made from spun sugar or something.'

'I still can't believe she's having a baby. It's like the Virgin Mary, but in real life.'

'Well, not exactly,' I say. 'Since Grace isn't a virgin.'

Grace lost her virginity to Dougie on her seventeenth birthday, and by all accounts it was romantic and perfect – rose petals on the duvet and Ed Sheeran on the iPod.

'You know what I mean,' Stella says. 'She's just so *not* the sort of person who gets caught out like that. I mean, how did she get pregnant in the first place? Wasn't she on the pill?'

I shake my head. 'The pill makes her insane. She took it for a bit when she was with Dougie and it turned her into a total crazy bitch. No, she reckons the condom broke and she and Sam didn't realize. Dad's already drafted his letter of complaint to Durex.'

Stella snorts.

The classroom is hot and stuffy. When we arrive Mrs Poots is opening all the windows with a long metal pole with a hook on the end. As she stretches, her slip shows beneath the hem of her tweed skirt.

'Ah, Mia,' she says, noticing me as I sit down. 'I saw the most wonderful documentary on Ancient Greece last night and it reminded me to ask if you've heard from Grace recently.'

Mrs Poots is one of Grace's biggest fans. She cried actual tears when Grace opened her envelope on A-level results day last year.

'She's already home actually,' I say.

Mrs Poots's eyes light up. 'Really? How lovely. And how is she? Is she well?'

'Oh, you know,' I say, keeping my voice purposefully casual. 'Six months pregnant.'

'Pregnant?' Mrs Poots repeats uncertainly.

'Yeah,' I say, unloading my folder and books onto the desk. 'You know, up the duff, got a bun in the oven, knocked up, with child . . .'

Mrs Poots gapes at me.

'It's true,' Stella confirms. 'With some guy she met in Greece. Broken condom apparently.'

Biting my lip hard to stop myself from laughing, I poke her in the ribs. She pokes me back.

'And Cambridge?' Mrs Poots says, her voice trembling with fear.

Grace is Queen Mary's first Oxbridge-bound student in over five years.

'Oh, don't worry, she's still going,' I say. 'She's going to take the baby to lectures in a papoose.'

Mrs Poots' cheeks are very red, her eyes drooping with disappointment. She looks devastated. She looks how my parents *should* look.

'I'll tell her you say congratulations, shall I?' I suggest brightly.

'Yes,' Mrs Poots stammers. 'Yes, please do, Mia.'

Next to me Stella shakes with silent giggles.

Mrs Poots is distracted throughout the entire lesson, stumbling over a Yeats poem and giving out the wrong homework, and I leave the classroom with the feeling that by lunchtime the entire staffroom will know that Amazing Grace is perhaps not quite so amazing after all.

After school I'm not in the mood to go straight home so I persuade Stella to walk into town with me instead. We try on nail varnishes in Boots, painting each nail a different colour, then sit in Starbucks, trying to make our frappuccinos last as long as possible until all we have left at the bottom are a couple of centimetres of milky water.

As usual we're on the Right Move app, looking at flats for rent.

'Check this one out,' I say, thrusting my phone under Stella's nose. 'It's got a Jacuzzi bath!'

She squints at the screen. 'The second bedroom is tiny though,' she points out.

I don't tell her I've already earmarked that one as hers.

After we finish our A levels next year, Stella and I are going to get jobs and move into a flat together, like Rachel and Monica in *Friends*. We've already registered our details with half the estate agents in Rushton, and folded down the corner of dozens of pages of the Ikea catalogue.

'How about this one then?' I suggest, clicking the next link. 'It's even got a little garden, look. We could have barbecues.'

A sun-drenched picture of Stella and I holding an epic barbecue pops into my head. In it everyone is laughing and drinking and having a good time, marvelling over what brilliant hosts we are.

'Do you even know how to light a barbecue?' Stella asks.

'No,' I admit. 'We can learn though. Or get a load of those disposable ones.'

'Do you reckon we'll really be able to afford somewhere like that?'

'Course we will. We'll have jobs, won't we?'

'I suppose,' Stella says, prising the plastic domed lid off her drink and tipping a couple of ice cubes into her mouth.

My phone vibrates in my hand. It's a text message from Mum asking if I'll be home for dinner. I haven't seen her since she said a sharp 'goodnight' on our return from the restaurant last night. By the time I dragged myself out of bed and down to breakfast this morning, she'd been gone for over two hours, down at the pool with Audrey.

'Stells,' I say, putting my phone away.

'Yeah?' she says.

'What's my thing?'

'Your thing?'

'Yeah.'

'How do you mean?'

'You know. Like Audrey's thing is her swimming, and Grace's is being really clever, and Kimmie's is her jewellery . . .'

Kimmie makes her own jewellery and sells it on Etsy.

'Oh, OK,' Stella says, nodding. 'I get it.'

'So?' I ask. 'What's mine?'

Stella chews on her straw as she thinks. 'You're really good at hair,' she offers eventually.

I slump back on my seat. 'Is that it? Being able to use a pair of GHDs? Wow, thanks.'

'Hey, don't knock it! People are always going to want to have their hair look nice.'

'It's not very impressive though, is it? It's not going to make me famous or anything.'

'I suppose not,' she admits. 'Unless you become one of those celebrity hair stylists with their own shampoo brand, like, I dunno, John Frieda or Trevor Sorbie or something . . . Why are you even bothered anyway?'

'It's just something stupid Sam said last night. He was asking me what my thing was and I didn't know.'

'Well, maybe you don't have one. Maybe some people just don't.'

'Maybe,' I mutter.

There's a pause.

'Do you think *you* have one?' I ask.

'What? A thing?'

'Yeah.'

'Of course I do. I've got my photography, haven't I?'

Stella's hobby is relatively new. The last time she saw her dad he gave her a really fancy camera and she's been learning how to take photos with it via YouTube tutorials. She uses me as her subject sometimes, lying on her belly and barking out instructions like she's David Bailey, stopping every few shots to fiddle with the settings. I didn't realize she was serious about it, though.

'Are you OK?' she asks, tilting her head to one side. 'You look annoyed.'

'No, I don't.'

'Yeah, you do.'

'Only because you're looking at me like that.'

'Fine,' Stella says, rolling her eyes and pulling her phone out of her bag. 'Then I'll stop.'

'Good,' I say, taking mine out too.

9

I get home to discover the entire family sitting on the living-room floor, the family photo albums open on the rug in front of them. It's rare we're all at home at once so I'm a bit overwhelmed by the number of bodies spread across the sofa and armchairs and carpet.

'Oh my God, Mia, I've just found the most hysterical photo of the three of us,' Grace says from where she's sitting on the floor, her legs stretched out in front of her. 'Come look.'

I hesitate before flopping onto the sofa behind her. Grace passes me up the album.

I immediately recognize the photo. It was taken outside Rushton Town Hall. I must have been about five at the time. I'm sitting on the edge of the fountain wearing a Hannah Montana T-shirt and eating a chocolate ice-cream cone. It's smeared round my mouth and dribbling down my chin and wrists. I don't seem to care though, grinning with both sets of teeth, half of which appear to be missing. Next to me, eight-year-old Grace is perched demurely, her ice-cream cone perfectly intact. Whereas I'd always eat mine in about a minute flat, Grace would make hers last for what seemed like hours, taking delicate little licks, never getting any round her mouth or on her chin. Even Audrey, aged eighteen months and sitting in her pushchair to the right of us, is making neater work of her cone than me. It isn't just the ice-cream, though – everything about me looks wild, from my tangled mass of hair, to my battered and bruised legs and scuffed sandals. I didn't know it at the time, but I was the odd one out, even then.

'Oh gosh, Mia, look at your hair,' Mum says, shaking her head. She turns to Sam. 'Mia never was terribly fond of having her hair combed when she was growing up.'

'You look almost feral!' Grace adds, giggling.

I make a face at the back of her head and resist the urge to give her smooth hair a sharp tug.

'Let's have another look,' Sam says, clambering up onto the sofa next to me. 'Aw,' he says, beaming at the three of us in turn. 'You guys were the cutest.'

He slides back onto the floor and kisses Grace on the top of her head. She positively glows. It's vomit-inducing. She turns the page, pausing on a photo of her as a baby. She looks like a doll with her plump pinky lips and saucer-round eyes.

I looked nothing like a doll when I was born. I looked like a baby rat.

'Oh, look at this!' Dad says, turning the page of the album he's holding.

He's pointing at a yellowed newspaper cutting, marking the one and only time my name has appeared in print, compared to Audrey (eleven times), and Grace (a whopping twenty-two).

I was born six weeks premature. Mum was at the supermarket when her waters broke. It must have been a light week for news because the story made page five of the *Rushton Recorder*. A few days later the supermarket sent Mum and Dad a hamper filled with talcum powder and baby wipes and nappy-rash cream. They often wonder what they might have been given had Mum actually given birth right there in the store, in the middle of the fruit and veg aisle, Kevin the trolley boy holding Mum's hand and urging her to 'breathe' and 'push', instead of Dad.

Dad turns the page again to reveal a set of photographs of me in the incubator where I spent the first six weeks of my life, hooked up to various wires and tubes, sticky white pads holding them in place. I'm pale and hairless, my eyes squeezed shut, a too-large knitted hat on my head. In one of the photos, Dad is lifting up Grace so she can see me. One of her chubby hands is splayed against the plastic cover of the incubator, the other reaching in through the hole in order to stroke my impossibly tiny fist. Compared to me, she looks huge – solid and healthy. Mum and Dad just look knackered; all dazed smiles and dark circles under bloodshot eyes.

'Causing us sleepless nights from the very beginning,' Dad jokes, not for the first time.

Mum is flipping through another album. 'Here we are!' she says, holding it up for us all to see.

It's a photo from the day Audrey was born – the five of us crammed on Mum's hospital bed. I'm refusing to look at the camera, pouting into my lap instead because Dad had just told me off for blowing a raspberry at Audrey, showering her big bald baby head with saliva.

'Our little family complete,' Dad says, smiling.

Mum flips back to a photograph of me when I'm about six months old. 'Oh, Mia, what a grumpy chops!' she says, laughing and passing the album to Sam, who is doing a very good impression of actually being interested.

I'm bigger in this photo, and less rat-like, the beginnings of my Afro sitting on the top of my hair like a mound of sooty candy floss. I'm glaring at the camera, my forehead all knots and wrinkles. I had a reputation for being a difficult baby, refusing to sleep through until I was over a year old, and catching every bug and infection going.

I hesitate as Sam peers at the hairy infant staring defiantly back at him. He looks up at me. 'You have almost exactly the same expression on your face in this photo as you do right now,' he says, smiling.

Everyone else turns to follow his gaze. I feel like a zoo animal.

'I'm going upstairs,' I say, standing up abruptly.

I've had enough nostalgia for one day.

'Don't go too far,' Dad replies. 'Dinner's in the oven.'

'What are we having?'

'Salmon en croûte.'

Otherwise known as Grace's favourite.

'OK,' I murmur, slinking away, leaving them to it.

*

I need a fag. Urgently. At dinner Grace and Sam held hands the entire time, forcing Sam to use his left hand to shovel food into his mouth. I kept trying to catch Audrey's eye across the table so I could pull a face and share my horror, but she didn't seem to notice me.

I rifle in my handbag for the lone cigarette I know is in there somewhere. I find it at the very bottom, covered in fluff. It's a bit crooked but will have to do. I push open my window and climb out onto the roof.

Although Grace and Audrey have access to the roof, they obey the rules and rarely venture out here. As a result I've come to think of the view – not that it's anything special, just the back garden and houses beyond – as mine and no one else's.

'Hey,' a male voice says, making me jump.

Sam is sitting outside Grace's window, his arms resting on bent legs, his face illuminated by the soft glow of light behind him.

'Jesus, you bloody scared the life out of me,' I say.

'God, sorry. Are you OK?'

'Yeah. Luckily. I could have fallen off the roof and sued the shit out of you.' I sit down, annoyed I'm not going to be able to smoke my cigarette in peace.

Sam lifts a cigarette to his lips. The tip burns orange.

'You smoke,' I say. 'But you're going to be a doctor.'

'I know, I know,' he says, smoke seeping out of the corner of his mouth. 'Do as I say and not as I do and all that jazz. For what it's worth, I'm giving up. I'm down to two a day now.'

'From how many?'

'Used to be a whole pack, a pack and a half some days.'

'Jesus,' I say, fumbling for the lighter I keep hidden under a plant pot. 'That's loads.' I straighten my cigarette out the best I can and light up.

'I plan to be down to zero by the time Bean arrives,' Sam says.

God, I wish they'd stop calling it that.

The sky in front of me is hazy and starless and the colour of scorched toast. My eyes trace the fuzzy silhouette of next-door-but-one's cat slinking his way across the top of our fence.

There's a pause. I notice Sam's cigarette has burnt down. I offer him the plant pot. He thanks me, tossing his cigarette butt in. For a few seconds I think he's going to go back inside and leave me to it. Instead, though, he angles his body towards me, so his knee is almost touching mine, forcing me to scoot backwards, the edge of the window frame digging into my shoulder.

'Can I ask you a question, Mia?' he says.

'You can ask,' I reply. 'No promises I'll answer, though.'

'Fair enough. It's just about *your* reaction to the baby.'

'What about it?'

'The fact you pissed yourself laughing. I'm curious as to what you found so amusing?'

It's funny; he doesn't seem angry or annoyed about it, more intrigued.

'Are you kidding me?' I say. 'Grace is like the last person on earth you'd expect to get pregnant by accident. How else was I supposed to react?'

Sam cocks his head to one side, like he wants more of an explanation.

'Look, it's just kind of how I roll,' I add. 'Totally inappropriate stuff comes out of my mouth sometimes, end of.'

'That must make life interesting.'

'Ha. Not everyone thinks so.'

'Who's everyone?'

'Who do you think? Mum, Dad. Grace.'

Especially Grace.

'Baby,' a female voice calls from inside. 'Are you coming to bed?'

Speak of the devil.

'A-ha, the lady hath spoken,' Sam says, standing up. He pauses, one foot resting on the windowsill. 'For what's it's worth, Mia, and I know I'm a terrible example seeing as until very recently I smoked like an absolute chimney, but you're far too young and beautiful to partake in such a thoroughly filthy habit.'

I raise an eyebrow. No one has ever called me beautiful before. I've been called hot and sexy and fit and gorgeous, but never, ever beautiful. Not that Sam meant it like that, but still, it's sort of nice.

'I mean it,' he continues. 'Quit now before you get totally addicted like I was, waking up in the middle of the night convinced I couldn't go back to sleep until I'd had a smoke.'

There's another pause. I can hear the muted roar of an aeroplane, thousands of feet above us, a dog barking, a baby crying.

'Night, Mia. It was nice chatting to you.'

I shrug.

He smiles before climbing back through Grace's window, pulling it shut behind him.

I'm in that weird half-sleep when I hear them – Sam's groans mingled with Grace's fluttery gasps, the occasional 'shhhhh!', the rhythmic squeak of Grace's bed on the other side of the wall. But what about the baby? Are you even allowed to have sex when you're pregnant? What about Grace's bump? Surely it's totally in the way? I yank my pillow from under my neck and wrap it round my head like a hat so it covers my ears. I stay like that for at least ten minutes, my eyes squeezed shut. When I finally remove the pillow, the house is silent again but it takes me ages to get to sleep.

10

Last lesson on a Tuesday is Religious Studies. There are only four of us in the class, so instead of sitting in rows Miss Linden gets us to arrange the chairs and tables so we're sitting in a semicircle, facing each other.

'Just look at Jesus's choice of disciples,' Owen Short is droning. 'Men – every last one of them. If that's not evidence of his wish for an all-male succession, then I don't know what is.'

Today's discussion topic is feminist theology and the ordination of women in the Christian Church, and as per usual it's descended into a debate between me and Owen, otherwise known as the most annoying boy on the planet, while our classmates, Heather Barnett (who never says a word), and Nathan Wint (permanently stoned), sit on and watch.

'What about Junia?' I ask, flipping through my notes. 'They reckon she was a full-on apostle.'

'Speculation,' Owen replies. 'They don't even know for sure that she was a woman.'

'Er, exactly how many blokes do you know called Junia?'

'The gender is irrelevant. The fact remains that Jesus favoured male disciples over female ones, and who am I to argue with the Son of God.'

'OK, so number one, the Bible was probably written by some arsehole bloke so no wonder the women got all the crap bits, and number two, what does any of this have to do with the ordination of women *today*?'

Owen's hand flies up in the air. 'Miss Linden, is Mia allowed to say "arsehole"?' he asks.

'She wasn't using it to address anyone in the room so I'm prepared to let it slide on this occasion,' Miss Linden replies.

I bite my lip to stop myself from smiling while Owen sulks.

Miss Linden is kind of the reason I took Religious Studies in the first place. She's one of the only teachers in the school who doesn't treat me like a massive disappointment every time I enter a classroom.

'Keep going, Mia,' she says.

I angle my body towards Owen. 'Look,' I say. 'Even if the bloke who wrote the Bible wasn't an arsehole, the idea that we should be living our lives by a three-thousand-year-old book is mental. Not to mention the fact people just seem to pick and choose the bits they like anyway.'

'Give an example,' Owen says.

'Easy.' I had known Owen would go down this road so I have a copy of the Old Testament ready, the relevant page

Q10. A new television competition

Si crees que tu madre es una gran cocinera con mucho talento, puedes participar en el concurso de la televisión que se llama "Mi madre cocina mejor que tu madre". Durante el concurso tendrás que cocinar con ella y podrá explicarte sus mejores platos. Ponen el programa todos los lunes en TVE.

El presentador es el famoso cocinero, Sergio Fernández, que tiene restaurantes no solamente en España sino también en el extranjero. Durante el concurso tienes que cocinar una especialidad española.

El ganador recibirá un premio de mil euros y la oportunidad de asistir a un curso de cocina en uno de los mejores restaurantes de Madrid. Después de esto, no vas a necesitar experiencia de trabajo para obtener un empleo en el futuro.

Write **T** (True)

      F (False)

      ? (Not mentioned in the text)

Higher

1 Each contestant must cook with his/her mother.

2 The TV programme lasts for an hour.

(1)

3 Sergio Fernández only has restaurants in Spain.

(1)

4 Part of the prize is to do work experience in a restaurant.

(1)
(Total 4 marks)

marked with my finger. 'From Leviticus,' I read. '"And all that have not fins and scales in the seas, and in the rivers, of all that move in the waters, and of any living thing which is in the waters, they shall be an abomination unto you."' I pause, lowering the book. 'The thing is, I could have sworn I saw you eating a prawn mayo sandwich at lunch today, Owen.'

'So what?' he splutters. 'I never said I believed in any of it myself. I think I've made it clear on several occasions that I consider myself an atheist.'

'In that case, you have no right to use the gender of Jesus's disciples to oppose the ordination of women. It's no different from me telling you to lay off the prawn sarnies.'

'I hardly think it's a fair comparison.'

'Well, *I* do. And if you're going to interpret the Bible to further your own sexist agenda, you can't act all wounded when *I* interpret it to make a point. The fact is you have no relevant or up-to-date evidence to back up your argument, and until you do, this debate just isn't even worth having.'

Owen opens his mouth to respond but the bell for home time drowns his words out.

'Hold that thought, Owen,' Miss Linden says. 'We'll pick up where we left off on Thursday.'

Owen scowls and shoves his folder in his bag. He hates not having the last word.

I stay behind to help Miss Linden put the tables and chairs back.

'I like your boots,' I say, as we work. 'Where are they from?'

'Office,' she replies. 'They hurt like hell though.'

'Really?'

'Yeah. They're rubbing on the heel. My fault for convincing myself I could squeeze into a size four.' She pauses to redo her messy bun. 'You know, you came up with some excellent theories today, Mia,' she says. 'You really should consider joining the Feminist Society next term.'

I make a face. On top of at least a dozen other extra-curricular activities, Grace used to be secretary of the Feminist Society. 'Extra-curricular activities are for nerds,' I say.

Miss Linden puts down the chair she was about to stack. 'That's a bit of a sweeping statement, isn't it?'

'Maybe. I just have better things to do with my time.'

'Like what?'

'Just stuff. Personal stuff.'

Miss Linden smiles. 'Look, I'm not trying to give you a hard time here, Mia. I just think the Feminist Society would be lucky to have you.'

I squirm on the spot.

'I'm serious,' she says. 'You're brilliant at expressing yourself, especially when it's something you're really passionate about. I have a feeling you'd be a real asset.'

I shrug and keep stacking.

'Think about it at least. Over the summer holidays.'

'Maybe,' I say, to shut her up more than anything.

'It'll be something for your personal statement,' she adds.

She's talking about the personal statement we have to write for our university applications. The deadline isn't until

January, but the teachers keep banging on about it any chance they get.

I almost open my mouth to tell her about my pact with Stella, about our plans to get jobs and a flat, but at the last second I change my mind. She'll only try to persuade me to reconsider my decision not to apply to university. It's sort of nice though, the idea that she thinks I'm clever enough to get in anywhere, even if she's totally wrong.

In the end, it's Miss Linden who changes the subject.

'I heard about Grace,' she says.

I stiffen at the mention of my sister's name. Miss Linden never taught Grace but (of course) knows who she is.

'That must have been quite a shock, I'm guessing,' she continues.

'You could say that.'

'And how are you feeling about it?'

I hesitate. It's the first time an adult has actually bothered to ask *my* opinion about the whole thing, and I'm kind of thrown.

'I feel . . .'

How *do* I feel? About a hundred different things all at once, none of them good.

'I feel, I don't know, pissed off, I suppose,' I say eventually.

'Pissed off. Why?'

'Because. Grace *finally* mucks up, and instead of getting into trouble, everyone treats her like she's this hero. It's just not fair, you know.'

I recount the events of the weekend, getting more and

more agitated as I build to the description of Grace and Sam's congratulatory cheesecake.

'Please tell me you think that's weird,' I say.

Miss Linden just smiles diplomatically, reminding me that no matter how cool her new boots are, at the end of the day, she's still a teacher.

'The thing you need to remember,' she says, 'is that Grace probably got an absolute roasting from your parents; you just weren't there to see it.'

'Well, it can't have been that bad if less than twenty-four hours later they were ordering bottles of prosecco and welcoming Sam the Spam into the family with open arms.'

'Sam the Spam?' she asks, laughing. 'God, is he really that bad?'

'No,' I admit, sighing. 'He's just a bit of a suck-up, that's all, acting like everything anyone says is totally fascinating.'

'He's probably just nervous. It's intimidating enough meeting your girlfriend's parents face-to-face for the first time, never mind having to explain you've got her pregnant while you're at it.'

'Maybe,' I say.

'Just give him a chance. You never know, you might end up being mates.'

I pull a face. As bloody if.

When I get home from school, the house is quiet and empty, a note on the fridge directing me to a portion of lasagne in the freezer. That's kind of how it is around here; either everyone is home or no one is.

88

I pour myself a glass of orange squash and wander into the living room. Pretty much overnight the mantelpiece has filled up with cards. I pick one up at random. On the front it says 'Congratulations!' in sparkly silver lettering. I open it.

To Grace and Sam, Congratulations on your wonderful baby news! All the best, Sue and Mike xxx

I frown. Who the hell are Sue and Mike?

I put it back and pick up another. It's from Izzy, one of Grace's friends from school.

To Grace,
You're going to be SUCH an incredible mummy. Can't wait to meet baby Bean!
Loads of love, Izzy xoxoxo

The last time the mantelpiece was this full was last summer, when Grace got her A-level results. Half of them arrived before she'd even picked her results up; that's how confident people were that she'd done well. The biggest one of all was from Mum and Dad. It was mocked up to look like the front page of a tabloid newspaper, the headline 'Amazing Grace!' splashed across the top, a photograph of Grace beaming underneath.

The following week, when I collected my GCSE results, I was presented with a normal card, from a normal shop. I was an idiot for expecting anything different.

As I look at the rest of the congratulations cards, all of them full of warm wishes, and praise and hugs and kisses, I can't help but wonder how many there'd be on the mantel-piece if I was the one who was pregnant.

I'm upstairs on my laptop when Mum and Audrey get home from the pool.

I can hear them in the kitchen below, chatting as Mum prepares their dinner. I think about going down to join them but then change my mind. They'll only be talking about swimming stuff. That's all anyone talks about in this house these days – that and the wedding. Oh, and the baby now too.

After about an hour, Audrey comes upstairs. 'What are you doing?' she asks, kicking off her pool sliders and squeez-ing next to me on the bed so I'm pressed right up against the wall. As usual, she smells of chlorine and the cocoa butter she slathers on after her shower at the pool.

'I'm designing T-shirts,' I tell her.

'Who for?'

'Stella, Mikey and Kimmie. For us to wear in Newquay.'

Weirdly, it was the memory of the personalized card Mum and Dad got for Grace last year that sparked the idea. I've based them on my 'It's All About Mia' T-shirt, substi-tuting my name with my friends'. I've spent the last two hours choosing fonts and colours, eventually plumping for red for Stella, turquoise for Mikey and purple for Kimmie, plus a new version for me in my signature hot pink. I'm just putting the finishing touches to Stella's – splashy red glitter letters on a white background. I angle the screen towards Audrey so she can see.

'They're really cool,' she says.

'I'm going to keep it a surprise, then hand them out the night before we leave so we can wear them on the plane.'

I keep having visions of the four of us walking down the airport concourse like a scene out of a film.

'I'm going to miss you while you're gone,' Audrey says, resting her head on my shoulder.

'Don't be such a sap.'

'But I mean it,' she says. 'I sleep better when you're in the room.'

'I thought you said I snore.'

'Only sometimes,' she replies. 'And anyway, I like it.'

'Sure,' I say, rolling my eyes.

'I do!' she insists. 'It's nice.'

I shake my head. 'You're a little weirdo sometimes, you know that, Nemo?'

There's a pause. Audrey takes a deep breath, like she's about to ask a question, then closes her mouth again.

'You OK, Auds?' I ask.

She shrugs and fiddles with the hair band round her wrist.

'C'mon, what's up?' I ask, pulling on the drawstring of her hoodie.

Another deep breath.

'I was just wondering, um, when did you start your period?'

By the time she reaches the end of the question, her cheeks are bright pink.

'When I was eleven,' I reply.

It was during the summer holidays, just before I started at Queen Mary's. I remember going into Grace's room and showing her the blood on my knickers and her taking me to the bathroom and pointing out the little wicker basket in the cupboard under the sink where the sanitary towels and tampons are kept, and showing me how to use them.

'Is that average?' Audrey asks. 'Eleven?'

'It depends. Grace was a bit older. Twelve, I think. Some people start later, though. I think Kimmie was nearly fifteen. You're not worried about it, are you?'

She hesitates.

'It's just that Lara got hers today. And Becca and Lottie both got theirs ages ago and now I feel like I'm the only one left.'

'Auds,' I say, putting down my laptop. 'Everyone's bodies are different.'

'But I'm the tallest by miles. Shouldn't I have mine by now?'

'It doesn't really work like that. Look, between you and me, you want your period to stay away for as long as possible.'

'Really?'

'Definitely. Everyone goes on about periods like they're this big deal, when to be honest they're kind of a pain in the arse.'

'How come?'

'Oh God, where do I start? They're messy, they're painful, you feel all bloated and moody . . .'

'Really? You're not just saying that to make me feel better?'

'I swear. They're well annoying. You should count yourself lucky you don't have yours yet. They're not giving you grief about it, are they?'

She shakes her head.

'Good. Because if they do, they'll have me to deal with.'

Audrey wraps her arms round my neck and buries her face in my hair. 'Thanks, Mia,' she says, her voice all muffled.

'No problem, Nemo,' I say, kissing her damp parting. 'Now, get off me already. I need to pay for these bad boys.'

11

I head downstairs for breakfast on Friday morning to discover Sam in the kitchen. He's standing in front of the open fridge wearing tartan pyjama bottoms and a white T-shirt, his hair flat on one side, sticking up on the other. I'm surprised to see what looks like a tattoo peeking out from under his right sleeve. I wonder what it's of. Something lame, I bet. His A-level results. Or his favourite element on the periodic table.

He hears my footsteps on the lino and glances up. 'Oh, hey, Mia,' he says, smiling broadly.

Ugh. He must be a morning person. The *worst* kind.

'I haven't seen much of you this week,' he adds.

He and Grace have been out most evenings, doing the rounds, meeting Grace's avalanche of boring friends.

'No,' I murmur, sleepwalking in the vague direction of the kettle.

'What have you been up to?' he asks.

Oh God, he's not going to expect me to make small talk, is he? Did he not get the memo that I prefer to avoid all non-verbal communication until after 9 a.m. at least? I'm especially knackered this morning. Grace barged into my room at 1 a.m., switching on the light and thrusting her weird veiny belly in my face because the baby was moving and she wanted me to feel it. I managed to get rid of her after about ten minutes, but it took ages to fall asleep again.

'Nothing much,' I mutter, flicking on the kettle and letting my upper body collapse over the counter, hoping he'll get the message and leave me alone.

'Is this you?' he asks.

I lift my head up a few centimetres and peer through my hair. Sam has shut the fridge and is holding a familiar piece of paper in his hand.

Suddenly I'm wide awake.

I lunge forward and reach to snatch it out of his hands but he's too fast, holding it high above his head.

'I'll take that as a yes,' he says, laughing.

'Whatever, *Dougie*,' I say, feigning nonchalance and pushing past him to open the fridge. This week it's hosting a massive Teenage Mutant Ninja Turtles cake, all our actual food shoved into the vegetable drawer or the shelves in the door.

'It was ages ago,' I say, grabbing for the milk and slamming the fridge door shut.

'So what's the story?' he asks.

'None of your business,' I reply, plucking the piece of paper from his hands and sticking it back on the fridge, knowing full well that, if I throw it away, a brand-new version will be up in its place by the end of the day.

I select one of the fancy boxes of granola that has appeared in the last few days (no doubt for Grace and Sam's benefit), and pour some into a cereal bowl, drowning the lot with so much milk it sloshes over the rim and onto the counter.

'Whoa there,' Sam says. 'That's a lot of liquid.'

'Yeah? And? I like my cereal soggy,' I tell him, sitting down at the breakfast bar. 'Any other interesting observations?'

He holds up his arms in surrender and sits down on the stool opposite. 'You know, that stuff looks good actually,' he says, pointing at my bowl. 'I might have some.'

'Copycat,' I mutter.

He pours himself a bowl and for about a minute we eat in silence.

'You don't like me being here particularly, do you?' Sam says eventually.

God, he's posh. It's a bit unnerving, like having breakfast with a member of the royal family or someone from the cast of *Made in Chelsea*.

'How so?' I ask.

Forgive me if I'm wrong, but I've been getting the vibes you'd perhaps rather I wasn't around. Am I right?'

'What makes you says that?'

'Um, the fact you keep calling me "Dougie"?'

I make a half-hearted attempt to hide my smile behind my spoon. 'Sorry about that,' I say. 'But hey, at least you know Grace has a type. Have you met Dougie?'

He narrows his eyes ever so slightly, like he's trying his very hardest to figure me out. 'Grace's ex-boyfriend? No, I haven't yet, funnily enough.'

There's a pause.

'Look, it's nothing personal,' I say. 'It's just that, in case you hadn't noticed, this house isn't exactly a mansion.'

'Understood,' he says. 'And I get how weird it must be for you having me here, I honestly do. The good news is, I'm starting a new job next week so hopefully I'll be out of your hair a bit more.'

'A job? Where?'

'Pulling pints at The Wheatsheaf.'

The Wheatsheaf is a pub at the rubbish end of the high street. It's a proper old man's place, full of smelly old blokes dribbling into their pints of bitter and playing darts. I wouldn't be seen dead in there.

'Ew. Why there?' I ask.

'It wasn't exactly my first choice either,' Sam admits. 'But beggars can't be choosers.'

'You're *hardly* a beggar,' I tell him.

I looked him up on Facebook the other day. There were loads of pictures of him on posh holidays, posing on skis at the tops of mountains, and riding horses, and jumping off rocks into tropical waters. I googled his old school too. The fees cost more than what Dad earns in an entire year as a paramedic.

'So, are you going to tell me about the picture on the fridge or not?' he asks.

'Do you have amnesia or something? I told you, it's none of your business.'

'It was taken in a hospital, right?' he says, undeterred.

'No shit, Sherlock,' I mutter. The hospital trolley I'm lying on and the exhausted-looking nurse in the background kind of give the game away.

'So, what's the story? 'Cos I'm guessing from your attire and what looks like vomit on your chin, you ended up there after a night out. Am I right?'

'Maybe, maybe not.'

'Would it be easier if I just asked Grace?'

I open my mouth, then close it again, realizing that if I don't tell Sam the full story behind the picture he'll only go and get Grace's second-hand version of events, which will no doubt be embellished to make what happened that night sound way worse than it actually was, which will be doubly unfair because she wasn't even in the country at the time. In fact, if you do the maths, there's a pretty decent chance that around the time I was being rushed to hospital, she'd already been impregnated by Sam.

'OK, fine,' I say, sighing. 'But only because you're getting on my nerves.'

Sam gets comfy on his stool, like a kid getting ready for story time.

'So, last New Year's Eve I had one too many drinks and ended up in A&E, and Mum and Dad thought it would be a good idea to capture the moment for posterity. Nothing more exciting than that.'

Sam gets up and re-examines the picture, his face literally

centimetres away from the fridge. 'How much did you drink?' he asks.

'No more than anyone else.'

He raises a quizzical eyebrow.

'It's true!' I cry. 'I don't know what happened. I mean, I know I was mixing my drinks quite a lot, but not enough to justify going to hospital. There's no point trying to tell Mum and Dad that though. They totally freaked out and didn't let me leave the house for six weeks. You'd think I was the first teenager in Rushton ever to get drunk from the way they reacted.'

'So the picture is, what, a deterrent?' he asks, sitting back down.

'Mum and Dad say they'll take it down once they think I've "learned from the experience".'

'And have you?'

I shrug and stir my granola, slowly turning the milk a pale brown.

Sam leans in. 'I once got so drunk I broke my arm and didn't even realize.'

I continue to stir.

'It was my seventeenth,' he continues. 'I'd been out with all my mates and got absolutely bladdered. I forgot my keys and had the bright idea of shimmying up the drainpipe and climbing in through my bedroom window. The next morning, my mum found me in the rose bushes with my arm broken in three places.'

I roll my eyes. Trust Sam to have a relevant anecdote to hand. It probably isn't even true.

'I know why you're telling me this,' I say.

He blinks in confusion.

'So we can "bond". Right?'

'Well, yeah,' he says, his cheeks tinged pink. 'Mainly.'

I hadn't anticipated such a straight answer.

He clears this throat. 'Like I said the other night, I've always really wanted sisters.'

I screw up my nose like I've just smelled something off. 'But why?' I ask. 'It must be great being an only child. You don't have to share a room with anyone, or wear hand-me-down clothes, or get shown up all the time.' I tick off each of the benefits on my fingers.

'True. It's still lonely though, especially when it's just the two of you.'

'The two of you?

'Yeah, me and my mum.'

'What about your dad?'

'He left when I was still pretty young. Married someone else and moved to Spain.'

'Oh,' I say, wondering if this is the part where I'm supposed to say 'I'm sorry'. Instead I ask him how old he was when his dad left.

'Seven. Old enough to get what was going on but not old enough to understand it.'

'What a tosspot.'

Sam smiles. 'Yeah, pretty much. Looking back though, I'm surprised they lasted as long as they did. That's probably why I'm so envious of you guys.'

'Us?' I ask, pulling a face. 'Why?'

'Your parents are so in love. Don't you find it inspiring?'

'More like emotionally scarring.'

'No, I mean it. It's really nice to see. You can get a bit jaded when you grow up with parents who do nothing but fight.'

'Maybe,' I say, wondering if Sam would change his mind if he had to witness his parents dry humping as regularly as I did.

'Aw, two of my very favourite people.'

I twist round in my seat. Grace is padding towards us, clearly naked under her silk dressing gown, her swollen boobs swaying beneath the thin material.

'What are you guys chatting about?' she asks, resting her elbows on the breakfast bar.

'Nothing very interesting,' I say, sliding off my seat. 'Right, Dougie?'

I glance at Grace for a reaction but she gives me nothing. Ever since our conversation in the garden on Sunday, she's been acting like everything is hunky-dory between us; stubbornly ignoring every eye roll, scoff and glare I dole out.

She snuggles under Sam's arm, her fingers lifting up his T-shirt, seeking out skin. I get an unwanted flashback to the other night, to their groans and gasps and moans.

'What do you want, babe?' Sam asks. 'Toast? Cereal? Eggs?'

'Don't get up, I can make it,' Grace says.

But Sam is having none of it, forcing her to sit down in his place as he sticks bread in the toaster and rifles through the cupboards for the marmalade the baby is apparently 'craving', while Grace witters on about some dream she's just woken up from, when everyone *knows* there's nothing more boring in the entire world than listening to other people talk about their dreams.

I rinse my bowl under the tap, dump it in the dishwasher, and leave the gross lovebirds to it.

12

According to the weather reports on TV, Saturday is going to be the hottest day of the year so far. Stella, Mikey, Kimmie and I decide to make the most of it and head to Rushton Lido.

'Do you see him, do you see him?' Kimmie asks, as we unload iPods and magazines and sun lotion and spread our towels out on the burning concrete. She's kneeling up, scouring the hordes of half-naked people for Aaron Butler.

Along with Stella's brother Stu, Aaron Butler was in the same year as Grace at Queen Mary's, and Kimmie has fancied him ever since she first clapped eyes on him back in Year 7. He didn't stay on for sixth form, so for the past three years Kimmie has had to rely on visits to the lido where Aaron works to satisfy her crush. I only hope this summer will be the one where she finally stops driving us mad with all her staring and squealing and actually tries talking to him.

Personally, I don't get what all the fuss is about. It's not like Aaron is all that; he never has been. He isn't even the nicest-looking lifeguard. He's as skinny as a rake with knobbly knees and has this stupid quiff that makes his pale blond hair look like a Mr Whippy ice-cream cone.

'There he is,' Stella says, finally locating Aaron in the throngs of people; he's patrolling the kid's paddling pool, a whistle dangling from his mouth.

'Don't point,' Kimmie gasps, slapping Stella's arm down. 'He might see us.'

'Isn't that the whole point?' I ask. 'That he actually notices we're here?'

'Well, yes, but not like that. It should happen naturally.'

I roll my eyes at the others and wriggle out of my denim shorts.

The paddling pool is predictably busy, dozens of children jostling for space in the shallow water. Their excited shrieks whizz me back to when I was six years old and slipped and fell on my way in, banging my head on the concrete path. I remember Grace cradling my bloody head in her lap while she screamed for Mum. I'm guessing adult help must have come pretty quickly because it was the summer holidays and the pool would have been crowded, but over the years, time has interfered with my memory, increasing the number of seconds Grace was holding my head and bleaching out the crowds of people that must have surrounded us, so that it's just the two of us – me and Grace, her desperate screams echoing into the abyss as I drifted in and out of consciousness in her lap.

I ended up going to hospital and having six stitches. And even though it hurt, I secretly loved every second. I loved the nurses fussing over me, the jelly and ice cream I was rewarded with for being 'so brave', the way Dad carried me to the car like a baby when he came to pick us up. I still have the scar. If I part my hair in the right place, you can see it, pale and shiny.

'Ooh, nice bikini, Mia,' Kimmie says, yanking me back into the present.

I look down. The bikini is a recent purchase. It's white with fringing on it, very Bond Girl and very, very skimpy. It's only from Primark but I'm not going to volunteer this information if I can help it. I bought it with my pocket money last month, smuggling it upstairs under my sweat-shirt so Mum and Dad wouldn't see. Tonight I'll have to rinse it out in secret in the bathroom sink and hang it to dry outside my bedroom window.

'I wish I could wear white,' Stella says, sighing and hold-ing out a freckled arm. 'But it does *nothing* for me.' Stella's skin is as pale as a porcelain doll's.

'I hear you, sister,' Mikey says, offering up his palm for a high-five of solidarity. He's stripped down to a pair of tiny blue swim shorts and is slathering his glowing limbs with what looks (and smells) suspiciously like cooking oil.

'What the hell is that stuff, Mikey?' I ask, scrunching up my nose.

'Just a little something to give my tan a head start.'

'Either that or skin cancer.'

'It's all right for you,' he says, glancing disdainfully at my legs. 'You have no idea the pain I have to go through to avoid people mistaking me for Boo sodding Radley. I'm telling you, I'm getting a tan this summer if it kills me.'

We lie in a tightly packed row, turning over every fifteen minutes, Kimmie constantly asking if Aaron is looking in our direction. By silent agreement, we all lie and say 'yes' to keep her happy.

After about an hour he comes to patrol the main pool, climbing the ladder to the elevated seat overlooking the deep end.

'Hey, maybe you should pretend to drown, Kimmie,' Mikey suggests. 'Get Aaron to give you the kiss of life.'

Kimmie blushes like mad. 'As if.'

'Mia would,' Mikey says.

'Yeah,' Stella agrees. 'Fake drowning to get a guy to kiss her is *so* something Mia would do.'

'I'm going to take that as a compliment,' I say. 'Mikey has a point though, Kimmie. You can't just wait for Aaron to notice you all summer – you need to be a bit proactive.'

'But I'm not like you,' Kimmie wails, sitting up and wrapping her arms around her legs. 'I can't just go up to him. What would I say?'

'Anything! Ask for the time if you have to. Just open your mouth.'

I turn onto my front and untie my bikini top so I won't get a tan line across my back. As I turn my head to the left, away from the others, I realize I'm being watched.

By Aaron.

The second he realizes he's been caught staring he looks

106

the opposite way, peering through his binoculars at the swimmers below. I pretend to close my eyes. Through my eyelashes though, I see him squeeze in another look in my direction; longer this time, his eyes daring to drift up and down my body. I resist a smile before turning my head back the other way.

Just before lunch we venture into the crowded pool. Stella announces she doesn't want to get her hair wet, which makes it Mikey and mine's mission to dunk her head under the water. We succeed shortly before the lifeguard (not Aaron, but his colleague who clearly has no sense of humour) blows his whistle at us.

'Relax, Stells,' I say, as we dry off. 'You're acting like we tried to drown you in a vat of acid or something.'

'If my highlights turn green, you're paying for me to have them redone, that's all I'm saying,' she says, pouting.

I shake my head. For someone with a really pretty ordinary head of hair, Stella manages to make *a lot* of fuss about it. It kind of annoys me, especially when *I'm* the one with the Afro and I don't make even half the drama she does.

Kimmie loses the coin toss and is despatched to the cafe. She returns with ice-cold Diet Cokes, assorted sandwiches and a giddy smile on her face because she passed Aaron on the way back and she's almost eighty-five per cent sure they made eye contact. I feel a bit weird about it but don't know why. After all, I don't control who Aaron looks at and when.

We sit in a circle to eat, the midday sun beating down on our backs.

'I think we should all learn to surf in Newquay,' I announce.

'Really?' Stella asks, wrinkling her nose. 'How come?'

Despite being super-skinny, Stella tends to avoid formal physical activity if she can help it. The one time she ran for the ball in PE, Mrs Cates almost fainted from shock.

'Duh! It's *the* way to meet hot surfer boys,' I say. 'I thought *everyone* knew that.'

Ever since Stella's mum booked our plane tickets I've been indulging in daily fantasies about boys with sun-kissed hair, six-packs and walnut tans.

'And I've found a club for us to go to on the Saturday night,' I continue. 'I've emailed them and asked if they can stick us on the guest list so we don't have to waste time queuing up. I was thinking we should start off with a few drinks at the caravan, then head into town around nine.'

'You should be a travel agent, Mia,' Kimmie says, peeling discs of cucumber off her tuna mayonnaise sandwich and lining them up on her napkin. 'You're really good at this stuff.'

'I'm so friggin' excited,' Mikey says. 'How many weeks to go again?'

'Six!' Stella and I chorus in unison.

'Jinx!' we crow, linking pinky fingers and giggling.

'How's Grace?' Kimmie asks once Stella and I have stopped laughing.

Her question instantly kills the mood.

'Still pregnant,' I say in a bored voice. Kimmie has been going on about Grace and the baby all week.

'Which reminds me,' Stella says, discarding her bread and eating only the slivers of ham and tomato. 'I went on her Facebook last night and checked Sam out. Why didn't you tell us he was so fit, Mia?'

I roll my eyes. Stella clearly has the same vanilla taste in men as Grace.

'Fit?' Mikey says. 'Seriously?' He grabs his phone. A few seconds later Grace's Facebook profile picture fills the screen. In it she and Sam have their arms round each other in front of some Greek ruins, the sun setting behind them. 'He's proper cute!' Mikey says. 'I thought you said he wasn't all that?'

'He's not,' I grumble.

'Let me see!' Kimmie cries, reaching for the phone.

Mikey holds it high above his head. 'Sorry, Kimmie, he's mine.'

She twists his nipple hard. Mikey swears loudly, prompting frowns and tuts from the family next to us, before surrendering the phone.

'Ooh, he looks lovely!' Kimmie says, studying it carefully. 'I love his glasses.' She holds the phone to her chest. 'Their baby is going to be sooooo cute, Mia. Grace should sign the three of them up to a modelling agency as soon as it's born, I bet they'd get loads of work.'

I snatch the phone from Kimmie's hands and inspect the photo more closely, trying to see what all the fuss is about. Sam is OK-looking, but nothing out of the ordinary, and definitely not my type.

'You really think he's hot?' I ask.

109

'Um, yes,' Stella says. 'He can impregnate me anytime.'

The three of them cackle away like Macbeth's witches.

'I thought you didn't *do* gingers,' I say.

'Never say never,' Stella replies.

'Does he have any brothers?' Mikey asks hopefully.

'No. He's an only child.'

'Is he nice?' Kimmie asks. 'He looks nice.'

'To be perfectly honest, he's kind of a try-hard.'

I tell them about getting home from school on Wednesday and discovering Sam sitting at the kitchen table with Mum, helping her cut out fondant snowflakes for yet another *Frozen* cake.

'Well, it must be weird for him, living with someone else's family all of a sudden,' Kimmie says.

'Weird for him?' I say. 'What about me? I'm the one who's had to give up my bedroom.'

'Um, not exactly. It was Grace's bedroom all along,' Stella points out.

'So? It's still rude of them to just turn up practically unannounced and expect everyone to shift around and make space for them both. Did I tell you about the bed?'

'Only about twelve times,' Stella says.

A brand-new double bed arrived on Thursday while I was at school. When I got home the mattress was propped up against the wall in the hallway, covered in plastic. Assembled, the bed takes up nearly the whole of Grace's room.

'I've been asking for a double bed for years,' I say.

Stella mimes playing a violin. I stick my tongue out at her.

'So, when can we meet him in the flesh?' Mikey asks.

'He'll be at the wedding, I suppose.'

'But that's ages away!'

'Are you really that desperate to meet him?'

'I am now that I've seen his photo,' Mikey says.

More cackling.

I check the time. It's not even 1 p.m.

I love my friends, I really do. But sometimes they totally do my head in.

I blink and open my eyes. At first all I can see is the sky – clear and perfect, the only interruption the crisscross of plane tracks, white against cornflower blue. Then a shadow in the form of Mikey's sunburnt face looms over me, and the picture is ruined.

'Mia,' he barks, spittle landing on my cheek. 'Phone for you.'

Frowning, I take it from him. 'Hello?' I say.

'Where are you?' Grace sounds annoyed.

'Why are you calling me on Mikey's phone?'

'Because I couldn't get hold of you on yours. I've been ringing and ringing.'

'Why? What time is it?' I ask, rubbing my eyes.

'Four o'clock. You were meant to be here half an hour ago.'

With my spare hand I fish my own phone out of my tote bag. Five missed calls from Grace, two from Audrey, two from Mum.

Shit, shit, shit.

'Sorry, I was asleep, I didn't hear it ring. I'm coming now.'

'Well, you'd better hurry, the shop closes at five.'

I hang up and struggle woozily to my feet.

'What's going on?' Stella asks, shielding her eyes from the sun.

'I have to go,' I say, looking around for my flip-flops.

'But why?'

'Remember that bridesmaid dress appointment I told you about?'

She nods.

'Well, I'm totally late for it,' I say, balling up my towel and forcing it into my bag. 'And that was Grace, being super-pissy about it.'

'Oooh, are you trying on dresses?' Kimmie asks, clapping her hands together.

'Meant to be.'

She lets out a little squeal.

'Ring us when you're done?' Stella asks.

'I'll try.'

I yank on my shorts and head for the exit, my good mood well and truly shattered.

13

Twenty minutes later I burst through the door of Reflections Bridal Boutique. The woman behind the counter, immaculate in a crisp white shirt, her hair swept into a silky chignon, looks up in faint alarm. When I catch sight of myself in the mirror behind her, I sort of understand why. I look a mess. My hair is even bigger than usual, glittery red heart-shaped sunglasses marooned in the mass of frizzy curls, my face damp with sweat from basically sprinting the entire way from the lido.

'Can I help you?' she asks, clearly convinced I've stumbled in here by accident.

'I'm with them,' I say breathlessly, pointing towards the back of the shop, where Mum is standing on a small plinth in her wedding dress, a woman with a mouthful of pins kneeling at her feet. Grace and Audrey are to her right, sitting on a white chaise longue. Mum and Grace are both shaking their heads at me, practically radiating disappointment.

After all the squealing and splashing at the lido, this place is bookshop-quiet in comparison, barely audible pan-pipe versions of classic love songs soundtracking my walk of shame towards my family. Pretty much everything in here is white. I swear, it's like being trapped inside a marshmallow. As I make my way across the pristine carpet, it is as if my very presence is contaminating the dresses one by one, staining them dirty yellow as I pass.

Grace tuts loudly as I sink down on the chaise longue between her and Audrey. I ignore her and try to focus my attention on Mum.

'Sorry I'm late,' I say.

Mum sighs. 'Well, you're here now, Mia, that's the main thing.' Her eyes drift down to my shorts. She frowns. 'Is that a new swimsuit?'

I look down; the tie sides of my bikini are sticking out over the waistband of my shorts. 'No,' I say quickly, tucking them in. 'I've had it for ages. You look really gorgeous by the way.'

Even though I'm totally trying to distract her with the compliment, I do actually mean it. Mum looks incredible, the strapless off-white dress with its beaded bodice and fish-tail skirt showing off her slim figure perfectly. She spends most of her life in jeans, T-shirt and apron, so it's fun to see her dressed up for once.

She puts her hands on her hips and twists her torso back and forth. 'You don't think I'm too old and saggy to go strapless?'

'Of course not,' I say. 'You look well foxy. Dad's eyes are

going to pop out of his head on stalks when he sees you coming down the aisle like this.'

Mum laughs and I know I'm off the hook. Not that Mum is in any danger of looking old *or* saggy anytime soon. She's only thirty-seven. Both she and Dad are younger than all my friend's parents by miles.

'Right, I think we're all done here,' the woman with the pins says, standing up and helping Mum off the plinth. 'Let's get you changed, and then we can move on to the bridesmaids.' She gives us a wink and escorts Mum behind a white curtain.

'Hey,' Audrey says in a low whisper, pressing her shoulder against mine.

'Hey,' I murmur back, pulling my mobile out of my bag. I scroll through the photos I took at the lido today, changing the filters and uploading the best ones to Instagram, secretly hoping Jordan might see them and mourn what he's missing. According to Stacey Khan, a girl in my year whose cousin goes to Toft Park, Hattie and Jordan are officially going steady now.

Mum, back in her denim skirt and vest top, emerges from behind the curtain.

'OK, girls, you're up,' she says. 'Grace and Audrey have already picked out a few styles they like,' she explains to me. 'So if you want to try something different you're going to have to grab them quick.'

Originally we were going to buy bridesmaid dresses off the high street, but now Grace is back earlier than planned and we have her big old pregnant belly to factor in, Mum thought we may as well go the whole hog and have proper froufrou bridesmaid dresses made up especially. I went online earlier in the week to check out the selection and quickly identified the dress I want the three of us to wear. It's crimson red and falls all the way to the floor in gorgeous silky folds. With its high neck and low scoping back, it shows just the right amount of skin, and is without doubt the most beautiful piece of clothing I've ever laid my eyes on. I showed Audrey online the other day and even she admitted it was lovely.

I head to the rack where all the bridesmaid styles are kept and reach for it, holding it up against me. It's even better in real life, the material smooth and luxurious against my bare legs.

'Don't you want to try on anything else?' the sales assistant asks.

To keep her happy, I select another couple of dresses at random and join Grace and Audrey in the changing area. We get dressed, one by one shuffling out from behind the curtain and lining up opposite the floor-to-ceiling mirrors.

Mum is already grinning. 'My gorgeous girls,' she says, clasping her hands together.

Stuck between Grace and Audrey, I feel short. 'Can I get some heels?' I ask the sales assistant.

She locates me a pair of size fives. They're white satin with jewels on the toe – proper wedding shoes. I slip them on and instantly feel better, striking a model pose, hands on my hips. My dress is by far the nicest in every possible way; I look like a proper grownup in it – womanly and sophisticated. Audrey's choice is a pale blue shift dress with embroidered flowers round the neckline. It's cute but nowhere special enough for a wedding, especially next to my red. She looks uncomfortable in it, one hand hanging limply across her body, the other tugging at the hem, the whole time her eyes looking anywhere but the mirror.

Grace has selected a lilac empire-line design with cap sleeves and a knee-length chiffon skirt. The only thing that stops it from looking like a little kid's party dress is the neckline; it makes her boobs look massive, like they've been inflated with air and might pop any second.

'So, what do you think?' I ask Mum eagerly.

'It doesn't matter so much what I think,' Mum says. 'I just want to find something all three of you will be comfortable wearing on the day.'

'In that case, I need to speak up now and say there's no way I can wear the one Mia's got on,' Grace says.

'Why not?' I ask.

'Well, it's backless for a start. How are you supposed to wear a bra with it?' She turns to Mum, who is sitting down on the chaise longue. 'Mum, please tell Mia that it's totally inappropriate for me to go braless right now.'

'You don't have to go braless,' I say. 'I already checked online and they can add an extra panel of material at the back if you want.'

'She's right,' the sales assistant says. 'It's really not a problem.'

I smile at her gratefully.

'That's all well and good, but where exactly am I supposed to put this?' Grace asks, patting her baby bump.

'Isn't that the whole point we're here?' I ask, appealing to Mum. 'To get made-to-measure dresses?'

Grace gives me a withering look, like I'm the most idiotic person on the planet. 'That's not quite how it works, Mia,' she says. 'It's obvious just from looking at that dress that it would never work as a maternity style. I'll be nearly eight months gone by the wedding, remember?'

'At least try it,' I say. 'It might look OK.'

But she just ignores my suggestion, harping on about Audrey now instead. 'Your choice is way too mature for her anyway. She's only thirteen,' she says.

'Exactly. It's not like she's a little kid any more. And it's not slutty or anything, it's really sophisticated. Right, Auds?'

We don't get to hear Audrey's stammered answer because Grace totally speaks over her.

'Mum said we all need to be comfortable and I'm not going to be comfortable wearing that in a million years. The end.'

'You haven't even tried it on!' I cry, throwing a desperate look at Mum, who is frowning up at us.

'I don't need to.'

'But, Mum, that's not fair!'

'I'm sorry, sweetheart,' Mum says. 'But Grace is right. You're going to be in these dresses for over twelve hours, so you've got to feel comfortable. All three of you.'

I glare at Grace. If it wasn't for her making such a fuss, I just know I could have won Mum over.

Mum clocks my face and laughs. 'There are plenty of others to try,' she says, gesturing at the remaining dresses hanging up.

But I don't want any other dress. I had my heart set on this one. I pull a face, which everyone seems to ignore, and stamp back behind the curtain.

We spend the next half an hour clambering in and out of boring dress after boring dress, my head pounding the entire time. I don't think I've drunk enough water today.

In the end the final choice seems to come down to Grace's bump. And of course, the only dress that satisfies her requirements is her favourite – the kids' party dress number. The sales assistant manages to find two more in the stockroom so we can try them on altogether.

The second we line up, Mum bursts into tears and I know my lilac-chiffon fate is sealed. I'm stupid for thinking the outcome would be any different. Pregnant belly or no pregnant belly, Grace would have got her way no matter what obstacles were in her path.

'Fantastic,' the sales assistant says, clearly relieved a decision has been made. 'In that case, let's get measuring. If we're fast we can get all three girls done before closing time.'

'Wonderful,' Grace says, smoothing down her skirt and smiling serenely in the mirror. 'I knew we'd get there in the end.'

It takes every ounce of self-restraint I have not to punch the glass with my fist.

I'm annoyed for the rest of the day. Mum notices on the drive home, asking me why I'm in 'such a grump' in the rear-view mirror, with Grace making some little dig about me always being in a grump, which isn't even true. Things were going fine until she turned up and ruined it all. It's Mum's oblivion that pisses me off the most. There's no point trying to explain, though. If I try to articulate why I'm fed up, I'll only sound petty. They'll think it's just about the dress.

'Which dress did you like best?' I ask Audrey as we're getting ready for bed.

'I don't know,' she replies, releasing her hair from its ponytail and pulling a brush through the tangles. 'I'm not really into that stuff.'

'I know that,' I say, adjusting my silk hairwrap. 'But if you were in charge and had to pick, which one would you have gone for?'

'Um, they were all OK,' she says unconvincingly.

'But which one was the *most* OK?' I ask, leaning forwards.

'I don't know. The one we ended up getting? The purple one?'

My shoulders slump. 'You mean Grace's choice?'

'Was it?'

'Yes.'

'Oh, OK. Well, yeah, that one, I suppose.'

Wrong answer.

I get in bed, pulling the covers over me and switching off my lamp.

'Are you OK, Mia?' Audrey asks, her voice quavering.

'Fine,' I mutter.

14

The following morning I sleep through my alarm. I'm late to work, where I'm forced to surrender an hour's wages to smug Jeremy. To make matters worse, it tips it down the entire shift and we're left with masses of sausages. Bye-bye, bonus.

My mood lifts momentarily when I get home and smell roast chicken. We haven't had a roast dinner in absolutely ages – 'too much of a palaver' according to Mum, who is always absolutely knackered by the time Sunday rolls round.

I'm hanging up my damp denim jacket on the peg in the downstairs loo when I hear Frankie's voice coming from the kitchen.

Frankie used to be Audrey's swimming coach until he retired last year and scary Steph took over. Even though Steph is a former Olympian and apparently an incredible coach, I know Audrey misses Frankie like crazy. Before he retired, he was a regular fixture at our breakfast bar, putting the world to rights with Mum and Dad over endless cups of tea.

I follow the smell of roast chicken to the kitchen. The entire family is sitting around the table, Frankie at its head.

'Hey, Mia,' he says, waving. 'Looking lovely as always.'

'Cheers, Frankie,' I reply.

I vaguely remember Mum mentioning his visit now. He can't make the wedding because his niece or nephew or someone is getting married that same weekend, but he wanted to wish Mum and Dad well and give them their present in person. A box wrapped in shiny silver paper sits at his elbow.

My eyes drift to the pile of dirty dishes next to the sink and a stripped chicken carcass sitting on a wooden board.

'Wow, thanks for waiting for me,' I say.

'Don't be silly. There's a plate for you in the fridge – you just need to pop it in the microwave,' Mum says before turning her attention back to Frankie.

I frown and open the fridge. Behind me, Frankie continues telling everyone about the house he's having done up in the Lake District.

'I'm so jealous,' Mum says.

'I'm not going to lie,' Frankie says. 'I'm absolutely loving it, even though the place resembles a bomb site right now. No running water, no electricity. I'm basically camping.'

I peel the clingfilm off my plate. 'Mum?' I say.

She swivels round in her chair, looking annoyed at the interruption.

'Mia, we're talking,' she says.

'Sorry,' I mutter, poking at one of the potatoes on my plate.

'What is it?' she asks, sighing.

'I don't have a Yorkshire pudding.'

'Really? I could have sworn I made enough for one each.'

'Oops!' Grace says. 'I think I took two by accident. Sorry, Bean was hungry!' She pats her tummy smugly.

'But Yorkshire puddings are my favourite bit.'

'Mia . . .' Dad says, his eyes narrowing.

Translation: Stop being a brat in front of our guest.

'Oh, forget it,' I mutter. I open the microwave, shove my plate in and slam the door.

By the time I turn round everyone's in stitches over something Frankie just said. It looks like a scene from a TV commercial – one big happy family. They're just missing the dog.

I eject my lukewarm food from the microwave and take it outside, even though it's still drizzling and all the garden furniture is wet through, heaving the patio door shut behind me. I can still hear them all through the glass though, their muffled chatter punctuated with frequent explosions of laugher.

'Do you not want pudding?' Dad asks as I return inside and dump my dirty dishes in the sink. 'I made an apple pie.'

I hesitate. Dad's apple pie is really, really good.

'With custard,' he adds, wiggling his eyebrows up and down.

'I can't,' I say, blocking out the sight and smell of the

fresh-out-of-the-oven pie cooling on the top of the hob. 'I'm going out.'

'Where?'

'Stella's.'

'Don't you two ever get bored of each other?' Grace pipes up.

'No. Don't *you* ever get bored of being permanently attached to Sam?' I ask, looking pointedly at their entwined fingers.

'It's not quite the same thing,' she replies.

'Of course it isn't. It never is, is it?'

She sits up straight. 'And what's that supposed to mean?'

But I can't be bothered to explain. That's half the problem; whenever I try to describe how I'm feeling, I always come off sounding petty and childish by bringing up stuff that happened years ago.

I sigh. 'Just forget I said anything.'

It's only once I've left the house I remember that Stella isn't around today. It's her dad's birthday so she's out for lunch with him, Stu and her stepmum. I know for a fact Mikey's out of action today too because he's stuck looking after The Accident while his parents go to a wedding, so I text Kimmie on the off-chance she's around. A reply pings back a few minutes later.

Yes! Come over anytime. K xoxo

I ring the doorbell. Unlike ours, Kimmie's actually works. A few seconds later, her older sister Sophie opens the door with her elbow. She's wearing a pair of red-stained plastic gloves, a purple hoodie I recognize as Kimmie's and star print leggings. I wouldn't dream of helping myself to anything from Grace's wardrobe: a) It wouldn't probably fit anyway; and b) Grace's clothes are dull with a big fat capital D.

'Come on up,' Sophie says, skidding across the wooden floor in her socks. 'I'm in the middle of dying Kimmie's hair.'

I follow her, pausing to wave 'hello' to Mr and Mrs Chu, who are sitting at the humungous kitchen table, reading the Sunday newspapers, classical music playing in the background. They smile serenely and wave back. Although we generally hang out at Stella's place because of the lack of parental supervision, Kimmie's house is actually the nicest of all my friends – all soft white walls and glass, and cupboards and drawers that shut themselves without making a sound. It's also massive; the ground floor alone is probably bigger than my entire house.

We head upstairs to the bathroom Kimmie and Sophie share. It's jammed full of products, every available surface littered with bottles and tubs and tubes. Sophie and Kimmie share pretty much everything, from shampoo and tampons, to each other's sentences.

Kimmie is sitting on the lowered toilet seat, her hair slick with dye. 'Hey, Mia,' she says. 'Sorry, won't be long.'

'No worries,' I reply, sitting down on the edge of the bath. 'What kind of dye are you using?'

Sophie tosses me the empty box. A glossy redhead pouts back at me. 'It won't go as red as that on KimKim,' she explains. 'It'll be more of a reddish glow.'

She squeezes the last of the contents from the dye bottle

on the top of Kimmie's head and carefully massages it in. Sixties music is leaking in from Sophie's bedroom. She and Kimmie automatically begin to harmonize, swaying their shoulders in unison and giggling over the same lyric.

Sophie pauses singing. 'I'm just gonna make sure I haven't got any on your skin,' she says, wetting a cotton wool pad and dabbing at Kimmie's hairline. She's working on the back of Kimmie's neck when she stands back and gasps.

'What?' Kimmie cries, her eyes wide with alarm. Sophie winks at me over the top of Kimmie's head.

'I'm sorry, Kimkim, but there's a massive red splodge on your neck and it won't come off!' she says.

'What? Where?' Kimmie asks, twisting her body awkwardly as she attempts to look in the mirror.

Sophie lets Kimmie sweat for at least ten seconds before gleefully yelling, 'Psych!' and creasing up laughing.

'Oi!' Kimmie says, grabbing a flannel and chucking it at her sister. 'That's so mean!'

She's laughing though, the same squawking laugh as her sister. I can't help but feel a bit left out as they shriek and lob cotton wool balls at each other, totally in sync. Kimmie chucks me a couple of cotton wool balls so I can join in but my heart's not really in it. I try to imagine the same scene with me and Grace, but it feels forced, two fakers just playing at being sisters.

'OK, twenty minutes, then we rinse,' Sophie says, once she and Kimmie have exhausted their supply of things to throw at each other. 'I'm going to get a drink. Want anything?'

'No thanks,' Kimmie and I reply.

Sophie leaves the room, singing the song from earlier, Kimmie unable to resist joining in until Sophie's voice has faded away.

We head into Kimmie's room where we clamber onto her king-size bed, sitting opposite each other with our legs crossed.

'How was the dress fitting?' she asks.

I fill her in.

'It sounds really nice,' she says when I describe the lilac dress.

I pull a face.

'It does!' she insists. 'And even if it's not, it won't matter because you'll make it look nice anyway.'

Even though it's a totally soppy thing to say, I can't help but smile. You can always rely on Kimmie for a compliment. She's nice that way.

Her phone beeps. She reaches for it, her eyes widening as she reads what's on the screen.

'What's up?' I ask.

She passes me the phone, her lips pursed tightly together.

Hey Kimmie. Hope ur having gr8 wkd. Coffee some-time? Daniel x

'Daniel?' I say. 'Who's Daniel?'

'Daniel Clark,' she says.

I continue to look at her blankly.

'Mia, he's in our sociology class!'

'Is he?'

As a rule, I don't really pay attention to the boys at school. Since breaking up with Jordan, I've sworn off guys my own age.

Kimmie sighs and takes back her phone, tapping at the screen a few times before handing it back to me. 'This is his Facebook profile picture,' she says.

The screen is filled with a photo of a vaguely familiar boy with curly brown hair and rosy cheeks, playing a guitar.

'Oh yeah,' I say. 'He sits next to Amir, right?'

Amir and I snogged a few times back in Year 10.

'That's him.'

'He's not bad,' I say, passing back the phone.

'You think?'

'Yeah. You'd look good together.'

He's not my type at all, but I can definitely see Kimmie with him. They both have that sweet, wholesome thing going on.

'Text him back then,' I say. 'Actually, don't. Leave it a few hours, let him sweat it out a bit.'

'You think I should say yes then?'

'Of course. Why not?'

'I don't know,' Kimmie says, tracing the floral pattern on the duvet with her fingertips. 'I mean, he's nice and everything but . . .'

'But what?'

'Promise you won't make fun of me?'

I narrow my eyes. I'm not very good at promises.

'Please, Mia.'

'Fine, I promise. Just tell me what the problem is.'

She takes a deep breath. 'Aaron.'

'Aaron?' I splutter. 'Are you serious, Kimmie? But he doesn't even know you exist!'

Her face crumples. 'You promised not to make fun of me!'

'I'm not making fun of you, I'm pointing out a fact.'

'What about the other day? At the lido? We totally had a moment.'

I wince, remembering the way Aaron stared at me as I sunbathed. I'd caught him at it later too, as I walked to the vending machine and back, his eyes on me the entire time.

'I don't know,' she continues. 'I just feel like something could actually happen between us this summer.'

'And you're worried if you do anything with Daniel, it'll rule that out?'

'I guess so. Does that sound mad?'

'Kind of, yeah. I just don't get why you can't see how stuff goes with Daniel in the meantime.'

Kimmie looks horrified.

'Oh, come on,' I say. 'You're seventeen. It's not like you've got to marry either of them.'

'It's just that if I'm going to have a boyfriend, I want to commit one hundred per cent and I can't commit to Daniel while I feel the way I do about Aaron. I've always said I want my first time to be with someone I really care about.'

'Er, slow down a bit, Kimmie, he's only asked you out for a coffee.'

'I know that. I'm just trying to think ahead.'

'Well, you're totally *over*thinking it.'

'Maybe,' she replies, chewing on her fingernail.

'Like, aren't you glad you lost yours to Jordan?' she says. 'Instead of some random guy?'

I try not to stiffen at the mention of Jordan's name.

'What was it like?' Kimmie asks. 'The first time you did it, I mean? Did it hurt or anything?'

'I don't really remember,' I say, shrugging.

'It was nice, then?' she asks hopefully.

'Look, Kimmie, like I just said, you're overthinking it. Trust me, once you've actually done it, you'll realize sex isn't the big deal people make it out to be.'

She continues to look unconvinced. Poor Kimmie. Sometimes I reckon she'd be happier living in the olden days, back when couples didn't kiss until after they were engaged.

'And for the record, I think you should go for that coffee with Daniel,' I say.

'Maybe in September,' Kimmie replies. 'I just want to see what happens this summer first, to find out if Aaron and I have something or not.'

'But what if Daniel meets someone else and you miss your chance?'

Kimmie lifts her chin determinedly. 'Aaron's worth the risk.'

I frown and wonder if I'll ever feel that way about someone, the way Kimmie feels about Aaron. No matter how hard I try though, I just can't quite imagine it.

15

The swimming pool is massive, 'Olympic-sized' according to Dad. My eyes attempt to seek Audrey out amongst the dozens of swimmers standing about in their different-coloured tracksuits, huddled around their individual coaches. I spot Steph first. Six feet tall with ice-white hair, she's pretty easy to pick out in a crowd. She's doing her usual super-intense thing, talking to each of the kids in turn with her hands on their shoulders. The whole time, Audrey stares up at her, her eyes wide and focused, her left hand tapping her thigh the way it always does when she's gearing up to race.

I rub my eyes, dislodging crispy bits of sleep from them. We had to leave the house at 5.30 a.m. to make it to Newcastle in time for Audrey's slot at the British Junior Championships. I totally forgot we were going until Mum rang last night and summoned me home from Stella's in the middle of an episode of *The Unbreakable Kimmy Schmidt*.

'It's been in the family calendar for months,' she scolded.

'But how are we all going to fit in the car?' I asked.

'Not to worry,' Mum replied. 'Sam's bringing his car.'

Grace and Sam have been in Cambridge staying with Sam's mum most of the week. They returned on Thursday in Sam's shiny red car, looking all grown-up and smug.

They're next to me now, unfurling the banner Sam had made up at the print shop on the high street. It has 'AUDREY FOR GOLD!' printed on it in bright blue lettering. It must have cost him a fortune. I can't help thinking he might as well just tattoo 'Please like meeeeeeee!' across his forehead instead; it'd probably be cheaper in the long run.

Audrey isn't in the first few races and it's hard to get very excited with no one in particular to cheer for so I go to the loo and re-do my eyeliner, then to the vending machine, where I dither for ages deciding which chocolate bar I want. By the time I return to my seat with my Double Decker, it's finally time for Audrey's first event – the 500-metres butterfly. Out of her tracksuit, she's easy to spot. One of only two non-white swimmers in the pool, her smooth brown legs gleam as she strides purposefully towards her starting block. She looks different in her swimsuit – strong and confident, a million miles away from the awkward girl trying on bridesmaid dresses last weekend.

She puts on her goggles, climbs onto her starting block and gets into position, knees bent, head tucked down low, eyes already fixed on the black line on the surface of the pool.

There's a moment of stillness before the gun fires and she chucks herself into the water.

As I leap to my feet to cheer her on, it dawns on me just how long it's been since I last saw Audrey swim. In the gap, everything has gone up a notch. She's not only noticeably faster as she slices through the water, but stronger too, powering down the lane and taking the lead quickly. By her ninth length, she's almost a full stroke ahead of the swimmer in second place. The whole time we're on our feet, Grace and Sam waving their banner madly over their heads and chanting Audrey's name. As I join in, I wonder if she can hear us, or if it's all just one big wall of noise. The racket builds to a crescendo as her fingers graze the wall, safely winning the race. She looks up at the scoreboard, pushing her goggles up onto her forehead, blinking, as if genuinely surprised by the result.

She goes on to win six of her seven events. In the seventh – backstroke, her weakest – she takes third place but still gets a personal best. As she's presented with her medals, shyly bowing her head so the adjudicator can hang them around her neck, my heart practically bursts with pride.

Afterwards we gather in the foyer to wait for her. When she finally appears, an angry red stripe across her forehead from where she's been wearing her swimming cap, I break free from the group, picking her up and twirling her round.

'Put me down, Mia,' she begs.

She's laughing, though.

I spin her once more, then set her down on the ground and give her a hug, as always bowled over at the realization the powerhouse in the water was actually my little sister.

'You were insane out there,' I croak in her ear, my voice hoarse from all the yelling.

'Thanks, Mia,' she replies, her Lucozade breath sweet and warm on my neck.

We go for a meal at Pizza Express to celebrate. All the sitting down has made Grace's feet swell up. As she plonks her foot on Sam's knee, I realize what her pregnancy toes remind me of – cocktail sausages. Fat porky cocktail sausages. I get the weird urge to impale each of them on sticks.

'Look!' she wails as we wait for the bill. 'I've got the feet of a seventy-year-old woman!'

As usual though, there's pleasure in her predicament.

'You should keep them raised,' Mum says. 'Why don't you swap with Mia for the return journey and come in our car? Then you can spread out on the back seat.'

I make a face. Four hours stuck in a car with chatty man? No thank you. But it's too late to protest; the decision has already been made – Grace will travel with Mum and Dad, and Audrey and I will go with Sam.

Sam's car is boiling and the metal clip of my seatbelt burns my thigh as I pull it on. Grace's pregnancy book is sitting in the footwell. I had another nose at it the other day. It's literally obsessed with fruit and vegetables. This week the baby is the size of a butternut squash, next week a cabbage. I'm struggling to remind myself that Grace is going to give birth to an actual baby in a couple of months' time and not a giant marrow.

'Can I move this?' I ask.

'Sure,' Sam replies. 'Stick it in the back.'

'I don't know why Grace brought it with her, to be honest,' he adds, grinning. 'She knows every word by heart.'

I chuck it onto the back seat along with a jumbo box of Grace's pregnancy vitamins and a stack of well-thumbed *Mother and Baby* magazines.

Audrey is asleep before we even leave the car park, her head resting against the window.

'She was incredible today,' Sam says.

'Yeah,' I agree softly.

Because he's right, she was. Cue the sting of jealousy at the reminder no one will ever be able to talk about me in the same way.

Sometimes I wonder what might have happened if I hadn't given up swimming lessons when I was eight. Would I be a champion by now too? Deep down though, I know I never had what it took.

I stare out of the window. Up ahead, a little kid has let go of a Pokémon balloon, wailing as it floats away.

'You know, fifty-two per cent of American presidents were middle children,' Sam says.

'Huh?' I say, turning to look at him.

'Yep. Also Bill Gates, Madonna, J-Lo. Um, let's see, who else? Er, Britney Spears, Anne Hathaway, Kim Kardashian . . .'

'And you're telling me this why?'

'I don't know, just making conversation. Interesting though, isn't it?'

'Not really.'

Unless any of them grew up with a do-gooding genius

and a swimming champion. Which I somehow doubt. That's the thing; there's usually only space for one remarkable child in any family. Trust me to get sandwiched between two.

'They reckon they have special powers,' Sam continues.

'Who?'

'Middle children.'

'No. Who reckons they have special powers?'

'I read an article about it online, from *Psychology Today*.'

'Oh.'

There's a pause.

'What kind of powers?' I can't resist asking.

'Lots of things. They tend to be really independent, creative, good negotiators, justice seekers, flexible thinkers . . .'

I switch off. It's just stupid psychobabble. Everyone knows all that stuff is crap. What matters is achievement you can measure – medals and exam results and mentions in the newspaper.

I look back out the window. The little kid is still crying, pointing up at the sky at the balloon, now a tiny speck. I can feel water building up behind my eyelids, threatening to spill. *What is wrong with me?*

'You OK, Mia?' Sam asks.

'Fine,' I mutter, keeping my head where it is so he can't see.

'Want to put some music on? I've got loads of stuff on my phone.'

'I might just sleep actually.'

'Aw, not you too,' he says. 'I was hoping you'd entertain me.'

'What ever gave you that idea?' I ask, balling my hoodie into a pillow.

I'm know I'm being rude, but after the brief excitement of Audrey winning all those medals, my mood has swung in the opposite direction and the last thing I want to do is chat.

'Night,' I say.

Before Sam can respond, I turn my head away from him and squeeze my eyes shut, worried that if I keep them open I won't be able to stop the tears from falling.

16

Over the next two weeks, the teachers are on our backs more than ever, banging on like broken records about the importance of us using our summers 'wisely'. At home, Mum and Dad are busier than ever. Mum has taken on some extra cake orders, so anytime she's not at the pool with Audrey she's in the kitchen, elbow deep in icing sugar. Meanwhile, the dining room is so full of stuff for the baby it's starting to resemble a branch of Mothercare, Grace squeaking with delight over every single new delivery.

I'm in a rubbish mood pretty much the entire time. At first I think it's PMT, but then my period comes and goes and I still feel crap. Not that anyone at home notices, apart from maybe Audrey who asks if I'm OK a couple of times. Everyone else is too busy obsessing about the wedding and the baby. It almost makes me miss the constant lectures I had to sit through following my New Year's Eve trip to

A&E. At least then I felt like Mum and Dad were vaguely aware of my existence.

'What you looking at?' Stella asks.

It's Friday lunch time and the four of us are lying on the bank outside the art block, perving at the bloke mowing the grass at the bottom. He's taken off his shirt and tied it to the belt loop of his cargo trousers. His face isn't much to look at ('like a bulldog chewing a wasp' according to Stella) but his body is lush.

I hesitate before passing her the phone.

On it, there's a photo of Hattie with Jordan's mum on Instagram. They're standing in Jordan's kitchen with their arms round each other's shoulders. The caption says 'My Favourite Ladies'.

'Barf,' Stella says. 'Why are you even following him still?'

I shrug. 'I didn't realize I was until this popped up.'

As porkers go, it's only a bite-sized one.

'Do you think her hair's real?' I can't resist adding.

'Hattie's?'

'No, Jordan's,' I say, tutting. 'Of course Hattie's.'

Stella peers at the screen. 'I don't know,' she admits. 'If they're extensions though, they're really good ones.'

It's not exactly the answer I was looking for.

'Let me see,' Mikey says.

Stella passes him the phone.

'Jesus, she looks like a friggin' Disney princess,' he says.

'Mikey!' Kimmie gasps. 'You can't say that!'

'Why?'

'Because. It's disloyal to Mia.'

'Whatever,' I say with a wave of my hand. 'Like I care. Jordan Latimer is dead to me.'

I take the phone back and look at the picture again. Hattie's hair *is* ridiculous. It's almost down to her bum and looks like it's been spun from real gold by a load of singing woodland animals. That isn't what's bothering me though, not really. What's bothering me is the expression on Jordan's mum's face. It's like she's posing for a picture with her favourite celebrity or something. She never liked *me* very much. She never used to offer me a drink or a biscuit or anything when I came round and used to tut at practically every word that came out of my mouth. Jordan always tried to make me feel better by saying she was 'like that with everyone'. She clearly isn't, though. I have the photographic proof right in front of me.

'I don't know why they're bothering,' Mikey says as we walk home from school later that day.

It's just the three of us. Kimmie has some family party to go to tonight and was picked up straight from school by her parents. Mikey is still managing to hog our communal bag of Haribo though, nicking all the fried eggs while he moans on about being roped in to babysit The Accident tonight while his parents go out for an anniversary dinner.

'They'll only end up arguing like they always do,' he continues. 'Anniversary or no anniversary.'

Stella and I make sympathetic noises, but both of us turn down Mikey's invitation to keep him company for the evening.

'Want to stay at mine?' Stella asks, once we've said good-bye to him.

'Why don't we go out instead?' I suggest.

'Out?' Stella says. 'As in out-out?'

'Yeah. It's been ages since we've gone out properly.'

'What about the Cuckoo Club?' Stella points out. 'That was only a few weeks ago.'

'Exactly. It's been ages. C'mon, let's get dressed up and have a dance.'

'What about Mikey and Kimmie? They'll be gutted if we go out without them.'

'Oh, don't be lame. They'll get over it.'

'I don't know, Mia, I was kind of in the mood for putting my jimjams on and slobbing out.'

I link arms with her, resting my head on her shoulder. Now the idea's landed in my head, I'm determined to see it through.

'Oh, come on, Stells, we can do that anytime. It's been for ever since we went out just the two of us, the originals.'

The Originals. We used to call ourselves that all the time because Stella and I went through the whole of primary school together, only making friends with Kimmie and Mikey when we started at Queen Mary's. We haven't used it in ages though, mainly because Mikey gets all pissy about it when we do.

'We'll have some vodka Red Bulls,' I add. 'That always perks you up, doesn't it?'

'I suppose so,' she admits.

'Is that a yes?'

She grins. 'Go on, then.'

I kiss her on the cheek. 'We are going to have the best night ever, Stells, I can feel it in my bones.'

A night out will fix everything, I just know it. It'll be like a reset; a few drinks and a bit of flirting and I'll be back to normal again, I'm certain. I just can't believe I didn't think of it earlier.

Stella's mum is in Dubai so we turn up her iPod speakers as loud as they'll go and mix stupidly strong vodka Red Bulls to drink while we get ready. We sing along as we do our makeup side by side, our elbows touching. Stu bangs on the door and bellows at us to shut up, but we ignore him and sing even louder, giggling hysterically as he gets more and more annoyed.

We turn down the music for a few minutes so I can ring Mum and tell her I'm sleeping over at Stella's.

'We're just going to watch Netflix, eat some pizza and chill out,' I say, when she asks what we have planned.

My words are already a bit slurred, but luckily she's too distracted by the massive wedding cake she says she's in the middle of stacking to notice.

I borrow a dress and shoes from Stella. The shoes are black with silver spikes on the heel and make me feel like I could rule the world in them. The dress is short, silver and skintight over my curves.

'Seriously, Mia,' Stella says once I'm dressed, 'your arse looks so hot right now I want to take a bite out of one of your bum cheeks.'

There's a pause before we both crack up laughing. Stella kind of has a point, though. My bum looks all kinds of amazing.

By the time we're ready to leave we're both a bit drunk. Stu shakes his head as we do shots in the kitchen. He's rolling a spliff at the table, hunched over his tin of Rizlas and weed.

'You two are a liability,' he says, his lank hair dangling over his forehead.

'Whatevs,' Stella replies, counting to three.

We go to clink our shot glasses together but miss and end up getting more vodka down ourselves than in our mouths. Stella almost falls over laughing as I attempt to lick alcohol from my cleavage.

Stu just sighs and shakes his head again. 'Like I said,' he says, heading off to smoke his spliff out on the patio. 'Total liabilities.'

'So where first?' Stella asks as we settle into our seats on the upper deck of the bus. 'If we want to get into the Cuckoo Club for free, we should make sure we're definitely in the queue by ten thirty at the latest.'

'We always go to the Cuckoo Club,' I say. 'How about we go somewhere different tonight?'

'Like where? The Union?'

'Ew, The Union is proper scuzzy.'

'Blue Bar, then?'

'Can't. The woman on the door hates me, remember?'

'Only because you gave her attitude when she wouldn't let us in that time.'

143

'She gave me attitude first!'

Stella sighs. 'Then where? It's not like Rushton has a billion options. Cuckoo Club is the best of a bad bunch.'

But I don't want to go to the Cuckoo Club. I don't want to have the same old dodgy blokes asking me where I'm from and trying to touch my hair and offering to buy me the same old boring drinks, all to the same old boring soundtrack. I want to go somewhere new, somewhere exciting.

'How about Flux?' I suggest.

'Ha ha, very funny,' Stella says.

'I'm not joking.'

'It's miles away. We'd blow all our money just getting there.'

Flux is a club in a massive converted factory way out of town, unreachable by public transport. It's supposed to be insane, floor after floor of the best DJs playing the coolest music.

'We'll get people to buy us drinks,' I say.

'If we even get in in the first place.'

'Why would we not?'

'Oh, c'mon, Mia, I know we can pass for eighteen at the Cuckoo Club, but Flux? No way.'

I won't be deterred, though.

'Please, Stella,' I say, taking her hands in mine and squeezing hard.

'I don't know, I think I'd rather just keep it local.'

'Oh, come on, where's your fighting spirit? Your sense of adventure?'

'At home. Watching Netflix in my PJs,' she replies.

'But just think about how jealous everyone at school will be if we actually get into Flux. We'll be heroes.'

Her face twitches. She's tempted, I can tell.

'What's the worst that could happen?' I continue. 'We get turned away and go back to yours. Life's bloody short, Stella, we should at least try.'

She takes a deep breath. 'OK,' she says. 'Let's do it.'

I squeal and chuck my arms around her. 'You won't regret this, Stells, I promise!'

17

We chug our usual jug of happy hour Blue Lagoon cocktail at Top Dogs then head straight for the taxi rank. On our way we pass the Cuckoo Club, the usual crowd queuing up outside. Amongst them are some girls from our year – April, Tamsin and Kat. They wave us over.

'Want to sneak in?' April asks, stepping aside to make room for us in the queue.

'No thanks,' I say, happily noting their disappointment. 'We're off to Flux.'

The three of them raise their eyebrows.

'You think you'll get in?' Kat asks.

'It's worth a try.'

'You know they're really strict with ID, don't you?' Tamsin chimes in. 'Passport or driving licence, that's it.'

'Yeah, I know,' I say, shrugging. 'I'm not worried.'

They exchange impressed glances.

'We should get going actually,' I say. 'Beat the queue.'

'Well, good luck,' April says.

'If you don't get in you can always come back here,' Kat adds, looking hopeful.

'Yeah, I suppose we could,' I say. 'I have a good feeling, though.'

We say our goodbyes and keep walking.

'Why did you tell them about Flux?' Stella asks as soon as we've turned the corner. 'Now when we don't get in, they'll think we're really lame.'

'We can worry about that if it happens,' I reply. 'If.'

The taxi journey to Flux takes just under half an hour, our eyes on the meter the entire time. The club truly is in the middle of nowhere, a vast brick building with virtually no signage and nothing else in sight other than a lone burger van. Even though it's still relatively early, there's already a queue snaking round the building, everyone in it utterly immaculate and noticeably older than us. Stella throws me a nervous look, which I pretend to ignore. The best thing we can do right now is to act as relaxed as possible; door people at places like this can sniff out underage nerves at one hundred paces. As we join the back of the queue, the group in front – a sextet of girls with long glossy hair in a variety of shades – give us the once over.

'I didn't know it was underage night,' one of them says.

The others titter.

'Excuse me?' I say, anger swirling in my belly.

The girl who spoke turns to look at me. Her face is so

expertly contoured I wouldn't be surprised if she could peel it off, like a villain in *Scooby-Doo*.

'I said I didn't know it was underage night,' she repeats.

'What makes you so sure we're underage?' I ask. 'Not that it's any of your business.'

'Would you like a list?' she asks.

Cue more titters from her friends.

'Just leave it, Mia,' Stella whispers, tugging on my arm.

I'm not scared of them though, with their fake hair and fake nails and fake tans.

'Look, even if they do believe you're over eighteen,' one of the other girls says, 'you won't get in unless you're on the guest list.'

'Says who?' I ask.

'That's just how it works at Flux,' she says, with a flick of her hair. 'Everyone knows that.'

She and her friends give us one final withering look before turning their backs on us to face the front of the queue.

I rise up onto my tiptoes. I can just about make out the two people manning the door – a woman with a severe ponytail, holding a clipboard, who appears to be in charge, and a muscly bloke in black, his arms folded across his chest.

'Do you think it's true?' Stella whispers. 'About having to be on the guest list? On top of them being really hot on checking IDs?'

'Nah,' I whisper back. 'They're just saying that to be bitches, to psych us out.'

I sound more confident than I feel, though. The fact is, I have no idea if the guest list thing is true or not. All I know

148

is that now we're so close, the throb of the music just metres away, the idea of not getting into Flux tonight physically hurts.

Ten minutes later, we're almost at the entrance, just the girls in front separating us from the door people. I hate to admit it, but they seem to be right about the guest list thing. Having witnessed four separate groups get turned away, I'm feeling increasingly pessimistic about mine and Stella's chances.

'We should be on the VIP list,' the girl with the weird mask face is saying to the doorwoman.

'Sorry, I can't see your name,' she replies.

'Are you sure? Let me see?' one of the other girls says, reaching for the clipboard.

The doorman grabs her arm to stop her, his beefy hand easily encircling her skinny wrist.

'Get off me!' she shrieks.

They all start yelling at once, stabbing angrily at the clipboard with their index fingers while the doorwoman attempts to shout over them. The doorman turns away and starts murmuring into a walkie-talkie.

That's when I see our chance.

'Run!' I whisper.

'What?' Stella says, her eyes widening.

'Run!' I repeat, grabbing her hand and dragging her past the commotion and through the main entrance.

We keep running, only stopping to have the Flux logo stamped on the back of our hands by a girl who looks like a supermodel.

'Have a good night, ladies,' she drawls.

'Oh, we will,' I say, grinning at Stella.

We wait until we're safely through the next set of double doors before daring to pause to scream in each other's faces.

'We did it!' I shriek. 'We actually did it!'

We join hands and practically skip down the corridor towards the thump of the music, the logo on our hands glowing triumphantly in the dark, before spilling out into a vast main room at least five times bigger than the Cuckoo Club. It's cool and industrial, with exposed piping and bare brick walls. All the bar staff are glossy and beautiful without exception. They wear tight black T-shirts, and toss glasses and cocktail shakers in the air and behind their backs with bored expressions on their faces, like they could do it in their sleep if they had to. It makes the Cuckoo Club, with its plastic red banquettes and cheesy light-up dance floor and drinks served in plastic cups, look like a kiddies disco in comparison.

My ribcage vibrates from the throbbing bass line as we make our way around the edge of the already packed dance floor, laser beams shooting from all directions, forming crazy patterns on the walls and ceiling.

'I can't believe it!' Stella shouts in my ear. 'We literally walked in!'

'Told you so!' I singsong.

We pause to take a series of selfies in front of the bar with Stella's phone, taking care to get the insanely hot barman behind us in the shot, before sending it to Tamsin and the others with the caption 'wish you were here?'

I elbow my way to the front of the crowd at the bar and grab a menu before returning to Stella. She whips it from my hand and opens it up, her eyes flickering down the page.

'Jesus Christ,' she says. 'A vodka and Coke is eight pounds fifty . . . Oh my God, look at this. They do a champagne cocktail with actual bits of gold in it!'

'Where? Let me see.'

'There,' she says, prodding the menu. 'The Gold Digga.'

'It's thirteen pounds!' I gasp.

'I know!'

'OK, that's our quest then, to find some blokes who'll buy us one.'

I search the rest of the menu for the cheapest alcoholic item on offer. 'Have you got nine quid?' I ask. 'That'll get us a bottle of Smirnoff Ice each.'

It takes for ever to get served. When we do, the barman tries to up-sell us.

'I can fix you an incredible lychee mojito,' he says.

'Sorry, but we're allergic to lychees,' I reply sweetly.

'Both of you?' he asks, his eyes flicking to Stella then back to me again.

'Yes,' I say. 'It's *such* a shame.'

'Do you think he thinks we're totally lame?' Stella asks as we fight our way back through the crowd with our drinks.

'Oh, who cares,' I say. 'Let's go explore.'

The club is like a massive grownups' playground. We career giddily from room to room, dancing to hardcore dance one minute, seventies funk the next. The R&B room is where it's at though, the compact dance floor heaving with a mass of undulating bodies, a DJ with her short Afro dyed platinum blonde dancing behind a set of decks.

Combined with the jug of Blue Lagoon from Top Dogs, the Smirnoff Ice is making me feel bold and buzzy. There are no drinks allowed on the dance floor so I down the rest of it and dump the empty bottle on the edge of the bar before strutting to the centre, my spiritual home, all thoughts of Jordan and Hattie and Grace and the stupid baby dissolving with every throb of the bass line.

I start to dance, quickly finding my rhythm, grinding and writhing and tossing my head back and forth. Even though the crowd here is achingly cool, and competition for attention is tougher than what I'm used to, I know people are watching us. Stella and I make a good team on the dance floor, her skinny frame and poker-straight blonde hair complementing my curvy body and wild black curls perfectly.

As we dance, I notice two blokes watching us from the edge of the dance floor. They look older than the majority of the crowd here, in their early thirties at least, and slightly out of place as a result. Not that I care. It's the older ones who tend to have the cash.

'C'mon,' I shout at Stella over the music. 'Let's go get another drink.'

'What with?' she asks. 'I've only got enough left for my half of the taxi fare home.'

'Just trust me.'

As I predicted they would, the blokes swoop in the second

we leave the dance floor. One of them is tall with dark hair and designer stubble, the other shorter and strawberry blond. They're both wearing well-cut suits and expensive aftershave.

'You girls must be thirsty,' the taller one shouts in my ear, tickling my eardrum. 'Can we buy you a drink?'

I throw Stella a triumphant look. 'That would be lovely, thank you,' I shout back.

'What are you having?' he asks. 'Beer, wine, cocktails?'

'Cocktails,' I say quickly.

'Anything in particular?'

'How about you surprise us.'

He smiles. 'No problem. We'll be right back.'

'Ew, Mia,' Stella says as soon as they're out of earshot. 'They're ancient.'

'Oh, don't be such a baby,' I say. 'It's not like we have to snog them or anything. We're just letting them buy us a drink.'

The guys return a few seconds later, pressing chilled glasses into our hands.

'Lychee mojitos OK?' the guy who's done all the talking so far asks.

'Perfect,' I purr, clinking my glass against his.

I take a sip. It's crazy delicious.

We head up onto the roof terrace where it's a bit quieter and we can talk without having to yell everything at least twice in order to be heard over the music.

'I'm Miles, by the way,' the taller guy says as we sit down. 'And this is Greg.'

In return I give them the standard fake names Stella and I use on a night out – Martine and Simone, after characters in our old GCSE French textbook.

They ask what we do and where we live. I tell them we run our own fashion label and live in one of the really cool converted warehouses over by the canal, ignoring Stella's elbow in my ribs as I talk. In return, Miles tells us that he and Greg work in sports PR and are here in Rushton on business.

'Do you know anyone famous?' Stella asks.

Miles reels off a ton of household names – footballers and rugby players and Olympic athletes. I consider telling him about Audrey but change my mind. Now maybe isn't the best time for bringing up thirteen-year-old little sisters.

I clock Miles's watch and decide it's probably worth more than Mum's motorbike. I grab a menu and point out the cocktail Stella was talking about earlier, the one with edible gold flakes in it. The Gold Digga.

'We were thinking of trying one of these next,' I say.

'I like your style,' Miles says, nodding approvingly.

'What can I say, I have very expensive taste.'

He laughs and I realize his hand is resting on the small of my back.

'Mia,' Stella hisses. 'Loo. Now.'

'Excuse us,' I say. 'We'll be right back.'

'What the hell are you playing at?' Stella asks as we squeeze into a cubicle together.

As cool as Flux is, the toilets are disgusting, the floor soaking wet and covered in wads of soggy toilet paper.

'What are you talking about?' I ask, pulling down my knickers and hovering over the toilet seat.

'Why are you flirting with them like that?'

'Like what?'

'You know what I mean. Letting Miles touch you and stuff.'

'Oh, come on, it's not like he's got his hand down my knickers or anything. He's just being friendly.'

'They're old enough to be our dads!'

'Hardly,' I bluff. 'Can you pass me some loo roll please?'

Stella rips off a few sheets and hands them to me.

'They're harmless,' I say. 'More importantly, they're loaded.'

I flush the loo and we swap places.

'I just feel funny about it,' she says, her skirt hitched up round her thighs.

'Oh, come on, you let blokes buy you drinks all the time at the Cuckoo Club.'

'That's different. I know where I am there.'

'Oh, Stells, please don't wuss out on me now. Just let them buy us another couple of drinks. I haven't got my buzz on yet.'

Who cares if they're kind of old and ever so slightly creepy? I'm having a good time and nothing on earth is going to persuade me to stop now.

Stella isn't saying anything.

Time to pull out my trump card.

'Miles has promised us the cocktail with gold flakes in it,' I say.

As I knew she would, Stella lights up like a Christmas tree. 'Really? But they cost a fortune.'

'Like I said, they're loaded. It's a no-brainer, Stells, I'm telling you.'

'OK,' she says. 'Just promise me you won't leave me alone with Greg. It's creeping me out the way he doesn't say anything.'

'Fine,' I say, rolling my eyes.

Stella can be *so* dramatic sometimes.

By the time we return, Miles and Greg have bought a round of Gold Diggas as promised. I pick one up and hold it up to the light. I can just about make out the flakes of gold mingling with the champagne bubbles. I finish it in three gulps, loving the slight sting as the liquid slides down my throat.

'I'm impressed,' Miles says.

'Good,' I reply.

He leans in. 'You're a very sexy girl, Martine,' he says, his breath tickling my ear. 'Did you know that?'

My stomach does a flip-flop. Not because I fancy him, because I don't. But because it feels so good to hear those words again, to get that kind of validation, to know I haven't lost my touch. It makes me want more.

More drinks.

More dancing.

More compliments.

More of everything.

We alternate drinking with dancing, stumbling back and forth between the bar, downing assorted cocktails in a few gulps, before returning to the dance floor. How many Gold Diggas have I drunk? I haven't a clue. All I know is that they taste amazing. Better still, they make me feel amazing. Like I could rule the world.

Another round of drinks.

Down in one.

Another in my hand. Like magic almost.

Stella is pulling at my arm, shouting in my ear. I can't hear her, though. It's too loud.

I shake her off. I go to leave the glass on the edge of the bar but I miss and it falls, smashing on the floor, the glass splintering into dozens of tiny pieces. I shrug and push my way back towards the dance floor, Miles right behind me.

I'd forgotten how much I love to dance, how good it makes me feel. Tonight it feels especially good, like all my limbs and organs are made of hot liquid and I'm sort of melting into the dance floor.

I jump on Miles's back.

'What are you doing?' he asks, laughing.

I ignore him and hitch one leg over his shoulder, then the other.

I love being up so high, floating above everyone's heads, like an angel. The entire time I'm laughing, harder than I have in ages. Because everything is beautiful and amazing. And so am I.

Stella is shouting at me to get down, tugging at my ankle, but I don't care. She can shout all she likes. I can do what I want.

I stretch out my arms. 'I'm the king of the world!' I yell.

Beneath me, Miles staggers about as he struggles to keep his balance. Then we're falling, the floor rushing to meet us.

We land hard but I don't feel a thing.

I just roll onto my back and laugh and laugh and laugh.

18

I want to die.

It's the only option.

Everything hurts.

My head, my stomach, my arms, my legs, my back.

Even breathing hurts.

I dare to open my eyes. This is easier said than done because they're glued together with a thick layer of gooey sleep and it hurts to even lift my arms off the mattress to wipe them clean. When I finally do I'm surprised to find myself looking at the familiar crack on my bedroom ceiling.

Hang on a second, why am I not at Stella's?

I tentatively turn my head to the left. The room is empty. The silver dress is hanging neatly over the back of my swivel chair, Stella's studded shoes tucked beneath it. I pluck up the energy to peek under the duvet. I'm wearing yesterday's knickers and my 'It's All About Mia' T-shirt.

What am I doing here? I seem to remember lots of noise, maybe even shouting. Did Stella and I argue? Is that why I didn't stay over?

Too many questions. They make my head ache even more than it already is.

I close my eyes and try to put everything I remember in order. I get as far as the cocktail with gold flakes in it that reminded me of a snow globe I had when I was little. But then what? After that it all goes blank. It's like that section of the evening has been wiped clean away. The sensation should feel fresh and clean but it feels the opposite – like my brain has been flooded with a thick grey fog.

I can hear people moving about downstairs, the buzz of the kitchen radio, the 'pop' of our ancient toaster.

A wave of dread washes over me, pinning me to the mattress. How drunk must I have been not to even remember leaving the bar? A lot drunk, that's how much.

An image crashes into my brain.

A car.

Yes! I remember being in a car; lying on the back seat and seeing the moon, big and full and yellow, through flickering eyelids.

But whose car?

Mum and Dad's?

Please God, no. I'll be grounded for life, especially after what happened on New Year's Eve. I get a flashback to the dark weeks of January and February, the disapproving looks I got every time I walked into the room, the constant phone calls and texts once I was finally allowed out again. Only this time it would be worse, way worse.

Why can't I remember? If I had the strength, I'd punch the wall in frustration.

I can hear a distant beeping. My phone. Of course, I should just ring Stella. She was there, she can tell me what happened. Maybe it wasn't so bad. Maybe I just got a taxi home and crept quietly up to bed. But why would I do that and risk Mum and Dad seeing me drunk when I'd already arranged to stay at Stella's?

I reach for my mobile phone but it's not on the bedside table where I usually leave it to charge. Instead, there's a pint glass of water, two aspirin and a folded-up piece of paper with 'Mia' written on it in unfamiliar handwriting. I open it up.

Hey,
Hope you slept OK. I told your parents you didn't feel well and so came home early this morning from Stella's.
Sam x

I read the note twice, my useless brain aching with confusion, then prop myself up on one wobbly elbow and down the water and aspirin.

I trace my beeping phone to my handbag on the floor at the end of the bed. It takes me three attempts to reach it. As I flop back on my pillows, a series of pictures explode in my head in quick succession like a film trailer on fast-forward.

A glass smashing.

A security guard standing over me.

Stella crying.

Being carried down a long corridor.

The cold night air hitting my legs.

I try to join the dots but the gaps are just too wide and the dots keep moving.

My phone is almost out of battery. With trembling fingers I plug it in to charge. I have seven missed calls, five voicemails, three texts and ten WhatsApp messages, all from Stella. Without listening to or checking any of them, I call her back.

She answers after one ring.

'Thank God for that!' she cries. 'Why haven't you been answering your phone? I thought you were dead or something!'

'Dead?' My voice is torn to shreds.

'Yes!'

'Why would I be dead?' Ow, ow, ow. Every word makes me feel like my throat is being attacked with industrial-strength sandpaper.

'Are you actually kidding me, Mia?'

'No.'

I tell her the dribs and drabs I've managed to cling on to.

'That's it?' she says. 'That's all you've got?'

'Yeah.'

She sighs heavily.

'Stells, what happened?' I repeat, a wave of dread rippling up my body.

'Where should I start?' she says, her voice thick with sarcasm.

'The cocktail,' I say. 'The one with the bits of gold in it.'

According to Stella I drank at least five of them ('like they were Ribena or something'). And that was only the beginning.

'I kept telling you to slow down,' Stella says. 'But you wouldn't listen. It was like you were on this crazy mission. And that Miles guy didn't help. He just kept buying you drinks and telling me to stop being a "such a spoilsport". Then all of a sudden you went completely floppy. It was like your bones were made out of mush, Mia. And I was so bloody scared. It was like New Year's Eve all over again, but worse because we were all by ourselves and in that massive club so far away from everything. I thought they'd drugged you or something. And I was hitting you round the face and stuff and trying to get you to wake up but you wouldn't even open your eyes. And then fucking Miles was saying he was going to put you in a taxi.'

My heart starts to beat very fast.

'I told him that wouldn't work because you were staying at mine, and he just kept telling me to stop worrying and that we could sort all that out later which I knew was all bullshit because he didn't even ask for my address.'

'And?' I say. 'Then what?'

I realize I'm whispering.

I realize I'm scared.

And not just because of the trouble I might be in. I'm scared of what I can't remember, of the memory of Miles's hands on my body and what might have come next.

'By this point the woman with the clipboard had appeared

163

and was being all pissy about you being in such a state in her precious club, and Miles was saying he was going to take you home. He picked you up and was heading for the exit, and I was screaming at him and telling the woman to stop him, but by then I was really drunk too and crying and my words were all coming out in a muddle and I wasn't making any sense and Miles kept talking over me, sounding all sober, and telling her that he had it under control, and she seemed to believe him, that you were with him and it was OK. And shit, Mia, I was so scared he was going to leave there with you and I'd never see you again, but then the clipboard woman was saying she was going to call the police if I didn't stop making such a fuss, and that must have spooked Miles and Greg because suddenly they just bolted, like one minute they were there and then they weren't. And that's when I called Grace.'

'You did what?' I cry, finally finding some volume.

'I had to, Mia! Flux were about to call the police on us!'

'Jesus, Stella.'

'Don't get snarky with me. You're the one who got so drunk you couldn't even stand up. What was I supposed to do?'

Silence.

'Exactly. So anyway, I called Grace but Sam answered instead and said he'd come get us.'

'Sam?'

I glance at the note. Things are slowly starting to make sense.

'Yeah. Grace was asleep so he picked up instead and said

he'd come get us. He was there in less than twenty minutes, Mia. I swear, he must have driven sooooooo fast.'

'Then what?'

'Sam wanted to take you to hospital but I literally begged him not to because I knew they'd probably want to ring your mum and dad. He only agreed when you came round and chucked up for about a minute straight.'

I close my eyes.

'The door people were being all shitty about it, making out they were going to try and bill you for vomming all over their fancy upholstery or some shit like that, and that's when Sam went mental at them, asking them why they were selling alcohol to sixteen-year-old girls in the first place and demanding to speak to the manager about their admission policies.'

'Shit.'

'I know. If he hadn't been there we'd have been screwed.'

A fresh wave of fear hits me. 'Does that mean Grace knows?' I whisper. Because if she does, there's no way she won't tell Mum and Dad.

'I dunno,' Stella says. 'Sam didn't say much in the car.'

There's a pause.

'I told you those blokes were bad news,' she says. 'I told you, Mia, and you wouldn't listen. You just kept saying you were having a good time, and the next thing I knew you were a total vegetable.' She bursts into tears.

I shut my eyes in an attempt to block out the guilt that's attacking my entire body. Stella may be a drama queen but she only cries when she's really upset.

'You're just so bloody selfish sometimes, Mia,' she continues, her voice all jerky.

'I'm sorry. I was drunk. You know what I'm like when I get drunk.'

'That doesn't make it OK. That's not your get-out-of-jail-free card, you know. I was really fucking worried.'

Her crying has been replaced with hiccups. It makes me want to hug her, to put things right somehow.

'I'm sorry,' I repeat, meaning it. 'I didn't want to worry you, I swear.'

She doesn't answer, just blows her nose loudly down the line. I chew on my tatty fingernails and wait.

'How are you feeling anyway?' she asks finally.

'Like my head's been stamped on.'

'Good,' she says.

It's not really very funny, but we laugh anyway. It hurts.

'He was really angry then?' I say. 'Sam?'

'Yeah. With the Flux people though, not with you. He was really sweet with you.'

A flashback. Sam rubbing my back as I threw up out of the window of his car. *'There you go, that's it, get it all out.'*

Another. Sam scooping me up like a baby, and carrying me up the stairs, my feet catching on the rungs of the banister.

I peek under the covers again, at my T-shirt and knickers. I vaguely remember holding my arms up over my head like I used to when I was a little kid, and something soft and clean-smelling slipping over my torso. I sniff my T-shirt. It smells of washing powder.

166

I can hear footsteps on the stairs.

'Stells, I've got to go.'

'OK. Ring me later?'

'Will do.'

'I'm glad you're OK, Mia.'

'Me too.'

'I'm still mad with you.'

'OK.'

I hang up and pretend to be asleep until the footsteps have passed my door and disappeared into the bathroom.

The next time I open my eyes, the light in the room has changed and over an hour has passed. My conversation with Stella feels like it happened in a dream.

Thirsty and desperate for the loo, I force myself to get out of bed. In addition to the series of small smudgy bruises on both legs, there's a massive monster bruise on my right outer thigh, purple and painful. I poke it with my finger and wince. I pull on an old pair of jogging bottoms I used to wear for PE and dare to venture onto the landing. In the bathroom I pee for ages. According to the chart that has been sellotaped to the tiles for as long as I can remember, I'm firmly in the 'dehydrated' range.

Gingerly, I head downstairs in search of water and carbs. Mum is in the kitchen, tapping away at her laptop. I can smell Dad's famous jerk chicken in the oven. Audrey is at the kitchen table, homework spread out in front of her. Out in the garden, I can see Grace in downward dog position, her belly almost grazing the lawn.

'You OK, sweetheart?' Mum asks, confirming my hunch she doesn't know what happened. 'Sam said you were feeling poorly.'

My body floods with relief. She doesn't know!

She places the back of her hand on my forehead. It feels nice to have her attention for once, and for a second I almost wish I had the flu or something for real.

'You don't have a temperature,' she observes.

'It's a stomach thing,' I say quickly, hoping Sam hasn't been too specific about my symptoms. 'Maybe a virus.' I reach for a glass from the cupboard.

'There's been a lot of that going around,' Mum says. 'Here, you sit down, I'll do that.'

She takes the glass from my hand and fills it up with water from the filter jug. I don't protest, sitting down at the table opposite Audrey, who is looking at me oddly, her head tilted to one side.

'What?' I ask.

She just shakes her head and returns to her homework. A few minutes later Grace wanders in from the garden, her rolled-up yoga mat tucked under her arm, her cheeks flushed.

'Gorgeous day,' she declares, propping the mat up against the side of the fridge and reaching for a banana from the fruit bowl. She notices me at the table, hunched over my water and the dry toast Mum insisted on fixing me when all I really want is a greasy old McDonald's breakfast. I brace myself for her full repertoire of disapproval; the stare, the raised eyebrow of disappointment, the sad shake of the head, but instead she just smiles and says, 'How you doing? Sam said you weren't feeling well.'

'Oh, a bit better, thanks,' I stammer.

'That's good,' she says, peeling the skin off her banana and humming.

'Where *is* Sam?' I ask.

'He's at work,' Grace says. 'Why?'

'No reason.'

Dad comes in from washing the car, his jeans and T-shirt damp and soapy. 'I hope Sam doesn't mind but I gave his a quick going over too,' he says. 'Some dirty bugger was sick all down his passenger door last night.'

Mum groans. 'Some people really are animals, aren't they?' she says.

'Disgusting,' Grace agrees, pulling a face.

I look down and concentrate really hard on my toast.

19

The rest of my day is spent in bed, drifting in and out of sleep. I ring Stella again but she doesn't answer.

I go through my phone. Of the hundreds of photos I took last night, only a handful are in focus. Miles and Greg look older than I remember, closer to forty than thirty. I delete every one they're in.

In order to add authenticity to my fake stomach bug, I miss dinner, sneaking some cake offcuts and a bag of crisps up to my bedroom while no one is looking, trying not to swoon over the jerk chicken smells floating up the stairs.

I take a long bath, staring up at the peeling paint on the ceiling as I lie in the water. I stay in the tub so long the pads of my fingers and undersides of my feet grow all wrinkly and spongy to the touch.

When I come out of the bathroom I walk slap bang into Sam. He's wearing the tartan pyjama bottoms he wears to breakfast most mornings, and nothing on top apart from a towel draped over his left shoulder. He isn't wearing his glasses and has pale grey rings under both eyes.

'I thought you were working today,' I blurt.

'I was. I finished at six.'

'Oh.'

I re-adjust the towel under my arms.

'How's the head?'

'Not great,' I admit.

'I suspected as much.'

I look over his shoulder. Grace's bedroom door is slightly ajar.

I beckon for him to follow me back into the bathroom. He hesitates for a moment before coming with me. Once inside, I lock the door.

'Sorry,' I say. 'Just a bit paranoid Grace might hear us.'

The room is hot and steamy from my bath and feels very small with both of us in it. I perch on the lowered toilet seat. Sam sits on the edge of the bath. The tattoo on his bicep reveals itself to be a tiny flock of birds. His body is pretty good, better than I thought it would be. I bet he grew up doing loads of sports – rugby and rowing and stuff. Posh sports.

'OK, two things,' I say. 'Number one, how did I get undressed last night?'

'Audrey helped me out,' Sam says.

Thank God. 'Number two, I, er, wanted to say thanks. You know, for coming to get me last night. Oh, and for not telling Grace.'

'About that,' Sam says. 'I'm really not comfortable about keeping this from her, Mia.'

'What? Why not?' I ask in a panic.

'She's my girlfriend. And you're her little sister. It just wouldn't be right.'

'But you can't tell Grace!' I cry. 'She'll tell Mum and Dad and they'll go mad. I won't be able to leave the house all summer.'

Which means no summer parties, no long lazy days at the lido, and definitely no Newquay.

'She won't necessarily tell,' Sam says. 'What if we explained?'

'Explained what?' I ask. 'That I went to a nightclub and some random old bloke got me totally trashed? That's hardly going to persuade her to keep the information to herself, is it?'

'She might understand.'

'No she won't. You know what Grace is like, she expects everyone to be as perfect as her.'

He winces slightly.

'You don't get it,' I mutter, frowning at the bruises on my legs. 'You're not her sister.'

I can sense him looking at me, really looking at me, like he's peeling back the layers and peering into my brain. It makes me feel weird, exposed. I go to stand up.

'Oh shit, your ankle's bleeding.'

I look. Blood is dribbling down my foot. I must have cut myself shaving. I rip off a few sheets of toilet paper and use them to soak the blood up.

'You need a plaster,' Sam says, jumping up and rifling in the medicine cabinet above the sink.

172

'It's fine. It'll probably stop in a minute.'

'Trust me,' he says, grinning over his shoulder. 'I'm a doctor.'

'Not yet.'

'A-ha!' he says, turning round, a box of Disney plasters in his hand.

'Oh my God, those are ancient,' I say.

Grace and I used to argue over the *Little Mermaid* ones. Or rather I did. Grace was always the martyr who backed down and let me have first choice, always taking care to make sure Mum or Dad were there to witness her selflessness.

Sam kneels on the bath mat and opens up the box. Two plasters flutter out.

'I can offer you,' he says, pausing to peer at them, 'Mulan or Pumba.'

'Mulan,' I say.

He nods and peels off the back of the plaster.

'It's probably lost its stick,' I say.

He tests it with his index finger. 'Feels OK to me.'

He applies the plaster to my ankle, smoothing it into place with his palm. His hands are warm.

'There,' he says.

'There,' I repeat.

He puts the Pumba plaster back in the box.

'Please don't tell her, Sam,' I say. 'Please. I'm honestly begging you.'

He sits back on his haunches and rakes both hands through his hair. 'I really don't know, Mia.'

173

'Please. I'll do anything you want.'

He thinks for a moment then sighs. 'If I don't tell Grace about this, I need you to promise me something, OK?'

'Anything.'

'You've got to promise me that you're going to stop getting into such a state. I get that you're going to want to drink every now and then, and that's fine, but you couldn't even stand up by the time I got to you last night. What if Stella hadn't been there to help you? What if you'd been all alone?'

'I'd have been OK,' I say.

My words sound hollow though, to both our ears.

'I just want you to be safe, Mia.'

'Why? Why do you even care?'

'Because I like you,' he says simply. 'And you're my girlfriend's little sister and I care about what happens to you.'

Tears prick my eyelids. I bite hard on my lip and will them not to fall. I refuse to cry over something so stupid. After all, what do I care if Sam *likes* me or not? He's just my sister's stupid posh boyfriend.

'Mia, are you crying?'

I shake my head hard. 'No. I'm just feeling a bit overemotional, that's all. It's the hangover.'

'Right,' he says. He doesn't seem convinced, though.

A single tear escapes before I can stop it, rolling determinedly towards my chin. I reach to wipe it away but before my hand can make contact with my cheek, Sam is hugging me.

I resist the natural urge to push him away, and let him

hold me, my face pressed against his bare stomach. He smells of the pub – of spilt beer and greasy food. It's weirdly nice. Comforting.

We've been hugging for maybe thirty seconds when there's a knock at the door. Sam's grip on me loosens instantly.

'Who is it?' I call, my voice all wobbly for some reason.

'It's Grace, Mia. Can I come in? I'm bursting for the loo.'

I glance up at Sam but he's already heading for the door. I wipe away my tears with the corner of my towel and stand up as he opens it.

'Well, this is weird,' Grace says as the door swings open and she takes in the scene in front of her. 'What's going on?' Her tone of voice is light-hearted but her eyes are alert with suspicion.

Sam opens his mouth as if about to reply but no sound comes out.

'What's going on?' Grace repeats, her voice less certain this time, her eyes flicking back and forth between us.

'Nothing,' I say. My voice doesn't sound like it belongs to me, though. It sounds weak, paper-thin.

Grace folds her arms. 'Mia, you're locked in the bathroom with my boyfriend, I think I deserve *some* kind of explanation.'

I open my mouth to respond but the words get stuck in my throat.

Sam sighs heavily and I know exactly what's coming next. I close my eyes and brace myself. So this is it. My summer down the drain.

'We can't tell you what we were doing,' Sam says.

I open my eyes. Huh?

'What do you mean?' Grace asks.

'We can't tell you,' he says, 'because it will ruin the surprise.'

'Surprise?'

'Yes. Mia and I are working on a little special something. For you and Bean.'

'You are?' she says, her mouth quivering upwards into a smile.

'We are,' Sam confirms. 'Right, Mia?'

'Right,' I echo.

There's a pause before Grace bursts out laughing.

'Oh my God, why didn't you just tell me that straight-away? I feel like *such* a dope, barging in here and demanding to know what's going on, like I'm in an episode of *EastEnders* or something. Wow, can I blame it on the hormones?'

Sam puts his arm around her. 'You don't have to blame it on anyone or anything. It's our fault for acting so shifty.'

'So can I have a clue?' Grace asks.

'A clue?' I repeat dumbly.

'Yes. About the surprise.'

'Absolutely not,' Sam says smoothly.

'Spoilsports,' Grace says.

She's smiling though, probably overjoyed because she thinks I'm finally making an effort with Sam, and showing some interest in the baby.

'I still don't see why you felt the need to lock yourselves in the bathroom, though,' she adds.

Sam hesitates and it's my turn to paper over the cracks in our story.

'Oh, come on,' I say. 'Where else are we going to get any privacy? This house is tiny.'

'Point taken,' Grace admits.

There's a pause. No one moves.

'Um, Mia, would you mind?' Grace asks. 'I really *do* need to pee.'

She needs to pee all the time these days.

'Oh right, sure,' I say, backing onto the landing, leaving the two of them together.

'Night, Mia,' she says, shutting the door on me.

'Night,' I murmur.

I'm getting into bed when my phone beeps. It's a text message from an unfamiliar number.

Friends? Sam x

I hesitate before texting back.

Friends. Mx

20

Last lesson of the day the following Friday is Sociology. Our usual teacher is off sick. For a few minutes we all get really excited and think we'll be allowed to go home early, until some bloke we've never seen before sweeps into the classroom and tells us he'll be taking the class. He's wearing a super-ugly tie – red with tiny green frogs embroidered all over it, and announces we're going to spend the lesson practising writing personal statements for our UCAS applications.

'Kill me now,' I whisper to Kimmie, who's sitting on my left.

'The January deadline may seem like it's a long way away,' Ugly Tie Man drones, passing out sheets of lined paper. 'But take it from me, it'll swing round faster than you think.'

Five minutes later, I'm peering over Kimmie's shoulder.

'What are you writing?' I ask.

She's filled an entire side of A4 already whereas I've barely written my name.

'All about my jewellery,' she says.

Kimmie wants to study jewellery design at university and have her own label one day. I crane my neck to try and see exactly what she's written, but she's hunched over her work and all I can make out is the odd word through the gaps in her fingers.

Ugly Tie Man makes his way round the classroom as we work. He stops by our desk and asks to take a look at Kimmie's statement. As he reads, he smiles and nods through his smeared glasses.

'Great stuff,' he says, handing it back. 'Very passionate.'

Kimmie beams.

He cocks his head to one side so he can read my name off the top of my piece of paper.

'Mia,' he says. 'Having a bit of trouble there, are you?'

I shrug.

He pulls up a chair and sits down next to me. I can smell his breath – coffee and Rich Tea biscuits. Classic teacher.

'Let's see if I can't give you a bit of inspiration. How about you start by telling me a bit about your interests, Mia.'

'What kind of interests?' I ask, fiddling with the zip on my pencil case.

'Well, do you play an instrument, Mia? Or do any sport?'

'Nope.'

I played the clarinet for about three weeks in Year 7.

'Are you in any school clubs or societies, Mia?'

I think of Miss Linden bugging me to join the Feminist Society and shake my head again.

'Do you write or draw or paint, Mia? Sew? Bake, maybe?'

God, he's really clutching at straws now. Plus, I hate the way he keeps using my name at the end of every question, like he knows me, knows what I'm about.

'Perhaps you collect something, Mia?'

'Like what? Stamps? I'm not ninety.'

'Do you have a part-time job?'

'I sell sausages,' I mutter.

Owen, who is sitting in front of me, snorts with laughter. I chuck my pen at his head. It bounces off and rolls under the desk. 'Ow!' he cries, clutching his skull with both hands.

'Oh, calm down,' I say. 'It was only a biro.'

Ugly Tie Man retrieves my pen from the floor, setting it down on the desk with a deep frown.

'OK, so you sell sausages, perhaps you can expand on that.'

'There's nothing to say. I. Sell. Sausages. The end.'

'Do you work as part of a team?' he ventures.

I think of smug Jeremy.

'Not really,' I say. 'Look, it's just a stupid Sunday job, OK?'

Ugly Tie Man sighs. 'Please, just help me out here, Mia, and perhaps tell me what you *are* interested in?'

I don't answer.

'Anything you think you're particularly good at?' he prompts.

'Going out with my mates? Having a laugh?'

He sighs again and takes off his glasses. They hang on a long chain round his neck.

'You asked,' I say, my body fizzing with irritation.

'Mia, your personal statement is your chance to sell yourself, do you understand that?'

'Of course I do. I just don't see what playing a musical instrument or baking cakes has to do with any of it.'

'Engagement in extra-curricular activities demonstrates relevant qualities, like resilience, problem solving, leadership, teamwork, creativity, critical thinking,' he says, ticking each of them off on his fingers.

Out of the corner of my eye I can see Kimmie listening in on our exchange. She looks sorry for me. I roll my eyes in an attempt to show her I don't care, but her expression stays the same.

'Mia, you have to see it from the university's point of view,' Ugly Tie Man continues. 'Who are they going to award a place to? The applicant with a full and varied personal statement, or the applicant with nothing to say for herself.'

'Look, I'm not even applying to uni,' I say. 'So this is all pointless anyway.'

'I beg to differ,' he says. 'What about job applications?'

I close my eyes and will him to move on to someone else.

'What is it you think you'd like to do for a living?' he asks. 'Because I dare say there'll be an application process you'll need to go through, whatever path you choose to go down.'

'I don't know yet,' I say through gritted teeth.

181

More people are listening now, turning round in their chairs and leaning in. I wish they'd all just piss off and mind their own business.

Ugly Tie Man frowns. 'Oh, come on, Mia, you must have *some* idea.'

Obviously not. Why can't he just get the message and bloody leave me alone?

He asks me to go through my A-level subjects and tell him why I chose each one.

'I don't know,' I say. 'They just seemed like the subjects I'd be the least rubbish at.'

'You're making my job really hard here, do you know that, Mia?' he says, rubbing his eyes now, like it's paining him to even talk to me.

That's when I finally lose it.

'Look, I didn't ask you come over here and interrogate me,' I explode. 'If I'm such a headache, then why don't you piss off and ask someone else your stupid questions?'

The classroom falls silent while Ugly Tie Man's face turns an unhealthy shade of deep pink.

'Head's office,' he says, standing up and pointing at the door. 'Now.'

'But I'm a sixth former!'

'I don't care,' Ugly Tie Man says. 'I won't be spoken to like that. Take your things and go.'

I screw up my empty sheet of paper and flick it off the edge of the desk before scooping up my bag and stamping out of the classroom. I don't look back.

*

Outside Ms Parish's office, I find Stella, Kimmie and Mikey sitting in a line on the seats outside. It's sweet of them to wait, but they're the last people I want to see right now. What I really want is some time to brood alone.

The second they see me, they jump up.

'What are you guys doing here?' I ask.

'Kimmie told us what happened,' Stella says, swooping in to give me a hug. 'Are you OK?'

'I'm fine,' I say, wriggling out of her embrace. 'The stupid supply teacher just wound me up a bit, that's all. No big deal.'

'Did you get into trouble?' Kimmie asks.

'Nah. Ms Parish was on my side actually, says he was bang out of order speaking to me like that.'

This is a complete lie. Ms Parish gave me a long lecture about respect, and ordered me to deliver a handwritten apology to Ugly Tie Man (whose real name is apparently Mr Montague) first thing on Monday morning.

'Come on,' I say, not wanting to remain on the premises for a second longer than necessary. 'Let's get out of here.'

21

We hang out at Stella's that evening. Her mum is having a girlie night in the living room, forcing us to camp out upstairs, eating kettle chips by the handful and arguing over what to watch on Netflix.

I argue even more enthusiastically than usual, to the point that Mikey, the undisputed reigning king of arguing over what to watch on Netflix, tells me to 'calm the fuck down'. I don't actually give a monkey's about what we watch; it just feels good to let off a little steam.

In the end we decide to watch some old episodes of *Pretty Little Liars* so we can chat over them without having to worry about missing any vital plot points. I'm doing an impression of my favourite character, Aria, when I accidentally knock Kimmie's glass of Diet Coke out of her hand. And of course, because I'm clearly having one of those days, it goes absolutely everywhere – on the duvet, up the walls, on the carpet.

'Mia!' Stella cries, jumping off the bed.

'Sorry,' I say grumpily. 'It was just an accident.'

Stella flies out of the room, returning a minute later armed with two sponges and a bottle of carpet cleaner. While Mikey and Kimmie strip the bed and Stella tackles the walls, I get down on my hands and knees and scrub at the irritatingly cream carpet.

'You're so clumsy sometimes, you know that?' Stella says.

'God, I said I was sorry, what more do you want from me?'

'It better not stain.'

'It won't. It's only Coke.'

She doesn't answer me. I roll my eyes at the back of her head and keep on scrubbing. That's when I notice them, underneath Stella's bed.

A stack of shiny university prospectuses.

They're pushed back quite far so that you'd only see them if you were on your hands and knees. I note the names on the spines – Canterbury Christ Church, Bath Spa, Sheffield Hallam, Manchester Met, etc. It's clear from their dog-eared corners and broken spines they've been read multiple times.

I realize my heart is beating very fast.

I look up. Stella is standing with her back to me, tutting at the wall, even though the Coke has come off just fine.

'What should we do with this?' Kimmie asks, the soiled duvet bundled up in her arms.

Stella turns round. 'Just leave it on the floor. I'll stick it in the wash in a bit.' She glances down at me. 'How's it looking?'

'All gone,' I say, sitting back on my heels.

She nods, although it's clear from her folded arms that she's still annoyed at me.

'Told you it wouldn't stain,' I add quietly.

Part of me wants to say something about what I've just seen, but what if Kimmie and Mikey already know? What if the three of them have already discussed Stella's post-school plans behind my back? A horrible image of them plotting to apply to the same university pops into my head. I imagine them coming back in the holidays, talking incessantly about people I don't know and cracking in-jokes I'll never have any hope of understanding.

Stella rewinds the episode and we all get back onto the bed. Ordinarily I like to quote along with the bitchiest lines, but I'm suddenly not in the mood, glazing over as the others chorus along in their rubbish American accents, wondering exactly when Stella was going to tell me her plans had changed. I think back to the last time we were on the Right Move app, how Stella managed to discount every single property I suggested. The idea that she's been humouring me all this time, just playing along to keep me happy, makes me feel hot and stupid.

Before the next episode kicks in we press pause so Stella can go downstairs to replenish our bowl of kettle chips and put her duvet cover in the washing machine.

'Where are you applying for uni again?' I ask Mikey while she's gone.

Mikey has wanted to study psychology for as long as I can remember.

'Not sure yet. Definitely Sussex,' he says. 'A few others. Why?'

I try to remember if Sussex was one of the universities

featured in the stack of prospectuses under the bed.

I'm about to ask Kimmie the same question when Stella returns with more crisps and a bag of popcorn.

We watch another episode but I can't concentrate. The moment the credits start to roll, I jump off the bed and start searching for my trainers.

'Where are you going?' Stella asks as I sit on the rug and loosen the laces.

'Where do you think? Home.'

'But aren't you staying over?'

'I can't. We have our final dress fitting first thing.'

This is a lie. The fitting isn't until midday.

'My mum could drop you off in the morning,' Stella says.

Her offer coincides with a burst of female laughter from downstairs.

'Like your mum is going to want to do that. Anyway, my mum and dad are expecting me.'

I finish lacing my trainers and stand up.

'Is it about what that teacher said?' Stella asks.

'Of course not,' I snap. 'I didn't even care.'

I'm sort of telling the truth. Because my bad mood isn't entirely about my conversation with Ugly Tie Man. It's also about Kimmie's embarrassment and pity as he grilled me. And Ms Parish's humiliating lecture about what a disappointment I am to the Campbell-Richardson name. And Stella's silence over the hoard of prospectuses under the bed. And the fact that, rolled into one, all these things have made me feel totally and utterly shit about myself.

*

By the time I get home, it's gone ten. I discover my parents sitting on the living-room floor, surrounded by a sea of Post-it notes.

'What are you doing home?' Mum asks in surprise. 'I thought you'd be sleeping over at Stella's.'

'I've got a headache,' I say, flopping down on the sofa behind them.

'You should have called me,' Dad says. 'I would have come to pick you up.'

'I didn't think,' I reply truthfully. Mum and Dad's schedules are so mental I rarely rely on them for lifts anywhere. 'What are you doing?' I ask.

'The table plan,' Mum says. 'It's a bloody nightmare.'

'Why don't you just let everyone sit where they want?' I suggest.

'I'm tempted, believe me,' Mum replies. 'But I think that might just give your grandmother a heart attack. You know how she is.'

This is true. Grandma Jules (Mum's mum) is just about the most organized person on earth and regularly despairs at the state of our messy house.

'Come on, Nikki, hang on in there, we're so close,' Dad says.

'No thanks to your family,' Mum replies. She turns to me. 'Did you know Great-auntie Joyce isn't speaking to Great-auntie Winnie?'

'No. Why?' I have about a thousand great-aunts on Dad's side.

'Apparently Winnie booked tickets to see *The Bodyguard*:

The Musical on tour and didn't ask Joyce along and Joyce took offence,' Mum says. 'Fair enough perhaps if this happened last week, but it was *two years ago*. And now I'm having to give up *my* Friday night moving Post-it notes around so neither of *them* feel "uncomfortable" on *my* wedding day!'

'Shouldn't that be *our* wedding day?' Dad suggests, a mischievous glint in his eye.

'Oh, shut up, you, you know what I mean,' Mum says, poking him in the belly.

'Do I now?' Dad leans in and kisses her on the cheek and, before I know it, they're full-on snogging, Post-it notes sticking to their clothes as they roll about on the carpet giggling.

'I'll be leaving then,' I say, heaving myself off the sofa.

Mum and Dad stop kissing and look up at me, surprised.

'You don't have to,' Mum says.

I make a face. As if I'm going to stick around to watch while my parents dry hump on the living-room carpet. 'I'm tired anyway,' I say.

'OK, sweetheart. There're pills in the medicine cabinet if you need one.'

'Sorry?'

'For your headache.'

'Oh, right. Thanks.'

'Night, darling.'

'Yeah, night.'

22

After the dress fitting on Saturday, instead of going home with Mum, Grace and Audrey, I head to meet Sam at Waterside. Ever since she caught us together in the bathroom last weekend Grace has been asking constantly about the 'surprise' we have planned for her and the baby, piling on the pressure for us to come up with something decent.

'Six quid for two pairs of socks that look like they could barely fit on my thumb?' I say. 'Are they having a laugh?'

'Very possibly,' Sam admits. 'Although you have to admit these definitely have the "aw" factor.'

I pull a face. I've never understood why people get all gooey about baby clothes. They're just little, that's all. We've been in the baby-clothing department of John Lewis for over thirty minutes now and I'm slowly losing the will to live.

I put the socks back and pick up a pair of denim dunga-rees. 'How come you haven't found out whether it's a boy or a girl?' I ask, looking at the price tag and quickly returning the dungarees to the rail.

'We want a surprise,' Sam says.

We. Ugh.

'*I'd* want to know,' I say.

'Really?'

'Of course.'

'You don't like surprises?'

'Only if they're good.'

'Call me cheesy if you want,' Sam says. 'But I really want to experience that magic moment where the midwife looks up and says "it's a girl" or "it's a boy", like they do on TV.'

'What do you want?' I ask, picking up an embroidered sunhat that fits almost perfectly on my fist.

'I honestly don't mind,' Sam says. 'As long as it's healthy.'

I mime a yawn. 'I *knew* you were going to say that. Come on, don't be such a boring cliché. You must want one more than the other.' I pause. 'I won't tell Grace,' I add in a sing-song voice.

Sam glances behind him as if he expects Grace suddenly to leap out from behind the display of dribble bibs like a trained sniper.

'OK,' he says. 'But you can't tell Grace I said this . . .'

'Cross my heart.'

'. . . but I'd secretly quite like a boy.'

'I knew it!' I cry, stabbing him in the chest with my index finger. 'I know you were lying when you said you didn't mind.'

'I'd love a girl too, of course I would, but . . . I don't

know, I've just always had this stupid fantasy about having a son I can impart all my "manly" wisdom to. I suppose there's a part of me as well that wants to do right all the things my dad did so wrong. Does that make sense?'

'I guess so.'

We drift into the toy department. I gravitate towards a huge wooden box filled with cuddly toys.

'So how about you?' Sam asks, absentmindedly playing with the ears of a pale grey bunny rabbit. 'Do you want a niece or a nephew?'

'God, I don't care,' I say, digging to the bottom of the box, tossing aside teddy bears and stuffed monkeys. 'Half the time you can't tell the difference anyway.'

'You think?'

'Yeah. Until they start walking and talking and stuff, all babies are basically just dribbly lumps.'

'Harsh words.'

'But true.'

Sam crouches down to pick up the cuddly toys I've rejected, gathering them up in his arms.

'Yes!' I cry.

'What?' he asks, straightening up.

'Found one.'

'Found what?'

'A lizard. Look!' I found him at the very bottom of the box, the lone reptile.

'Are you sure he's not a crocodile?' Sam asks.

'No. Look at its tongue.' I thrust the lizard in Sam's face. 'See. One hundred per cent lizard.'

'But why lizards?'

'Because. Lizards hardly *ever* get to be cuddly toys. They're the total underdog of the cuddly toy world.'

'You gonna buy him for Bean, then?' he asks.

The mention of the baby throws me, reminding me why we're actually here. I hesitate, holding out the lizard so it's facing me, its red felt tongue dangling out of its mouth hopefully.

'Nah. It'll get a ton of cuddly toys when it's born,' I say, shoving it back on the pile.

We continue round the toy department, struggling to find anything unique enough to warrant a secret bathroom meeting.

'How about a baby shower?' I suggest eventually. 'That's what they always do on the reality TV shows I watch.'

'That's a brilliant idea!' Sam says, chucking his arm round my shoulder. 'Mia, you're a genius! We can do it in August, after the wedding.'

We abandon John Lewis and head to the massive twenty-four-hour Tesco superstore. I usually hate supermarkets, but shopping with Sam is actually kind of fun, even if it is all for Grace's benefit, and for a bit I forget about how horrible yesterday was. It probably helps that we're buying fun stuff – bunting and banners and balloons – and that Sam (who has already offered to pay for everything) lets me put whatever I want in the trolley, no questions asked. I sit cross-legged in the bottom and shout out orders as he steers. A couple of other shoppers throw us disapproving looks, but we ignore them, Sam pushing me even faster down the wide aisles, jumping on the back of the trolley so it almost tips up.

In the party aisle, as we argue over what colour napkins to buy, I find myself wondering if this is what it would be like to have a big brother. I'm so *used* to sisters, to living in a house so full of oestrogen you can almost see it in the air – pink neon sparks crackling like lightning. All I know is, it's nice to hang out with an older boy and not feel the need to flirt or show off or act sexy. It just feels, I don't know, easy and relaxed. Nice.

The feeling doesn't last long.

We're heading for the checkouts when I see them.

Jordan and his mum.

They have their backs to me, but I know it's them right away. They're loading their shopping into bags. Jordan's wearing the maroon hoodie he used to drape round my shoulders when I got cold. I swallow hard. It's the first time I've seen him in the flesh since we broke up. With him suddenly only metres away from me, it seems miraculous I haven't run into him before now – Rushton isn't a small town but it isn't a particularly big one either. I'm suddenly very aware of the fact I haven't had a shower or bothered to put on eyeliner or cover up the spots on my forehead or do anything to my hair, which is currently in two wonky bushy pigtails on either side of my head. Not to mention the fact I'm sitting cross-legged in the bottom of a shopping trolley like a little kid.

'This one?' Sam asks, about to steer into the checkout next to theirs.

'No,' I say in a low voice. 'Let's try further down.'

I dare to peek over my shoulder as we pass. Jordan is stuffing a Kellogg's Variety Pack into a bag for life. He likes Coco Pops the best, he once confessed. I remember finding his childish taste in breakfast cereal cute at the time. What a sucker.

'What are you looking at?' Sam asks.

'Nothing,' I say, facing forwards.

'That boy?'

'No.'

'Who is he? Do you like him?' Sam teases, tugging on one of my pigtails.

I bat him away. 'He's my ex.'

'Oops. Sorry.'

'Don't be. It's not a big deal. I just wasn't expecting to see him, that's all.'

'Fair enough.'

I can't relax though, not until Sam is able to report Jordan and his mum have definitely left the building.

I'm still in a funny mood when we leave the shop ten minutes later, laden with bags, my eyes automatically scanning the car park for Jordan's mum's Mini.

'You hungry?' Sam asks. 'Maccy Ds drive-in? My treat.'

'Grace hates McDonald's,' I say, as we park up again shortly afterwards, removing our seatbelts and unwrapping our food on our laps.

'Why do you think I suggested it?' Sam asks. 'I've been craving a Big Mac ever since I arrived in Rushton.' He sinks his teeth into his burger and sighs with pleasure.

'Does she email you links to articles about thirty-year-old hamburgers that still haven't decomposed?' I ask.

'Yes!' Sam says. 'All the time. I thought I was the only one.'

'Nope. She's being doing it to me for years.'

We laugh.

I peel the bun off my cheeseburger and remove the two slithers of gherkin.

'You not eating those?' Sam asks.

'Uh-uh. Gherkins are rank.'

'Sacrilege! They're the food of the gods!'

I flick them into his burger box.

'So, do you want to talk about it?' Sam asks, arranging the gherkins on top of his patty.

'What?'

'The guy in Tesco.'

'Jordan? Not especially.'

'You sure?'

I hesitate. It's weird, because part of me *does* want to talk to Sam about Jordan. I haven't really talked about him to anyone, not even Stella and the others.

'There's nothing really to say,' I say eventually. 'We went out, then we broke up. Isn't that how most relationships go?'

'Who called time on things?'

'Me.'

'Do you regret it?'

I shake my head hard.

'But you still miss him, right?'

I pick up a napkin and begin to shred it into ribbons. Do

I miss Jordan? Most of the time we were going out, I wasn't even sure if I liked him. We only really got together because that was what was expected of us. I was cool and popular, and so was he. People had been shipping the two of us as a couple since Year 9. Getting together was just a matter of time. But it never felt right. For a start we argued all the time, about anything and everything. But it wasn't just that. I kept waiting to feel something more, the stuff they describe in books – fireworks and butterflies. But I never did. I just figured maybe I'd never be one of those girls who just 'fell in love'.

I realize Sam is still waiting for my answer.

'I dunno if I miss him. Does it sound really messed up if I say I want him still to be heartbroken over me? Even if I don't necessarily want him back?'

'No, I don't think so. In fact, I think that's probably a pretty natural response. When did you guys break up?'

'The beginning of May.'

'Were you together a long time?'

'A bit less than a year,' I say, shrugging. 'I just hadn't bargained on him getting a new girlfriend so quickly, you know.'

'It'll get easier. You do know that, don't you, Mia?'

'I suppose so. I just wish it would hurry up . . . You won't tell Grace about any of this, will you?'

'Not if you don't want me to.'

'Thanks.'

'Can I ask why?'

'I just don't like her knowing my business,' I say.

197

'How come?'

I don't really know. I used to tell her everything. I'm not quite sure when I stopped. I don't think it was really like that. It wasn't like there was ever a big betrayal or argument or anything that marked the breakdown in communication. It was more of a slow fade. If I was forced to pinpoint when things started to change though, it would have to be when I started at Queen Mary's. The teachers' eyes would light up the moment they realized I was Grace's little sister, their excitement dissolving the moment they cottoned on to the fact a shared surname is pretty much all we had in common. It was different when we were little kids, back when things like grades didn't matter so much, but with us both at Queen Mary's, the differences between us were impossible to escape.

Grace is clever, I am not.

Grace is good, I am not.

Grace is going places, I am not.

'It's complicated,' I say eventually.

I'm relieved when Sam doesn't push me on it.

23

That night Mum and Dad are off on their respective hen and stag dos. Mum is going to a pole-dancing class (cringe), followed by tapas, while Dad is going on a pub crawl. They have the monopoly on the bathroom, which means I don't get the chance to finally have a shower until gone six. By the time I'm done, I have to start getting ready to go to Paul's next door. I'm about to pull on my usual babysitting 'uniform' (tracksuit bottoms and a T-shirt), when I find myself reaching for my denim mini skirt and a black vest top instead, and taking extra care with my hair and makeup.

'You look nice,' Grace says when I stick my head behind the living-room door to say goodbye. She and Audrey are sitting on the sofa watching a nature programme about penguins. 'Where are you going again?'

'Next-door. I'm babysitting.'

'Bit dressed up, aren't you?'

'I'd hardly call a denim skirt and a vest top dressed up,' I say. 'It's a hot night, what am I supposed to wear?'

Grace points the remote control at the TV to turn down the volume. 'What is with you today, Mia? You've been moody since the second you got up.'

'Er, no I haven't.'

'Yes you have. You were miserable as sin at the fitting earlier.'

'No I wasn't. I just don't see why you need to make snarky comments about what I'm wearing.'

'There's kind of a big difference between being snarky and making an observation.'

'Yeah, well, it doesn't feel like it sometimes.'

She sighs. 'Look, I'm sorry if it felt like a criticism; it wasn't meant to be. You look really nice.'

I inspect my fingernails. The mint-green polish is all chipped.

'So how was shopping with Sam?' she asks. 'You guys have fun?' With Sam at work tonight, she's been bugging me for clues ever since I got home.

'I told you, fine.'

'I love how close you two have become.'

'We're hardly BFFs,' I mutter, wrinkling my nose.

Grace just smiles this incredibly annoying smile, like she's somehow masterminded some deep friendship between Sam and me.

'I'm gonna go,' I say, backing out of the room.

'OK, night,' Grace says, her eyes still lingering on my skirt.

'Night,' Audrey echoes, looking worried for some reason.

*

'Mia, you're early,' Paul says when he opens the door. I guess he's just finished in the bathroom because he smells strongly of minty shower gel and has a smear of shaving cream on his neck.

'Do you want me to go away and come back?' I ask.

'Of course not,' he says, smiling. 'Come on in.' He steps aside to let me pass.

Duncan is already in his bedroom from the sounds of it, the faint noise of explosions and gunshots just audible from where I'm standing at the bottom of the stairs.

I step out of my flip-flops and follow Paul into the living room where I perch on the edge of the sofa while he fastens on a pair of silver cufflinks.

Paul's house has the exact same layout as ours, only it's the opposite way round and about a thousand times tidier. Paul has a cleaner who comes every Monday afternoon. I see her sometimes when I get home from school – a squat Portuguese woman with silver-streaked black hair, vacuuming the curtains or polishing the TV. All of Paul's furniture and decor is brand-new and what Mum would probably describe as 'tasteful' with a wrinkle of her nose. The sofa I'm sitting on is an L-shaped chocolate-brown corduroy number, dotted with coordinating scatter cushions and a cream cashmere throw. A flat screen TV, three times the size of ours, is mounted on the opposite wall and the lights are artfully dimmed, bathing the entire room in a soft romantic glow. Being at Paul's is the closest I'll probably ever get to stepping inside a Galaxy Bar commercial.

'Off anywhere nice?' I ask.

'Work do,' Paul replies.

I realize I have no idea what Paul does for a living, only that he wears a suit, drives a company car and earns enough money to have a cleaner, the latest iPhone and weekly Ocado deliveries.

'A work do on a Saturday?' I ask.

'It's the company's fiftieth anniversary. The CEO is taking the entire staff out for dinner.'

'Does that mean you don't have to pay for anything?' I ask.

'That's right.'

'Drinks and everything?'

'As far as I know.'

'Nice.'

'Dangerous, more like.' Paul's phone bleeps. 'Excuse me,' he says, picking it up off the coffee table. There's a pause as he taps at the screen, before sliding it into the back pocket of his trousers.

I like his outfit; a powder-blue shirt teamed with well-cut grey trousers. Grownup but not too stuffy.

'Paul, can I ask you something?' The question leaves my lips before I can stop it.

'Of course you can,' he says, sitting down on the sofa beside me. 'What's up?'

'Er, OK, this might sound stupid, but what did you want to be when you were in sixth form?'

Even though I've tried to shove it to the back of my mind, yesterday's showdown with Ugly Tie Man keeps invading my thoughts.

'I never made it to sixth form,' Paul says.

'You didn't?'

'No. I left school at sixteen with four GCSEs to my name.'

'Really?'

'Yep. A combination of undiagnosed dyslexia and spending too much time showing off in front of my mates.'

'But you've got a really good job,' I say.

'Well, yeah, but that's now, twenty-four years on. There's been a lot of hard graft in between.'

I do the maths in my head. That means Paul is forty.

He tells me all about his first job, how he started out selling printer cartridges over the phone before rising up through the ranks. It's a bit boring to be honest and I switch off after a while, glazing over as he reminisces.

'And now I'm sales director for the entire region,' he says, puffing out his chest.

'Wow, sounds great,' I say automatically.

'Why'd you ask, Mia? Something bothering you?'

I find myself telling him about my confrontation with Ugly Tie Man. I hadn't planned to at all, but it actually feels good to get it off my chest and have someone listen patiently and nod and make sympathetic noises in all the right places.

'He just made me feel so stupid and, I don't know, insubstantial almost,' I say. 'Like there's nothing more to me than big hair and attitude.'

Paul sits back and folds his arms. 'Now, Mia, come on, your hair isn't *that* big.'

It takes me a second to realize he's making a joke, albeit

a *very* lame one. 'Are you taking the piss?' I ask, poking him on the bicep and noting its firmness.

'Only a little bit,' he says, grinning.

I stick out my lower lip in an exaggerated pout.

'Seriously though, Mia,' he says, swapping his grin for a straight face. 'You can't let wallies like this supply teacher bloke get you down. You're a bright young woman. You'll figure out what your thing is, I have no doubt.'

No one has called me a woman before. I like it.

I notice Paul's eyes drift away from me and over to the clock on the mantelpiece.

'Shit, it's nearly half past. I'd better get a move on,' he says, standing up.

I can't help but feel disappointed.

'Now, I shouldn't be back too late, but it's hard to know with these things.'

'That's OK,' I say.

I watch as he moves about the living room, scooping up his wallet and keys from the arm of the sofa and pulling on a matching blazer.

'Duncan!' he yells up the stairs. 'I'm off. Be good for Mia.'

'OK!' Duncan yells back.

'Are you not going to come down and give your old man a kiss goodbye?'

'No thanks!'

Paul laughs and rolls his eyes. 'Kids.'

'Kids,' I agree, mimicking Paul's eye roll.

'As always, help yourself to anything from the fridge,'

Paul says. 'And if you need me for any reason, don't hesitate to call.'

The smear of shaving cream is still on his neck. I stand up, rising onto my tiptoes to wipe it away with my index finger. His skin feels both rough and smooth at the same time.

'Shaving foam,' I explain.

'Oh, I see,' he says, his face and shoulders relaxing. 'Thank you, Mia.'

I shut the door behind him and go back into the living room, flopping on the sofa and scrolling through the Sky Planner. Paul clearly has a thing for moody American crime dramas because they make up the majority of his watch list, along with the odd football match. I find a couple of films I wouldn't mind watching and a heap of trashy reality TV stuff, before heading to the kitchen to investigate the contents of the fridge. It's packed with olives and wheels of brie and three different kinds of hummus and those little cheesecakes that come in their own glass ramekins. I load up a plate and head back into the living room.

I select an episode of mine and Stella's favourite reality TV show, dunk an artisan cheese straw into a tub of taramasalata and wait for my mind to empty.

I'm lying on the sofa watching one of the films I earmarked earlier when I hear a car in the driveway. Paul's back already? It's not even eleven. I grab the compact mirror from my bag and quickly check my reflection.

'Hey, Mia,' Paul says as he comes into the room. 'Everything OK?'

'Fine, thanks,' I say, tossing my hair over my shoulder. 'Duncan OK?'

'Yeah, all good,' I say, even though I haven't given Duncan a single thought all evening. 'You're back early,' I add.

'I've got a rule when it comes to work dos,' Paul says, taking off his blazer. 'Quit while you're ahead.' He drapes the jacket over the back of the sofa. 'I already predict some rather red faces on Monday morning,' he continues, laughing as he removes his cufflinks and rolls up his sleeves to the elbow.

An extra couple of buttons have come undone on his shirt. His chest is hairy. Manly. Nothing like Jordan's – he used to wax the tiny bit of chest hair he had with a kit from Boots. What a loser.

Paul's eyes flicker towards the TV. 'Oh, I love this film,' he says, sitting down on the sofa next to me. 'Has it been on long?'

'Half hour or so.'

'There goes the rest of my night then,' he says, propping his feet up on the coffee table.

For a few seconds we watch together, laughing out loud in unison. And it feels nice. Like we're a couple almost.

Paul glances at me. 'God, sorry, Mia, what am I thinking? You must be wanting to get home to bed.'

He arches his back to get his wallet out of his pocket. I can smell his aftershave. It smells nice, expensive. Paul is going through all the compartments in his wallet and muttering something about how he could have sworn he had another twenty on him. As he talks, I stare at his arms. I love the way his muscles strain against the pale blue cotton, how strong and safe and reassuring they look. They make Jordan's arms look pathetic and weedy in comparison. In fact, everything about Paul makes Jordan look like a silly little boy.

I imagine him wrapping his arms around me and kissing me, telling me how beautiful and sexy I am.

He turns to me, a roll of notes in his hand. I realize I'm holding my breath.

'I've only got thirty on me,' he says apologetically. 'All right if I pop round with another ten tomorrow?'

I scoot along the sofa a little. He turns his head to look at me, his lips only centimetres away from mine. It's now or never. Before I can change my mind, I lean in and press my mouth hard against his.

'Dad?' Duncan's reedy voice suddenly floats down the stairs.

Paul shoves me away and leaps to his feet, the money he was holding fluttering to the ground. The straps of my vest top have slipped off my shoulders. I rearrange them and tug at the hem of my skirt.

Duncan appears in the open doorway, his *Star Wars* pyjamas rumpled and riding up his skinny little legs, snow-white hair sticking up on end. Paul has shot over the other side of the room faster than the Road Runner. He's pressed up against the fireplace, his neck and face flushed pink.

'Hey, buddy!' he says a bit too loudly, sounding like an overexcited children's TV presenter. 'What you doing up?'

'I heard you talking,' Duncan says, sticking out his lower lip.

Paul shoots me a look, but it's too quick for me to have a decent stab at interpreting what it might mean.

'Sorry, kiddo,' he says. 'Didn't mean to wake you up. C'mere, I'll come up and tuck you back in.'

He swoops over to Duncan, draping an arm round his shoulder and guiding him back out into the hallway. I plop down onto the sofa and listen as they climb the stairs together, Paul speaking to Duncan in a low voice.

I lift my fingers to my lips. A few minutes later, I hear Paul's footsteps on the stairs. I sit up straighter, arching my back so my tits stick out.

Paul enters the room hesitantly. I wait for him to rejoin me on the sofa but he doesn't. Instead he returns to the spot in front of the fireplace, raking his hands through his hair before placing his fingers on his temples like he's trying to communicate with the dead.

'Look, Mia, you're a lovely girl, you really are . . .'

Girl. So all of a sudden I'm a girl again.

'. . . but you can't go round doing things like that.'

I feel like I've been slapped. Hard.

'But I thought you liked me,' I say. I hate the way my voice sounds, like a sulky little kid denied their share of the sweets.

Paul smiles this sad sort of smile that makes my cheeks burn with humiliation.

'Of course I like you,' he says. 'But not like that, Mia, not ever like that. I'm, what, twenty-odd years older than you?'

'So? Age is just a number,' I babble. 'If you like someone, you like someone, age shouldn't even have to come into it.'

But do I even like Paul? I don't know any more. All I know is that I hate the way he's looking at me, with this excruciating mix of pity and confusion that makes me want to curl up in a ball and have the sofa cushions swallow me up.

'Oh God, Mia, if I've given you the wrong idea somehow, then I'm truly sorry. That was never my intention, OK?'

My brain is spinning. I try to rewind, get the details straight, but the kiss is already a blur, my thoughts all jumbled up.

'I think we should call it a night,' Paul says. He's still glued to the fireplace. 'And perhaps it's best if I find someone else to look after Duncan from now on,' he adds.

'Right,' I mutter, standing up and grabbing my handbag.

I want to go home. I don't want to be in this room, this house, a second longer.

Paul picks up the money he dropped and puts it on the coffee table for me. God, he can't even bring himself to hand it to me. 'I'll stick that extra tenner in an envelope and pop it through your letterbox tomorrow,' he says.

'Don't bother,' I snap, snatching up the money.

'Mia, don't be like that.' His voice is condescendingly gentle. I half expect him to pat me on the head and say 'there, there'.

'Are you going to let me out or what?' I say, my eyes on the door.

He sighs and digs in his pocket for his keys. I just want him to hurry up.

Ordinarily, he'd walk me to the bottom of the driveway, his hand resting on the small of my back, but tonight he stays inside. The air outside is oven-warm, but I'm trembling like I've just been shoved into a walk-in freezer. Hugging my bag to my chest, I stalk down the driveway, praying to see my house is in darkness so I don't have to face anyone. All I want to do is creep up to bed, fall asleep and forget tonight ever happened.

24

'Hungover, are we?' Jeremy asks the following morning at work.

'No. What makes you say that?' I snarl.

'Number one, you're wearing sunglasses when it's overcast. Number two, you're on your third can of Coke. And number three, you just gave that woman change for a twenty when they only gave you a ten.'

'What? Who?' I ask, scouring the playground for disgruntled customers.

'Don't worry, I sorted it.'

'Oh.'

'Do I get a thank you?'

'Thank you,' I mutter.

'Sorry, what was that? I couldn't quite hear you.' He cups his hand to his ear, his eyes dancing with amusement.

'Thank you,' I growl.

Jeremy smirks. It doesn't help that he looks annoyingly

healthy today, his face tanned and freckly from a cycling trip to France he's been banging on about all morning.

The fact is, I'm not even vaguely hungover, just knackered after a crap night's sleep. I spent hours tossing and turning, reliving the shame and humiliation of Paul's rejection.

When I get home after work today though, I can hear him out in their back garden, playing Frisbee with Duncan. Part of me wants to brazen it out, go and lie in the hammock in my white bikini and show Paul what he's missing. The other, bigger part of me never wants see him ever again. All I know is, I can't concentrate on anything with their stupid voices floating in through the patio doors.

Dad is still in bed, sleeping off his stag do hangover. I was still awake when he stumbled in at almost 5 a.m., tripping on the stairs and frantically shushing himself. I stick my head behind the living-room door. Mum is lying on the sofa with the curtains drawn.

'Good night?' I ask, nodding at the pint glass of Berocca she's sipping from.

'Not so loud,' she says, wincing.

'Sorry,' I say, adjusting my volume to a loud whisper. 'Did you have a good night?'

'Hmmmm, probably a bit too good.'

'Did they get you a stripper?'

'No. Thank God. I have absolutely no desire to have to see anyone's dangly bits other than your dad's.'

'Ew, Mum.'

She smiles. 'Come sit with me for a bit,' she says, patting the sofa. 'We haven't had a proper chat in ages.'

I hesitate, tempted. When I was younger I used to tell Mum everything. We'd sit at the breakfast bar every day after school and I'd tell her all about who fancied who and who had fallen out with who and she'd listen patiently and ask lots of questions, and not in an annoying patronizing way, but like she was actually interested. I imagine telling her about the events of the last two days, how it might feel to let it all just pour out. I know I can't, though. If I tell her about last night she'll go bananas, and somehow the idea of sharing an edited version of events seems worse than saying nothing at all.

'I can't,' I say eventually. 'I'm going out.'

'Where?' she asks.

'Stella's. We're going to revise.'

'OK, sweetheart,' she says, stretching. 'What time will you be back?'

'I'm not sure. When we're finished, I suppose.'

'Well, let me know your dinner plans so I know how many pizzas to order, OK? I can't face doing any proper cooking today.'

'OK.'

She blows me a kiss. I pretend to catch it and blow one back, feeling a bit sad but not really knowing why.

I leave the house with no real intention of heading to Stella's. I'm still pissed off with her about the prospectuses and I'm too tired to have it out with her and too tired to pretend everything's fine.

I head into town instead, wandering aimlessly from shop

to shop. In WHSmith I flip through magazines until one of the shop assistants asks if she can help me, which of course is unsubtle code for 'buy a magazine or bugger off'. I tell her 'no thanks' and shove the copy of *Heat* I've been looking at back on the shelf. I can feel her eyes boring into my back as I sashay out of the shop and it takes all the strength I have not to turn round and give her the finger.

Having exhausted all the browsing possibilities on the high street, I find myself skirting the perimeter of Rushton Park. The weather has brightened up. Maybe I'll go lie down in the sun for a bit. Yeah, I'll listen to some music on my phone, try to relax a bit and forget about last night.

I stop at the newsagent's near the park gates and buy a Twister ice lolly. When I open it, it's all mushed-up and wonky, like it's melted then been frozen again. I eat it anyway, but it tastes sort of funny.

I wander into the park with no real aim or destination. I just know I don't want to be at home listening to Paul and Duncan do their father and son act in the garden. The park is busy, kids swarming the adventure playground like locusts.

I'm passing the little wooden hut that sells bird feed when I spot Aaron.

He's sitting with a bunch of other boys in a raggedy circle, a beer cooler in the centre, a couple of scratched-up guitars scattered on the grass. I contemplate texting Kimmie to alert her, knowing she'd be down here like a shot. But after the other night at Stella's, I'm not in the mood for seeing Kimmie either. I'm not in the mood for seeing anyone I know today.

I veer off the path and walk towards the boys. One or two of them look familiar but the majority I don't think I've seen before. A couple of them notice me approaching and are already sitting up to attention like meerkats by the time I arrive. After what happened with Paul last night, their reaction feels good, really good.

'It's you,' Aaron says, standing up.

My heart does an unexpected little leap. Not that I fancy him or anything, it just feels nice to know that he *has* noticed me before, that I didn't imagine his lingering stares; that I've still got it after all.

'It's me,' I confirm, my lips curling into a smile.

'Aaron,' he says.

I resist the urge to say, 'I know'. Instead, I tell him my name and ask if he and his friends can spare a beer, cocking my head to the side and biting my lip. It has the desired effect and at least half of the group scramble to be the one to hand me a can from the cooler. Aaron gets in there first though, triumphantly pressing it into my hands, his long, skinny fingers purposefully brushing mine.

The rest of the boys open up the circle so I can sit down. I hold the can against my forehead for a few seconds, before transferring it to my chest, multiple sets of eyes tracking my every move. I open the can and take a long sip.

One of the guys picks up a guitar, strumming it a couple of times and asking if I have any requests. I name a Taylor Swift song. Everyone laughs. They think I'm being ironic. He plays some gloomy song I've never heard before instead. I pretend to listen carefully to the wanky lyrics, nodding

215

along with everyone else and adopting the same vaguely stoned expression. Aaron grins at me across the circle. I hold his gaze in return and try to ignore the guilt tugging at my brain cells.

The song ends. I realize my can is empty. As if by magic, Aaron passes me a new one, open ready.

'You're a mind-reader,' I say.

He performs a little bow. 'At your service.'

Someone else has the guitar now – a boy with scruffy brown hair and cut-off jeans. He plays a never-ending version of 'Hey Jude', with Aaron sitting astride the cool box, drumming on it with his palms. I join in on the endless 'na na na na's'. The next song is fast and upbeat and one of the other boys pulls me up to dance. The two beers have stripped away my inhibitions. Along with the added incentive of ten eager pairs of male eyes, I grind and writhe in time to the music. At the end of the song everyone begs me not to stop. I do, though. Best to keep them wanting more.

The sun is starting to go down. I find my phone and text Mum, and tell her I'm going to eat dinner at Stella's. Without my noticing, everyone has changed places and Aaron is next to me now, lying on his side, propped up on his elbow. I mirror him, knowing my body looks extra hot this way. I'm pleased when I notice Aaron's eyes trace my curves from head to toe and back again.

'I didn't know you were a drummer,' I say, nodding over at the cool box. 'Are you in a band?'

'Nah,' he says.

'Why not?'

'Dunno. I just play for fun.' He pauses. 'If I was in a band, would you come watch me play?' he asks.

'Maybe. Depends how nicely you asked.'

He grins. 'You're Grace Campbell-Richardson's sister, aren't you?' he says, inching closer.

The mention of Grace's name sobers me up for a second. 'Yeah,' I say. 'So?'

'You're really different from her.'

'Different how?'

'Oh, good different,' he says quickly. He leans in so his lips are only centimetres away from my right ear. 'Sexy different.'

His breath tickles and makes me shiver. It feels good to hear him say that. It feels safe. Because being sexy is one thing I've always been good at, the one thing I can beat Grace at.

'You come to the lido sometimes, don't you?' Aaron adds.

'Sometimes.'

'I'm a lifeguard there.'

'Oh, really?' I bluff. 'I don't think I've seen you.'

'Yeah, you were there a few weeks ago, with a really camp guy and a blonde girl who kept screaming about getting her hair wet.'

Mikey and Stella.

'And Kimmie,' I say quickly. 'Our friend Kimmie was with us too.'

Aaron looks blank.

'Super-cute Chinese girl?' I add. 'Shiniest hair on the planet?'

He shrugs. 'To be honest, it wasn't really your friends I was looking at,' he says, fixing me with a meaningful look.

I glance away, down the rest of my beer and try to push Kimmie's face out of my head.

With the sun steadily dipping in the sky, it feels cold suddenly, goose pimples breaking out on my arms and legs and stomach. I sit up, wrapping my arms round my knees. Aaron notices and whips out the hoodie he's been lying on, placing it round my shoulders. It stinks of his aftershave. After a bit I slip my arms through the armholes and zip it up to my chin. The sleeves are too long, just the very tips of my fingers poking out.

'Aw, you look well cute,' Aaron says.

I roll my eyes towards the sky.

'You do!' he insists.

A couple of girls turn up, each of them carrying blue plastic bags full of more beers. They glare at me, the interloper. I ignore them and rest my hand on Aaron's thigh as I reach into one of the bags for another can of beer. The taller of the two girls sucks in her breath but doesn't say anything. Someone starts playing the guitar again and we all sing along. The whole time Aaron draws on my back with his index finger.

A few songs in, I realize I need the loo. I stand up, wobbling a little. Aaron jumps up to steady me.

'Hey there, Bambi,' he says, not letting go of me until he's satisfied I'm capable of remaining vertical without his assistance.

We're miles away from the toilet block so I stagger into

218

the bushes and pull down my shorts and knickers, squatting down. I seem to pee for ages. It feels good. I can see the group through the foliage, their faces illuminated by cigarettes and mobile phones.

I'm making my way back towards the group when someone grabs hold of my arm and pulls me back into the bushes, leading me to a small clearing.

'Hey,' Aaron says.

'Hey,' I murmur back.

As he puts his arms around me, I think of Kimmie. I know I should probably shake him off, return to the others, give Aaron back his hoodie and go home, but I can't resist the look in his eyes, the look that says 'I want you'. He kisses me. I kiss him back and do all the things I know boys like. I sigh and moan and run my hands through his hair and trace them round the waistband of his jeans, and wrap one leg around his. He responds, groaning and murmuring my name into my hair. He smells of grass and beer and sweat.

It's not like he's ever paid Kimmie any interest. It was me he was looking at both those times at the lido, not her. He doesn't even know who she is, he admitted as much when I described her just now and clearly had no idea who I was talking about. It's not like if I walked away now, it would change anything, that he'd magically start fancying her.

His hand sneaks under the hoodie, under my top, my bra, seeking out skin.

'You want to come back to mine?' he asks breathlessly, as his cold palm cups my left boob.

And even though I don't actually fancy him, and even

though I know Mum will be expecting me home in a bit, and even though I know Kimmie would be devastated if she could see me right now, letting Aaron Butler, love of her life, kiss my neck and try to undo my bra strap, I tell him 'OK'.

Because, sod it, I'm having fun and feel good about myself for what seems like the first time in ages.

25

Not bothering to say goodbye to the others, Aaron and I stumble back to his place. The whole time, he can't keep his hands off me, stopping every few metres to kiss up against walls and bushes and shop windows. I manage to hold him off long enough to text Mum and tell her I'm still revising and that I might as well stay over at Stella's. She texts back to say OK. No questions, nothing. I stare at the screen as Aaron slides his hands under my top. Is that it? It seems so easy. Too easy.

Aaron lives in a house share with a couple of guys and a girl, all students, he explains as he fumbles for his keys. The house is Victorian with high ceilings and picture rails. Even though it's a warm night, it still manages to feel damp and draughty. The hall is narrow, crowded with battered bicycles and piles of unopened post. The carpet is threadbare, revealing the wooden floorboards beneath.

Aaron takes me through to the kitchen at the back of the

house where my flip-flops stick to the lino and I have to make extra effort to lift my feet. A girl with long dirty-blonde hair is sitting with her feet propped up on the table eating a bowl of cereal and watching YouTube videos on her phone. She pauses to look me up and down, her lips curling upwards in unfriendly amusement, before returning her attention to the screen.

'Mia, Cara, Cara, Mia,' Aaron says, opening the fridge.

'Nice to meet you,' I say, not meaning it one bit.

Cara doesn't even bother to answer.

I let my eyes wander around the room. The fluorescent tube lights are too bright, illuminating the tomato sauce splatters on the yellowed wall tiles, the overflowing bin, the water stain that covers at least a quarter of the ceiling. It makes me long for the shadiness of the bushes at the park.

There's a heap of unwashed dishes in the sink. An upside-down bottle of economy washing-up liquid and a grotty sponge lie redundant on top of the pile. On the draining board there's a bottle of tequila. It's about a third full. The bottle itself looks sticky and is covered in fingerprints. It doesn't stop me wanting some, though. The effects of my last beer are already wearing off.

Aaron opens a beer for me and pushes it into my hand. 'Cheers,' he says, pressing his can against mine before taking a long swig.

'Cheers,' I repeat.

There's a pause. The only noise is the tinny music coming from Cara's phone. I try to work out what she's watching, but I'm at the wrong angle to see properly.

'You wanna . . . ?' Aaron says. He jerks his head towards the ceiling.

I nod and follow him out of the room.

'Well, she was friendly,' I say as we climb the creaking stairs.

'Who, Cara? Yeah, sorry about her. Let's just say she's a bit possessive.'

'Possessive? How come?'

'We sort of have history.'

'What kind of history?'

'Weird history. When I first moved in here we had a bit of a drunken snog, and I don't think she's ever really gotten over it not going anywhere.'

I smile, enjoying the one-upmanship. Mia 1 – Cara 0.

Aaron's room is on the first floor. There's no living room, he explains, because it's been converted into a fourth bedroom. The landlord doesn't know though, so every time he comes round, they have to move the bed into one of the other rooms so he doesn't twig they're subletting.

Aaron's room is small and square and mostly taken up by a double bed so he has to crawl across it to turn on the lamp. The mattress is bare.

'I'll be right back,' he says.

I perch on the end of the bed and slurp my beer, putting it between my thighs while I shrug out of Aaron's hoodie, shivering slightly.

Aaron returns with a load of bed linen draped over his arm. 'Can you give me a hand?' he asks.

I put down my can of beer on the floor and help him

make the bed. It feels weird. Wrong. It's the sort of thing married couples do together. Aaron's sheets are navy blue, his duvet cover and pillowcases white with grey stripes. I turn my back and slide on the pillow cases one by one. Aaron's pillows are flat and sad-looking, tinged yellow. I'm glad the sheets are clean, though. Aaron puts on some music and pulls down his blind. I down the rest of my beer. There are film posters Blu-tacked to the wall – *Pulp Fiction* and *The Godfather* and *The Usual Suspects*, the edges curling up. As Aaron lowers me back onto the duvet, the ceiling feels very far away. Cobwebs cling to the paper lampshade, fluttering slightly as if caught in the breeze. I'm not drunk enough. I need to be drunker than this.

'Can I get another beer?' I ask, sitting up, the blood rushing to my head. 'And maybe some of that tequila I saw.'

'The tequila's not mine, it's Cara's.'

'Oh, that's a shame.'

'But let me see what I can do.'

He seems to be gone for a long time. There isn't a mirror so I check my reflection on my phone instead. I look tired, dark shadows under my eyes.

Aaron returns a few minutes later. 'Ta-da!' he says, looking pleased with himself. He has a couple of fresh cans of beer wedged under his left armpit, and two plastic beakers of what I guess must be tequila in his right hand. I wonder how he persuaded Cara to let him have it. From what I could gather, she didn't seem like the sharing type.

I down the tequila in one. It's warm and stings my throat,

going to my head immediately. I open the beer and take a gulp of that too. It's warm too.

'Yeah, sorry, they haven't been in the fridge,' Aaron says, noticing my grimace.

'No worries,' I murmur.

We put our drinks on the narrow mantelpiece and lie down. I need the toilet but feel too lazy and drunk to move. Instead I let Aaron kiss my neck and collarbone and stomach and tell me how sexy I am. His lips are a bit dry, dragging against my skin.

'You OK?' he whispers.

'Course.'

He grins and leans across me to snap out the light. I long for pitch black but there's a street lamp right outside, its glow leaking in round the edges of the flimsy roller blind that hangs at the window. I squeeze my eyes shut instead.

Immediately, Aaron starts pulling at my shorts. I arch my back to help. Then he's tugging my top over my head and tossing it across the room. I hear it hit the door.

Time to even things out. I remove Aaron's T-shirt and undo his belt, chucking it on the floor where it lands with a loud clatter. We're both just in our underwear now. He fiddles with my bra. On the third attempt he manages to take it off. Then he's yanking at my knickers while I use my foot to slide his boxer shorts down his legs.

'Nice move,' he whispers in my ear. 'Want to get under the covers?'

'OK. Hang on a second.'

I pause and take off my peacock feather earrings, setting

them on top of the chest of drawers next to the bed before wriggling under the duvet.

Aaron's hands are warm and slightly clammy. As he runs them up and down my body, he tells me how sexy I am and how much he fancies me and all the things he wants to do to me, and I start to relax into it a bit and remember to play my role, arching my back, gasping in all the right places, whispering in Aaron's ear as we roll about on the mattress.

He pauses to lean across me and rifle in the chest of drawers. I hear the sound of a package being ripped open, the snap of plastic against skin.

It makes me flinch.

What am I doing? What am I actually doing? I don't even like him. I barely even know him, I just think I do because Kimmie goes on about him so much.

Oh God. Kimmie.

I need to say something; make up an excuse and get out of here, but then he's climbing on top of me and kissing my neck and it all feels OK again.

You can do this, Mia, I tell myself. You can.

I wrap my legs around the tops of his to prove it. He groans in response and says my name.

'You ready?'

Ready for what? I want to ask. I don't, though. Instead I whisper 'yes' and gently bite his earlobe, making him groan.

The pain as he pushes into me is sharp and unexpected. I let out an involuntary gasp. He stops.

'You OK?' he asks.

I bite my lip hard and nod. 'Fine. Sorry.'

He hesitates before pushing again. I squeeze my eyes shut in preparation, trying to block out the pain.

Aaron stops again, propping himself up on his elbows. 'Mia, you're not a virgin, are you?' he asks.

'Of course not. It's just been a while.'

He frowns.

Another push. I grit my teeth and try not to cry out.

He swears under his breath and rolls off me.

'What are you doing?' I ask, wrapping the duvet around me, embarrassed by my nakedness suddenly.

'You should have told me you were a virgin, Mia,' he says, pulling the condom off and letting it drop on the floor. He leans over the side of the bed and reaches for his phone from the pocket of his discarded jeans, the screen lighting up his face.

I open my mouth to respond but realize I don't have a clue what to say. I could try to deny it but what would be the point? Aaron is absolutely right. I am a virgin. I've just spent so long letting my friends think I'm not, that I did it with Jordan, that I'd almost tricked myself into believing it too.

'I need the loo,' I say eventually. 'Do you have a T-shirt or something I can wear?'

Aaron opens a drawer and tosses me one. I pull it on over my head. It smells fusty, just like the house.

I can't find my knickers.

'Can you turn on the light please?' I ask, holding the T-shirt down over my thighs.

He switches on the lamp. The duvet is all twisted and our clothes are scattered over the floor. The abandoned condom lies on top of Aaron's jeans. Just the sight of it makes me feel hot with shame.

I snatch up my knickers, pulling them on before stepping out onto the landing. The bathroom is on the opposite side, near the stairs. It smells of mould. I pee for what seems like for ever. The shower curtain has the map of the world on it. I find Jamaica, then Greece, then New York City. There's no soap to wash my hands with. Eventually I spot a sliver of a bar at the bottom of the bathtub but it's all grey and veiny. I make do with a rinse of lukewarm water instead.

I don't like the look of the single towel hanging on a hook on the back of the door, so I wipe my hands on Aaron's T-shirt instead, leaving dark handprints on the navy-blue cotton.

I stare at my reflection in the smudged mirror. My mascara has run and I have a love bite on my neck, purple and ripe. I rearrange my hair so I don't have to look at it.

Back on the landing, I run into Cara. She smiles at me, eyeing my neck. It's a mean smile though, one that doesn't reach her eyes.

'Got a problem?' I ask.

She just shakes her head and disappears into a dimly lit, weed-scented bedroom, slamming the door shut behind her.

By the time I get back to Aaron's room, he's asleep or at least pretending to be. Either way I'm glad. I gather up my clothes and start to put them on. As I fasten my bra, I stare at the mole on Aaron's temple. It looks like a chocolate chip. I hadn't noticed it before. Kimmie probably worships that mole.

A tear rolls down my cheek.

No, I tell myself. None of that.

I wipe it away with my fist and fold Aaron's T-shirt. I put it on the edge of the bed and leave the room without looking back.

26

'Shouldn't you have left by now?' Grace asks the following morning as I search for my English folder amongst the mess on the kitchen table.

'Slept through my alarm, didn't I?' I say.

The truth is I've been awake for hours. I'm going purposefully slowly so I don't have to walk to school with my friends.

'What is that?' I ask. 'It absolutely stinks.'

'This?' she asks, holding up her mug.

I nod.

'It's red raspberry leaf tea,' she says in this weird, serene voice she's taken to speaking in any time anyone brings up the birth. 'It's supposed to help ease labour by strengthening the walls of the uterus.'

I pull a face. 'Well, it smells rancid,' I say, knocking a pot of pens off the table.

I swear under my breath and drop to my knees to pick them up.

'I didn't think you were even here,' Grace says. 'Mum said you were staying at Stella's.'

By the time I got back last night, everyone was in bed.

'Yeah, I was going to,' I say. 'But then I remembered I needed my PE kit.'

'Couldn't you have just borrowed something off Stella?'

Trust Grace to think of that.

'Didn't think.'

I straighten up and put the pot of pens back on the table.

Grace slides off her stool and adds a splash of cold water to her tea. 'What were you revising for?' she asks.

'Huh?'

'At Stella's.'

'Oh, Media Studies.'

It's the first subject that pops into my head.

'Stella takes Media Studies?' Grace says.

'Yeah. Why?'

'I could have sworn when I chatted to her last summer, that she said she was doing English, Geography, Art and Economics.' A pause. 'I must have got it wrong,' she adds.

'Yeah, you must have,' I say, finally finding my folder under a pile of Mum's work invoices.

But Grace never gets it wrong. She knows that and I know that.

I glance up at the clock. 'I'd better get going,' I mutter.

I walk to school slowly. If I time it right I can go straight to English and won't have to see Kimmie until lunch time at the earliest. I don't quite know why, but until I've seen her face-to-face, it's almost as if I can trick myself into thinking what happened with Aaron wasn't so bad, that I'm not a completely horrible person after all. In the cold light of day, I feel even worse than I did last night, stumbling home in the dark, feeling dirty and sore and numb.

I arrive a few minutes before the bell, dropping off my stupid letter of apology for Ugly Tie Man at the admin office before ducking into the toilets and sitting in one of the cubicles until it rings. I wait for the corridors to empty before sprinting to English, slipping into my seat just in time for Mrs Poots to call my name on the register.

At break time, I make an excuse about unfinished homework and hide out in the library instead of heading to the sixth form common room. I'm staring out of the window when I notice someone waving at me from over the other side of the library out of the corner of my eye.

Kimmie.

My heart starts to beat faster as she makes her way towards me with a big smile on her face. She looks extra cute today in a corduroy dungaree dress layered over a T-shirt with cherries embroidered all over it.

'Hey,' she says. 'Stella said you were in here.'

'Yeah,' I say, swallowing hard.

'What homework are you doing?' she asks, looking at the empty table in front of me.

'Oh, RS,' I say. 'I've just finished it actually.'

She nods and slides into the seat opposite. 'Are you mad with us?' she asks.

'Mad? Why would I be mad?'

She draws circles on the table with her finger. 'It's just that none of us heard from you pretty much all weekend.'

'I was busy.'

'What doing?'

'Just stuff.'

The guilt physically hurts. Sort of like a nettle sting, only a hundred times worse.

'Is everything OK, Mia?' she asks. 'You seem a bit funny.'

'I'm fine,' I say. 'It's probably just PMT, you know how I get.'

She nods, but doesn't look convinced.

'Oh my God, what the hell is that?' Stella cries.

It's the last period of the day and we're getting changed for PE.

'What's what?' I ask.

I've been spaced out since my conversation with Kimmie in the library earlier and am not remotely in the mood for Stella's theatrics.

'That big fat vampire bite!' she says, pointing at my neck.

Shit. I reach to untie the ponytail I've just scraped my hair into, but it's too late. I've been rumbled.

'Jesus Christ, Mia,' Stella continues, forcing my head to one side to get a closer look. 'Where did you get it?'

'Get what?' I ask, shaking her off.

'Oh, come on, like you don't know it's there.'

I go over to the mirror and pretend to notice the love bite for the very first time. Despite about twelve layers of concealer, it's shining out for all to see.

Idiot.

'Oh my God,' I say. 'Where the hell did that come from?'

Stella and Kimmie crack up laughing.

'You are *such* a bad actress, Mia,' Stella says.

'I'm serious, I have no idea where I got this,' I protest, prodding at it for good measure. 'It's probably just an allergic reaction or something. Come to think of it, Audrey had Beyoncé up in our room like all day yesterday, I bet it's that.'

'I didn't you know you were allergic to guinea pigs,' Kimmie says.

'Yep,' I say. 'Really, really allergic.'

Stella snorts. 'Oh please, Mia, you're no more allergic to guinea pigs than I am Kate and Pippa Middleton's long-lost little sister.'

'But it's true,' I whine.

'Honestly, do you think we were born yesterday? Just tell us already! Who gave you the hickey to end all hickeys?'

'No one,' I say, loosening my hair from its ponytail.

Mrs Cates barges into the changing rooms and tells us to hurry up, forcing the group to disperse.

'Hair up please, Mia,' she barks as she strides the length of the lockers.

'I've lost my bobble,' I lie.

'No you haven't, it's on your wrist,' Kimmie says.

'Thanks,' I mutter, reluctantly tying my hair back up, yanking down a few tendrils in an attempt to disguise the love bite as best I can.

'That's better,' Mrs Cates says, shoving a load of wooden rounders bats into my arms.

Mikey is waiting for us outside the changing rooms.

The first thing Stella does is instruct him to 'check out Mia's epic love bite'.

'Fuck me,' Mikey says, screwing up his face as he peers at it. 'Someone went to town on you.'

'Do you have to be so loud?' I hiss, nodding at the group in front.

'And since when are you coy about this stuff?' he asks.

'I'm not being coy,' I mutter.

'Come to think of it,' Stella says, scampering along beside me like an excited puppy dog. 'You do look pretty knackered. I thought so earlier.'

'Wow, thanks a lot,' I reply.

'I'm just being honest,' Stella says, like that somehow makes it OK to go around telling people they basically look like shit warmed up.

'She's got a point,' Mikey says. 'You're not looking your hottest this morning, Mia.'

'Well, *I* think you look really pretty today,' Kimmie says, offering me a sweet from the bag of Haribo Star Mix she has hidden under the stack of bibs Mrs Cates gave her to carry up to the field.

'Suck-up,' Mikey says, disguising it as a cough.

'Oh, piss off,' I say, taking a fried egg and popping it in my mouth, swallowing it whole. I can feel it making its way down my windpipe. Kimmie offers me another. I shake my head, a fresh crop of guilt creeping up my body like climbing ivy on fast-forward, winding round my ankles and wrists, threatening to drag me to the ground.

235

'So, come on then,' Stella says. 'What *were* you doing this weekend?'

'Or more accurately, *who* were you doing this weekend?' Mikey adds, looking disproportionately pleased with himself.

'I told you, nothing,' I say.

'Whatever! That thing on your neck is a textbook love bite. Plus, how else do you explain the crazy hair? The dark circles? The elusiveness? You've blatantly been shagging all weekend!'

'You must think we're total idiots,' Stella adds.

I open my mouth and then shut it again. Because I can't admit what I did this weekend. Any of it.

'Oh my God, I can't believe you weren't going to tell us!' Stella continues to squawk. 'I would never dream of not telling you if I got it on with someone.'

'Who is he?' Kimmie asks, her eyes shining. 'Someone we know?'

The guilt morphs into a thousand little knives attacking every centimetre of my body. Stab, stab, stab.

'Yeah, someone from school?' Mikey asks.

'Ew, no,' I say. 'I've had it with boys my age, you know that.'

'Then who?' he cries.

I hesitate, my brain whirring as I start to panic, my clammy hands struggling to hold onto the rounders bats in my arms.

'You may as well tell us the gory details now,' Stella says in a singsong voice. 'Because you know if you don't, we'll only find out some other way.'

She's right. They'll never let me get away with not dishing the dirt. And I can't risk them finding out the truth. Not ever.

'Paul,' I blurt. 'It was Paul.' The words leave my mouth before I can stop them.

'Wait, Paul who?' Mikey asks.

His words are overlapped with a gasp from Stella. 'Oh my God, as in Paul your next-door neighbour?' she cries.

I don't have to say anything else. They join the dots all by themselves, squealing and gasping, full of questions, all of which I answer in startling detail, the lies flowing easily.

Too easily.

27

I'm not quite sure who's to blame (although the smart money is on Mikey and his stupidly loud voice), but by the end of PE our entire class seems to know about my 'affair' with my forty-year-old next-door neighbour.

'My cousin is going out with a twenty-five-year-old, and I thought *that* was old!' Tamsin says as we troop back to the changing rooms at the end of the lesson.

'Does he look forty?' Kat chimes in.

'Do your mum and dad know?' Stacey adds.

'No,' I say, trying and failing to disguise the panic in my voice. 'And they really can't, OK? So please just stop going on about it.'

Despite my classmates' promises not to breathe a word to anyone (whatever), I still can't get rid of the sicky feeling in my stomach. I keep waiting for it to go away, but it shows no signs of leaving me alone. It's there as I get changed back into my clothes, my classmates not even bothering to hide their excited whispers. It's there as I walk home, fielding yet more questions, inventing more and more lies. It's there as I eat dinner, and help Mum put sugared almonds in little gauzy bags for the wedding favours, and sit on my laptop scouring social media for evidence of my presence at the park yesterday. And even though I don't find a thing, and so according to the internet at least I'm in the clear, the sicky feeling remains. It's there as I lie in the bath, and brush my teeth and toss and turn in bed, unable to fall asleep. And the next morning it's there the moment I wake up, a big fat tangled knot deep in my belly.

At Thursday-afternoon registration, our teacher, Mr Costa, hands out our school reports. We usually rip them open immediately (apart from Kimmie, whose parents always insist she brings it home in its sealed envelope), but today I shove mine straight to the bottom of my bag without looking at it.

I forget about it until later that evening when I'm searching through my bag for a rogue cigarette.

'Is that your report?' Audrey asks from over the other side of the room.

I shrug and push it under my mattress.

'Aren't you going to read it?' she asks.

'What's the point? It's only going to be shit.'

'It might not be,' she says. 'It might be really good.'

'Oh, come on, Auds. Get real.' It's no secret I'm making a right mess of my A levels. I was stupid to think I was up to them in the first place. My GCSEs were clearly a fluke, a red herring.

'Won't Mum and Dad want to see it though?'

'I doubt they'll even remember it's due.'

'I bet it's not as bad as you think.'

I sigh. 'Thanks, Audrey, but it's probably worse.'

On the last day of term, for probably the first time ever, I'm glad to have an excuse not to go to the pub with the others.

'I've got to get home and pack,' I explain at the school gates.

The venue for Mum and Dad's wedding is a big hotel on the edge of town and it's our base for the next two nights.

'Can't you just come for one?' Mikey asks.

'Yeah,' Kimmie says. 'You don't have to stay long.'

Even though the guilt has faded a bit, I'm still struggling to look Kimmie in the eye properly, directing most of my conversation at her eyebrows instead.

'Sorry, I can't,' I say, pretending to check my phone. 'My mum will go mad if I'm not home on time.'

'Er, since when does Queen Mia care about keeping people waiting?' Stella points out.

'Oh, shut up, Stella. It's my mum and dad's wedding. Do you really think I'm such a cow that I'd mess it up for them?'

Stella frowns. 'God, it was supposed to be a *joke*,' she says.

I smack myself on my forehead with my right palm. 'Stupid me,' I say. 'There I was assuming you were just being a bitch.'

I'm being a moody cow, I know I am, but somehow I

can't bring myself to apologize. I just need to have a break from the lies I've told, the chance to reset. For about the thousandth time, I regret letting them believe it was Paul who gave me the stupid love bite. Why didn't I just make up a random boy? If I had, they'd have probably forgotten about it by now. I wish I had a time machine I could climb inside so I could put it all right. I try to decide when I would go back to. Getting ready for PE on Monday? The moment just before Aaron kissed me in the park? The moment just before I kissed Paul? Or further back still? When exactly did everything start to unravel?

'What's with you this week?' Stella asks, putting her hands on her hips. 'You've been in *such* a mood.'

'Is it Paul?' Mikey butts in. 'Did something else happen?'

'No,' I say. 'I told you, I haven't seen him all week.'

'But how? He lives next door, for God's sake.'

'Oh my God, just drop it, OK?'

'But, Mia—'

'I said, drop it.'

They exchange looks, ranging from concerned (Kimmie), to bitchy (Mikey) and exasperated (Stella).

I take a deep breath. 'Look, I'm sorry if I've been in a bit of a shit mood this week,' I say. 'Things are just a bit stressful at home right now, you know, with the wedding and everything.'

This is a lie. Even though I'm not exactly looking forward to it, my bad mood has barely anything to do with the wedding. My explanation seems to do the trick though, both Stella and Mikey quickly apologizing for having a go at me.

'I'll see you guys tomorrow, OK?' All three of them are invited.

The mood lifted, we hug goodbye. I'm still relieved though, when we can finally go our separate ways and I can breathe that little bit easier.

As I walk away, I try to shove everything that's happened from my mind and focus on the weekend ahead. It's going to be full-on and if I'm going to get through it, I *need* to be on form.

28

The introduction to 'Isn't She Lovely' by Stevie Wonder blasts through the overhead speakers.

'Go, Audrey,' Grace says. 'Go!'

Because Grace is wearing flats, Audrey is the tallest for a change, wobbly and uncertain in her high heels as she creeps round the corner and down the aisle towards the music like a cautious baby deer in lilac chiffon.

As rehearsed, I count to five before following her.

The room is packed, kids piled on laps, several people forced to stand at the back because there are more guests than available chairs. There are so many strings of fairy lights I feel like Father Christmas is going to emerge any second yelling, 'Ho, ho, ho!' and tossing presents from his sack. Audrey must have legged it because the aisle is entirely clear. As I walk down the centre, the faces on either side are a blur. All I can see are teeth and camera phones and humongous hats until I spot Stella, Mikey and Kimmie waving madly at me and I'm able to focus for a few seconds and give them a grin in return.

There's a collective sigh from the entire crowd. I turn round just in time to see Grace and her 'adorable' baby bump advancing down the aisle towards me, followed by an even bigger sigh for Mum's entrance. Dad's eyes are already wet, and by the time Mum joins him they're both openly wailing at each other, milky mascara tears running down Mum's face.

The ceremony is being conducted by a woman called Charmaine. Even though Mum's family is officially Catholic and Dad's family are super-Christian, neither of them wanted a religious service. The compromise is a single reading from the Bible performed by one of Dad's billions of great-aunts, offset by Mum's sister Ali reading a passage from *Captain Corelli's Mandolin*.

'And now I'd like to invite Grace and Sam to the front,' Charmaine says as Ali returns to her seat.

Huh?

Mum and Dad look equally surprised as Grace and Sam get up, Sam taking a seat at a keyboard I hadn't even noticed was set up, Grace smiling serenely at us all as Charmaine adjusts the microphone to her height.

'This is a special surprise for Mum and Dad,' Grace says breathlessly. She turns towards them. 'Thank you for being the most incredible parents I could ever wish for.'

She nods to Sam, who begins to play the introduction to 'Back for Good' by Take That. It was number one in the charts when Mum and Dad met and is their official song.

Pleasure ripples through the audience as Grace begins to sing, her soprano voice as clear as a bell. Mum and Dad beam, their arms wrapped round each other, Mum's head resting on Dad's shoulder. I glance behind me. Everyone is spellbound, snapping pictures and swaying in time with the music. Stella and the others have been reeled in, joining in on the chorus. Kimmie even cries.

'Did you know about this?' I ask Audrey in a low whisper.

She shakes her head.

At the end of the song the room breaks into thunderous applause. At Mum and Dad's insistence Grace and Sam hold hands and take about ten bows.

'How long have you been planning that?' I ask once Grace has returned to her seat.

'Just a few weeks,' she replies, facing front and not looking at me. 'We practised while you were at school.'

'You should have said something.'

'We wanted it to be a surprise, silly.'

'Not to Mum and Dad, to me.'

'Why?'

'I might have wanted to do something special too.'

'Like what?'

'I don't know,' I mutter.

'No one was stopping you, Mia,' she says, stroking her bump.

I try to concentrate as Charmaine moves on to the final vows, culminating in her announcement that Dad and Mum are now 'man and wife' and he may 'kiss the bride'. They snog for about a minute straight while 'Happy' by Pharrell plays and the crowd goes wild. The doors at the front of the room are flung open and we're ushered out onto the terrace for drinks and photos. Within seconds I'm hijacked by aunts and uncles and family friends I haven't seen in ages. Instead of their usual comments about tall I am and how grownup I look, all they're interested in is Grace and the baby.

'You must be so excited,' they say, over and over again.

I smile and tell them what they want to hear, that 'I can't wait' to meet my niece or nephew.

The photographer rounds us up for endless photographs on the lawn, the group combinations gradually getting bigger and bigger until all 150 guests are assembled together on the damp grass. It takes for ever to make sure everyone is looking in the right direction and can be seen, heels sinking into the lawn and tempers fraying.

It's as we're waiting for my cousin Tanisha to persuade her three-year-old, Dante, to stop screaming and smile nicely for a final shot, that I notice her, standing on the steps wearing a crisp white skirt tucked into black trousers, a tray of Pimms resting on her palm, a weird little smirk on her face as her eyes clock me in the crowd. It's the exact same smirk she wore when I bumped into her outside Aaron's bedroom last weekend, his T-shirt barely covering my bum.

Cara.

The photographer seizes his moment. 'Everyone say, "Best wedding ever!"' he yells.

'Best wedding ever!' the crowd crows back obediently.

Everyone apart from me. I open my mouth and make the right shapes but I'm pretty certain no actual words come out. There's only one thought on my mind – what the hell is Cara doing at my mum and dad's wedding?

'You OK, sweetheart?' Dad asks once the photographer has dismissed the crowd. 'You look like you've seen a ghost.'

'I'm fine,' I stammer. 'Just hungry, I think. I only had a bit of breakfast.'

'Well, not long now until we eat,' he says, giving my shoulder a squeeze.

The photographer beckons Mum and Dad to join him for a few more shots. Dad kisses me on the forehead and takes Mum's hand.

As the terrace swarms with thirsty guests, I try to think about the situation logically. It's not as if Cara's going to march up to Kimmie and tell her I shagged her housemate – that would make no sense whatsoever. She doesn't even know who Kimmie is, never mind the fact that Kimmie fancies Aaron. I remember what Aaron told me, about him blowing Cara off that time and how badly she took it. She was probably only giving me evils because she's jealous. Yeah, that must be it. Feeling slightly better, I smooth out my dress and go look for Stella and the others.

I find them gathered around Grace and Sam, their hands fixed to Grace's bump, even Mikey's, who claims to hate kids as much as I do.

'Hey,' I say.

'Hey,' they reply, barely even looking at me, their hands still stuck to the bump.

'Oh my God, I can feel it moving!' Kimmie gasps, crouching down and pressing her right ear against Grace's belly like she's listening to a bowl of Rice Crispies go 'snap, crackle, pop'.

'Me too!' Stella says. 'Loads!'

'Of course it's moving,' I say. 'It's a foetus. That's what foetuses do. They move. Big fleshy deal.'

'Not today, Mia,' Grace says, sighing. 'Please.'

'What do you mean?' I demand.

'You know what I mean.'

We're interrupted by some of Mum's mates, all eager for their turn to touch Grace's fat belly. I swear from the way everyone's acting you'd think she was about to give birth to the future king or queen of England or something.

Reluctantly my friends peel away, making room for another three sets of hands.

'Grace looks *so* beautiful,' Kimmie says, looking over her shoulder as we walk away. 'Pregnancy properly suits her. And Sam is *so* nice too. I can't believe how perfect they are together.'

'Hashtag relationship goals,' Mikey chimes in.

'Oh, please,' I mutter.

'You look really nice too,' Kimmie adds, looking guilty. 'I knew your dress wouldn't be horrible.'

'Horrible is exactly what it is,' I say, glaring down at the lilac chiffon. 'I look like a little kid at a birthday party.'

But Kimmie isn't listening. She's too busy squinting up at the terrace, her hand shielding her eyes from the sun.

'Oh my God,' she says.

248

'What?' Mikey asks. 'What are you looking at?'

Kimmie grabs my wrist and bounces on her heels, her bitten-down nails digging into my skin. 'Aaron's housemate is here!' she squeaks.

'What?' I say.

How on earth does Kimmie know Cara? How?

'Where?' Stella asks.

'Over there,' Kimmie says, pointing. 'Holding the tray. She must work here.'

'No shit, Sherlock,' Mikey quips.

'Wait, how do you know she lives with Aaron?' I ask, trying to keep my voice steady while attempting to ignore my flip-flopping stomach.

'He posts pictures of his housemates online sometimes,' Kimmie says. 'And I'm like ninety-five per cent sure that's the girl he lives with. Her name's Cara and she's a student at Rushton uni – Art, I think. Should I try talking to her, do you reckon?'

'No!' I cry, probably a bit too loudly.

'Why not?' Kimmie asks, frowning. 'You're the one always telling me I need to be more proactive. And she looks nice. You never know, she might put in a good word for me.'

'I just think it's a bad idea, that's all,' I babble. 'What if she tells him and he thinks you're a mad crazy stalker? You wouldn't want that, would you? I just think it's a really, really bad idea, Kimmie, honestly.'

I look to the others for backup.

'I hate to say it but I think Mia's probably right,' Stella

249

says. 'I mean, won't she think it's totally weird that you know she's Aaron's housemate in the first place?'

Thank you, Stella Fielding, thank you, thank you, thank you.

'Maybe,' Kimmie admits.

'There's no maybe about it,' I say. 'Seriously, I'd just leave it if I were you. You'll only regret it if you say something. I mean, what if she goes running to Aaron and tells him what a mentalist you are, then you'll have blown your chances for good.'

'Maybe you're right,' she says, chewing on her lower lip.

'Of course I am. You need to trust me on this one.'

She nods, resigned, and I breathe an inward sigh of relief.

'In the meantime, does anyone fancy a tipple?' Mikey asks, producing a hip flask from his inside pocket and waggling it about.

I snatch it from his hands and hug it to my chest. Because a drink is *exactly* what I need right now.

'I love you, Mikey Twist,' I say, unscrewing the cap.

'Tell me something I don't know,' he replies.

'What's in it?' Stella asks.

'Vodka, of course,' he says. 'The drink of champions.'

I glance over my shoulder. Grace and Sam are still surrounded and Mum and Dad are posing for photographs on a bench further up the terrace. We huddle in a tight circle and pass round the hip flask.

'Oi!' Mikey cries as I take my turn. 'Leave some for the rest of us.'

'I am,' I say, sneaking in another sip.

Kimmie is last, wincing as she takes her first taste. 'It's really strong, Mikey,' she says.

'Of course it is, dummy,' he replies. 'It's neat vodka.'

'Don't worry, I'll have your share,' I say, whipping the bottle from Kimmie's hands and downing the contents.

'Hey!' she cries.

'Oh, please,' I say. 'As if you were going to drink it all anyway. You'd be chucking up all night and you know it.'

Kimmie is an infamous lightweight.

I hand the empty hip flask back to Mikey.

'Bloody hell, Mia,' he says, turning it upside down. 'This was supposed to last all night.'

'Sorry,' I say, batting my eyelashes.

Not sorry.

29

We're interrupted by the master of ceremonies (one of Dad's mates from work) banging a gong and booming that it's time for the wedding breakfast.

Instead of a traditional long top table, the bridal party are seated at a round table like everyone else. Cara is serving tables on the other side of the room, far away both from my table and the table my friends have been assigned to. Still, I can't help but track her movements as she goes back and forth to the kitchen, holding my breath every time she interacts with any of the guests for longer than a few seconds. At the same time I sense she knows exactly where I am too. I try to ignore her, but there's something about her sly little glances in my direction, so tiny I doubt anyone else would ever clock them, that stops me from being able to relax properly.

I'm allowed a small glass of wine with my meal and a flute of prosecco for toasting, but that's it. When I appeal to Mum and Dad across the table, they raise their eyebrows in unison as if to say 'not now, Mia', forcing me to shrink back down in my chair in defeat while the waiting staff top up everyone else's glasses.

The main course has just been cleared away when Mum stands up and taps her glass with a knife. A hush falls over the room as she murmurs 'one, two, one, two' into the microphone she's holding.

'Rejecting the tradition that dictates men do all the talking at weddings, *I'm* going to be the one kicking off the speeches this afternoon,' she says.

A couple of her friends whoop in noisy appreciation, and everyone laughs.

'On behalf of my husband and I . . .'

A cheer erupts, followed by more fuzzy laughter. Mum, grinning wildly, waits for it to die down before continuing. 'On behalf of my husband and I,' she repeats, 'I want to thank you all for being here and sharing our special day with us. I can't tell you how incredible it is to look around the room and see all our favourite people in the same place. Thank you as well for being so patient with us. As most of you know, Jase and I have had what you could call a pretty long engagement.'

Cue more laughter, and knowing nods from both sets of parents.

'We just hope the wait is worth it. I, for one, know it most definitely is.'

She leans down to kiss Dad on the lips before passing him the microphone.

Dad gets up, slipping his spare arm around Mum's waist

before proceeding to thank pretty much every person he's ever met.

'Finally, though,' he says. 'We need to thank our three beautiful daughters. Stand up, girls.'

Grace, Audrey and I get to our feet. I don't realize how drunk I am until I'm standing up and my head starts to spin. I grip onto the edge of the table to keep myself steady.

'Are you OK?' Grace whispers.

'Fine,' I mutter, reaching for a glass of water and taking a big gulp.

Camera flashes are going off all over the place. I scan the room for Cara, but all the waiting staff seem to have disappeared. Good. Hopefully she'll go home after this and I can put the whole Aaron thing behind me once and for all.

Dad addresses Audrey first.

'Audrey,' he says. 'Our little fish. Your drive, commitment and discipline impresses and inspires me every single day. You have no idea how proud we are of you. In and out of the water.'

Audrey bows her head, shy and proud at the same time. She looks pretty in her dress and with her hair down for once.

'And then we've got our Grace,' Dad says.

Here we go.

'Grace, you're the proof that sometimes the best things in life just can't be planned for. From the moment we met you, we were besotted, and you've ensured we've stayed that way, astonishing your mother and I with your ability to turn your hand to absolutely anything. I can't say I'm thrilled at the prospect of becoming a grandfather at the age of forty, but any thoughts of vanity are cancelled out by how bloody proud I am of the way you and Sam – hang on a second, Sam, you stand up too.'

Sam clambers to his feet, smiling bashfully as people hold up their phones to take another round of photos.

'Sam,' Dad continues. 'I'm so proud of the way you've handled this situation with such maturity, positivity and determination, and how you've slotted into our family with such ease. I have no doubt whatsoever that the two of you are going to make wonderful parents. If you do even half as good a job as Nikki and I did with Grace, we'll be over the moon.'

I stare down at my fingernails as the room choruses, 'Aw,' and wonder where I might be on that scale. Am I considered a job well done? Or did Mum and Dad drop the ball with me, hastily plunging all their energy into raising Audrey in an effort to make up for it.

'And last but certainly not least, Mia.'

I brace myself, getting ready to plaster on the smile everyone expects.

'Our fiery, funny, spirited girl,' Dad says. 'As many of you may know, almost seventeen years ago, Mia gave Nikki and I a bit of a shock by arriving six weeks early. I don't think I got a wink of sleep until we finally got her home and she's been causing us sleepless nights ever since.'

Lots of laughter.

'Say what you like about Mia,' he continues. 'But there's never a dull moment when she's around. From the 2 a.m.

phone calls from Rushton Central Hospital, to her – let's just call them "interesting" – wardrobe choices, she certainly keeps Nikki and I on our toes. I'll tell you one thing though, we wouldn't swap her for the world.' He raises his glass. 'Love you to bits, baby.'

More laughter and a smattering of applause. I hold my smile as best as I can, my lips trembling from the effort. For a few horrible seconds I'm worried I might cry. I don't though, keeping my eyes as wide open as possible to stop any tears from forming.

The rest of the speeches go by in a blur of clinking glasses and laughter. I pretend to listen, smiling and laughing where I'm supposed to, when all I really want to do is escape from the table and get drunk with my friends. The second the dessert plates are cleared away, I bolt in the direction of the bar, only to discover Cara on duty.

'I'll get the drinks in,' I tell my friends quickly.

I take their orders and shoo them back towards the main room, waiting until they're firmly out of sight before taking a deep breath and walking towards the bar. Cara is waiting for me, wearing her trademark smirk.

'Can I help you?' she asks with over-the-top politeness.

I reel off my order.

'Sorry,' she says. 'I can't serve you.'

'Why not?'

'You're underage.'

'No, I'm not. I'm eighteen.'

She rolls her eyes. 'Give it up. You're still at Queen Mary's. Aaron told me.'

I swallow at the mention of his name. 'But this is my mum and dad's wedding,' I say.

'So? You're still underage and that means I can't serve you.'

She's full on grinning now. I can't let her know she's got to me, though. I won't.

'Fine,' I say, moving to the other end of the bar and trying to attract the other bar person's attention. 'I'll ask someone else then.'

'Oh, I wouldn't bother,' she says, producing a laminated piece of paper from behind the bar and handing it to me.

On it are the faces of all the underage guests at the wedding, average age twelve. My face flames with humiliation. I can't believe Mum and Dad have done this to me. To make matters ten times worse, the picture they've used is last year's school photo.

'Nice uniform,' Cara adds.

I stalk into the foyer, bashing straight into Sam.

'You OK?' he asks.

'No,' I growl.

'Why? What's up?'

I tell him about my mugshot behind the bar, leaving out the details of my connection to Cara.

'It's just so humiliating,' I say. 'How am I supposed to "grow up" when they insist on treating me like a little kid all the time?'

'Sorry, dude,' Sam says.

'Thanks,' I mutter, rubbing my shoulder.

That's when I realize how idiotic I'm being. *I* may not be able to get served tonight, but Sam can.

'Sam?' I say sweetly.

'No,' he replies, taking a step backwards. 'Absolutely not.'

'You don't even know what I was going to ask!'

'Yes, I do. And the answer is no.'

'But why?'

'Your parents would go mad, not to mention Grace.'

'They won't even need to know,' I say. 'We'll just say it's Coke if anyone asks.'

'I'm sorry, Mia, I just don't feel comfortable with it.'

'Just one drink, please!'

I clasp my hands together in prayer position and flutter my eyelashes.

'Pretty please with a cherry on top,' I singsong.

'I said "no", Mia.'

I let my arms fall by my sides.

'I thought we were friends,' I say.

'We are.'

'No we're not. Friends help each other out.'

'Oh, don't be like that, Mia,' he says, reaching for my hand.

I shake him off and stomp towards the toilets, my heels clacking against the marble floor.

I push open the door and walk straight into Patrice, a friend of Grandma Sapphire's.

'Mia!' she cries. 'I haven't seen you properly in ages. Excited about becoming an auntie, are you?'

It's a variation on the same boring question I've been asked at least twenty times today.

'Well?' she prompts.

That's when I realize I can't be arsed to pretend any more. 'No, not really,' I say.

Patrice laughs a big hearty laugh. She thinks I'm joking.

'I mean it,' I say. 'Grace's stupid baby is the worst thing that ever happened to our family.'

Patrice gawps at me.

'Excuse me,' I say, turning round and walking straight back the way I've come.

'Where are the drinks?' Stella asks when I find them outside on the terrace.

'Bad news,' I say. 'They're being really tight at the bar. You have to show ID to get served.'

'No way,' Stella says. 'That's so unfair!'

'Yeah, it's your mum and dad's wedding!' Mikey adds.

'It's hotel policy apparently,' I lie. 'They have to ID anyone who looks under twenty-five. Sorry, I had no idea.'

'I told you not to drink all the vodka at once,' Mikey scolds.

'Oh, relax,' I say. 'There's booze absolutely everywhere. We'll figure something out.'

Inside, the evening guests are starting to arrive – colleagues of Dad's, old schoolmates of Mum's, friends of the family – and the tables and chairs are being put away to make room for dancing. That's when I notice that there are still loads of half-drunk glasses of wine on the tables, left over from dinner.

Bingo.

Quickly I lead my friends round the room, giggling as we down as much wine as possible before it's cleared away, only Kimmie refusing to join in 'in case we get caught'. Zzzzzzzzzz.

By the time the master of ceremonies announces Mum and Dad are about to cut the cake, I'm feeling nice and tipsy again and about a million times better.

Stella has brought her fancy camera with her. As Mum and Dad giggle and feed each other slices of cake, their arms entwined, she flits around them, snapping from every possible angle, before following them as they make their way to the dance floor for their first dance. It's to 'Back for Good', the original version this time, thank God. They don't do a choreographed routine or anything like that, instead they just hold onto each other tightly and sway in time to the music while everyone else lines the edge of the dance floor and takes yet more photos.

I glance behind me. Although all the wine from dinner has now been cleared away, the tables are littered with abandoned drinks as everyone watches Mum and Dad. I slip away and help myself to a shot of Baileys and the dregs of what I think is a gin and tonic.

Ha. That'll show them.

The next song is fast and upbeat. Stella rushes to put her camera down on one of the tables and we immediately start leaping around like idiots. The alcohol is properly kicking in now and I finally feel like I'm having some actual fun, Cara and the stupid list behind the bar shoved further and further to the back of my mind with every cheesy song the DJ plays.

For the next hour, we dance to every single song, whether

we know it or not, until Mikey announces that he's sweating his 'arse off' and needs some water.

'I'll come with you,' Stella says. 'I'm bursting for the loo.'

Kimmie and I stay behind and are having a proper laugh dancing to 'Uptown Funk' when we spot Stella and Mikey racing towards us, their faces alight with scandal.

My heart plummets.

Cara. They must have spoken to Cara at the bar.

'Oh my God, Mia!' Stella cries, crashing into me, grabbing hold of both of my wrists and shaking them hard.

'What? What's wrong?' I stammer, paranoid fear shooting down my arms and legs.

'Paul's here!' she gasps.

Paul?

I didn't even know Mum and Dad had invited him.

'Where?'

I follow Mikey's pointed finger. Paul is standing on the edge of the dance floor wearing a dark suit. The sight of him makes me feel hot and embarrassed and childish, especially in my stupid flouncy dress. Next to him is a pretty woman around Mum's age. Paul's hand is resting very gently round her waist. I didn't know he had a girlfriend. I've certainly never seen anyone at the house. I can't decide if it makes me feel better or worse.

'But he's meant to be with you!' Kimmie gasps.

'Did you know he was bringing someone tonight?' Stella demands.

'What a scumbag!' Mikey cries.

'Look, can you guys please just shut up?' I beg,

desperately trying to get my story straight in my head. 'My mum or dad might hear you.'

They may be totally wrapped up in each other right now, but my parents are literally a metre away from us.

'I can't believe he's flaunting her in front of you like that,' Stella continues, her voice still carelessly loud.

'Oh, for God's sake, will you just shut up,' I hiss, grabbing her arm and dragging her off the dance floor, Mikey and Kimmie following close behind.

'He didn't even look at you!' Stella cries as we spill out into the busy foyer.

'Shut up,' I repeat. 'Please!'

My eyes fall on the photo booth Mum and Dad hired for the night.

I pull aside the curtain, relieved to discover it empty. Inside, it's slightly bigger than a normal passport-picture booth, but instead of a swivel chair, there's a plastic bench with space for three or four people to squeeze their bums onto. We clamber in.

'Are you OK, Mia?' Kimmie asks.

'I'm fine,' I insist.

'I wonder if she knows about you?' she adds.

'As if,' Stella chimes in. 'What woman in her right mind would put up with her bloke giving love bites to teenage girls?'

'Maybe he's going to suggest a threesome?' Mikey says.

'Oh, Mikey, don't be so gross!' Kimmie cries. 'People don't actually do stuff like that.'

'Oh, sweet, sweet Kimmie,' Mikey says, patting her on the head. 'You're *such* an innocent sometimes.'

262

The bright yellow light is making me feel dizzy. I just want them to shut up and leave me alone and for this entire day to be over.

'Seriously though, Mia,' Stella says. 'What are you going to do? Are you going to say something?'

'No,' I say. 'Last weekend was just a one-off. I don't know why you guys are even bothered. *I'm* not.'

'So you're OK with Paul parading his new girlfriend in front of you, then? Jeez, I didn't have you down as such a pushover, Mia.'

'I'm not a pushover,' I say. 'It's just not worth the energy. I told you, it's you lot making the big deal out of it, not me.'

'I just don't get how you can switch your feelings off like that,' Kimmie says. 'I know I couldn't.'

'It was easy,' I reply loudly. 'Because there were no feelings. It was just sex, that's all. If you'd actually done it, Kimmie, maybe you'd understand.'

Kimmie's face reddens and I feel a stab of guilt I really don't have the time for.

I just need this conversation to be over. Now.

As if on cue, the introduction to our anthem, 'Shake It Off', starts to play in the distance.

'Listen!' I say. 'Our song! C'mon, let's go dance.'

I lean across Mikey and whip open the curtain, only to reveal Grace, her mouth hanging open in a perfect 'O' shape, the expression on her face leaving me in no doubt she just overheard every single word.

30

'You had sex with Paul?' Grace whispers. 'As in Paul who lives next door?'

Sam is standing just behind her, shifting his weight from one foot to the other.

'Mia, answer me,' Grace says. 'Did you sleep with Paul?'

'No,' I say, my voice wobbling like mad as I try to fight my way out of the booth, my heel getting stuck in the curtain. 'Of course not.'

'Then what were you talking about just now?'

'It's none of your business. In case you hadn't noticed, that was a private conversation.' I try to push past her but she doesn't let me, her grip on my left wrist surprisingly strong.

'Mia, I can't just ignore something like that. He's more than twice your age!'

'So?'

'What do you mean, *so*? He totally took advantage of you!'

I have a flashback to what happened on Paul's sofa. I've replayed the scene so many times I can't remember what's real and what's not any more. All I do remember is how crap I felt, how small and childish and stupid.

'No, he didn't,' I say. 'Why do you always assume that? Why can't you just trust me to look after myself?'

'Because you blatantly can't!' she gasps. 'Oh my God, is that why you were acting so shifty on Monday morning? Is that where you'd been the night before? With Paul?'

'Hang on a second, you were with Paul Sunday night as well as Saturday?' Mikey asks, frowning.

Shut up, Mikey. Shut up, shut up, shut up.

'No,' I say.

'So where were you on Sunday?' Grace asks.

'I told you, revising at Stella's,' I say, praying Stella will play along with me, at least until we've managed to get rid of Grace.

'No you weren't,' Stella says. 'You didn't answer my texts the entire day.'

'In that case, where were you?' Grace repeats.

'Yeah, where were you?' Stella says, a strange look on her face.

'Excuse me, I'm sorry to interrupt.'

Everyone looks round to see who is speaking.

It's Cara. Smiling her horrible smug smile. I wonder how long she's been listening in, how long she's been plotting to bring me down. Because that's surely what comes next.

'Hello again, Mia,' she says. 'I'm so sorry, I totally forgot that I was supposed to give you a message. From Aaron?'

265

Kimmie lets out a tiny gasp.

'He would have called you,' Cara continues. 'But you didn't leave a number. Anyway, last Sunday you left your earrings on his bedside table. The peacock ones? I just thought you might like to know.'

I'd forgotten about my earrings. Kimmie made them for me for my last birthday. They're one of my favourite pairs. I glance over at her. Her face is flushed, her eyes flooded with water. Next to her, Mikey and Stella's mouths are hanging wide open.

'Lucky I bumped into you really, isn't it?' Cara adds, her voice sickly sweet. She smiles, flips her limp ponytail over her shoulder and walks back towards the bar.

Nasty. Evil. Interfering. Bitch.

Everyone is in a little semicircle, looking at me, hemming me in.

I turn my attention to Kimmie, whose lower lip is wobbling dangerously.

'Don't listen to Cara, Kimmie,' I say desperately. 'She's full of crap, just stirring. She fancies Aaron and he blew her off and now she wants revenge. Just ignore her.'

'But that doesn't make any sense,' Kimmie says slowly. 'Why would she drag you into it? She doesn't even know you.'

'I don't know,' I stammer. 'She's crazy, isn't she? Totally batshit.'

'Exactly what is going on here, Mia?' Grace asks. 'Did something happen between you and Paul or not?'

I hesitate. 'No.'

'You lied, then?' Stella says, blinking in disbelief. 'But why?'

'It wasn't my fault. You asked about the love bite and I panicked.'

'Because Aaron gave it you,' Kimmie says in a tiny voice. 'Didn't he?'

'Nothing happened,' I cry quickly. 'I was going to tell you all about it, Kimmie, but I thought you might be upset because I got to hang out with him and you didn't. I don't even fancy him, you know that.'

She takes a step towards me, breaking the semicircle formation. My back is pressed right up against the booth now.

'So why were you at his house?' she asks. 'Why did you take your earrings off? Why were they on his bedside table?'

'It's not as bad as it sounds.' But it is.

'Oh, come on, Mia, we're not total idiots,' Stella says, her voice impatient. 'Just admit it. Did you shag Aaron Butler on Sunday night or not? Yes or no?'

'I don't know.'

She pulls a face, like she's totally disgusted with me. 'You don't know? How can you not know, Mia?'

But I can't put it into words. Because then I'll have to admit I never slept with Jordan, that I've never slept with anyone properly.

'Oh my God, just tell the truth!' Stella cries.

'Me? You're the one applying to uni behind my back!' I explode.

'What?'

I describe what I saw under her bed last weekend. It

sounds petty when I say it out loud though, silly and insignificant.

'Seriously?' Stella says, folding her arms. 'You're comparing what you've done to me sending off for a few university prospectuses?'

'But we pinky swore on it,' I say, my voice verging on a whine.

'It's nowhere near the same,' Stella spits. 'You outright lied to us, Mia. The end.'

'It's not that simple,' I say.

I turn to Kimmie. She backs away, like she can't stand to be anywhere near me right now.

'Kimmie,' I say. 'Just wait . . .'

'You knew how much I liked Aaron,' she says, talking over me. 'And you don't even fancy him – you've said so at least a thousand times.'

'It's true, I don't. It wasn't like that.'

'Then why did you do it, Mia? Why?'

Because I felt stupid.

Because I felt sad.

Because I wanted to feel sexy.

And beautiful.

And like I mattered.

But I don't know how to explain any of that. It's all way too complicated.

Kimmie gives me one final look, like I'm a smear of dog poo on her foot, before bursting into tears and running towards the exit, Stella and Mikey shooting glares at me before rushing after her, leaving me alone with Grace and Sam.

'What the hell, Mia?' Grace asks.

I look up. She has her arms folded across her chest and is shaking her head at me in disappointment. The sight makes my blood boil. It's her fault I got into this mess in the first place.

'Why do you always have to stick your nose into my business?' I hiss.

'Excuse me?' she says, actually daring to pretend she doesn't know what I'm talking about.

'I had things under control before you opened your big mouth.'

'Under control?' she scoffs. 'Are you sure about that?'

'Yes! And then you came in and totally ruined it.'

She laughs. 'Oh my God, are you actually trying to blame *me* for all this?'

As she turns to Sam as if to say 'can you believe her?', I'm flooded with hate. I hate how neat her hair still is; how glowing her stupid pregnant face looks; how she always gets to play the role of 'Little Miss Perfect' no matter what the situation.

'You just don't get it, do you?' I say.

Over Grace's shoulder, I notice Audrey coming towards us.

'There you are,' she says, her face falling the second she clocks the expressions on our faces. 'Is everything OK?' she asks, her eyes round with worry.

'It's fine,' Grace says smoothly.

I almost burst out laughing. Not because it's funny, but because it's so ridiculous. Everything is *not* fine. It's the opposite of fine; it's a fucking disaster.

'Mum and Dad have been looking for you,' Audrey says, her eyes flicking from me to Grace and back again. 'They want to do a family picture in the photo booth before it gets too busy.'

'Good idea,' Grace says.

She turns away from me and starts searching through the box of props and costumes next to the booth. All I can do is stare at her back as she crouches down to select a feather boa and pair of oversized plastic sunglasses.

'Here they are!' Mum's voice rings out. 'My beautiful girls.'

I look up. She and Dad are walking towards us, arm in arm.

I stand rigid as Mum plonks a pair of Minnie Mouse ears on my head and a massive plastic medallion round my neck, while the others squeeze inside the booth.

'C'mon, you two,' Dad says, sticking his head out. 'We're waiting.'

Mum takes my hand. I have no choice but to follow her, grit my teeth and play Happy Families.

31

'There you are,' Sam says. 'I've been looking for you everywhere.'

At least I think it's Sam. It *sounds* like Sam anyway.

I'm right at the end of the terrace, slumped on the stone steps leading down to the lawn, my body sort of folded in half. I dunno how long I've been out here. Half an hour? An hour? Longer?

I get up, kicking over an empty wine bottle. It clinks as it rolls over the paving slabs. The person who I'm now almost eighty-five per cent sure is Sam picks it up and sort of peers at it like he's never seen a bottle of wine before.

'Mia, did you drink all of this?' he asks.

'What's it to you?'

I sound all funny, like I've lost half the letters in the alphabet. It makes me giggle.

'Oh my God, you did, didn't you?'

'Maybe. Maybe not,' I say, prodding him in the chest.

Oh God, there are two of him now. Sam and Sam. I don't know which one to look at so I settle for somewhere in the middle which makes me giggle even harder.

'Shit, Mia.'

I tut. 'It's my mum and dad's wedding. Am I really not allowed to have one 'ickle drink?'

'You've had more than one, Mia.'

'*You've had more than one, Mia,*' I repeat, in an exaggerated version of his posh accent. 'You know what, Sam? I like you and everything but you're a right spoilsport sometimes.' I prod him in the chest again, harder this time, forcing him to stumble backwards a couple of steps. 'Whoops!'

'You promised me you'd stop getting in this state,' he says. He looks all serious, his mouth set in a straight line.

'What state? I'm not in a state. Look.' I jump up on the wall and pretend it's a tightrope. 'See,' I say, balancing on one leg. 'I'm *fine*.'

'Mia, get down.'

'No,' I say, running along it, going faster and faster.

'Mia, seriously, get down,' Sam says, jogging alongside me, his arms outstretched as if primed to catch me. It sets off a fresh wave of giggles.

'Oh, don't be such an old lady, Sammy!' It's not even like I'm that high up. I do a leap. It feels good. Like I'm flying almost. I do another. 'Look at me, I could be in the circus!' I squeal.

'I mean it, Mia, get down,' Sam says. 'You might hurt yourself.'

'Or the Olympics!'

'Mia, I'm not joking!'

I blow a raspberry at him and do another leap, then change direction and run back the way I've come before transferring to the steps, jumping up and down them in rhythm as I sing. 'So, do, la, fa, mi, do, re!' I bellow, pretending I'm all the Von Trapp kids at once.

I get to the end of the song, the bit where they run up and down the steps while Julie Andrews sings a really high note. Only halfway down, I catch my foot on something and go flying, landing on the grass with a thud.

'Shit,' I hear Sam cry. 'Are you OK?'

The next thing I know he's kneeling over me, his face centimetres from mine. I can smell the smoked salmon starter from dinner on his breath.

'I'm fine,' I say.

'Gimme your hand,' he says, standing up.

I reach out an arm, but instead of letting him help me up, I pull him onto the ground. He lands on top of me hard, the flower attached to his lapel squishing against my cheek.

'Mia,' he says. 'What are you doing?'

'Rolling!' I cry. 'Let's roll together!'

I wrap my arms around him and push off with one foot to get us going.

'Mia, stop mucking about,' he says, trying to prise my fingers apart.

I'm on top of him now, pinning him to the lawn, my hair all in his face, in his mouth, making him cough and splutter.

'Stop it,' I say. 'I'm doing that thing. That thing where you roll down a hill together.'

'But there is no hill. It's totally flat.'

I stick out my lower lip in a sulk. 'You're no fun, Sam Castle. Sam Castle,' I repeat, dissolving into giggles. 'Sam bloody Castle!'

'Just let me get up, Mia, I'm serious now.'

'No, you're not. You're boring. Boring snoring!'

'What's going on?'

I can't work out where the voice is coming from. Only that there's a light shining right in my eyes suddenly, making me go all squinty.

'What's going on?' the voice repeats.

It sounds strict.

Grace.

Perfect Grace being all perfect.

I pretend to snore loudly.

'Nothing,' Sam says, wriggling free. I stay where I am, lying on my back, the wet from the damp grass soaking through my dress as I stare up at the stars. They look *so* pretty tonight. All twinkly and shiny and magical, like something out of the Nativity.

'She was on top of you, Sam,' Grace is barking.

She sounds annoyed. More than annoyed. Angry.

Ha. Now she knows how I feel half the time.

'She's been drinking,' Sam says. 'She fell and when I went to help her up, she pulled me down. Mia, for God's sake, get up and tell Grace what happened.'

I'm not getting up. I'm having a perfectly good time lying on the grass, thank you very much.

Sam grabs my arm, forcing me to stand up.

I'm all floppy though, and fall straight back down again. 'I don't want to get up! I want to stay down here and look at the stars and moons and planets.' I lie on my back, my arms and legs spread wide.

'Tell Grace,' he says. 'Tell her you were just being silly.'

Inside they're playing 'At Last' by Etta James. I spring up, the blood rushing to my head, and wrap my arms round Sam's neck.

'Dance with me, Sammy,' I say.

'Mia, no,' he says, pushing me away. I lose my balance, tumbling backwards onto the grass. I don't mind though. I like being on the grass. I like how it feels, how it smells. I cling on, digging my fingernails in the soil.

'Going for the hat-trick, is that it?' Grace asks. 'Paul, Aaron *and* Sam?'

What *is* she on about?

'God, I'm stupid,' she continues. 'I should have known all along. All those secret meetings were nothing to do with a surprise for me or the baby, were they? You were trying to nick my boyfriend the whole time.'

Me and speccy Sam? As bloody if. I start to laugh hysterically, the laughter fizzing through my body. I laugh so much my stomach actually hurts.

'Grace? Mia?' a voice calls.

What now?

It's Audrey, peering down from the terrace. I roll over, lying my cheek against the grass. It feels nice. Cool. If only everyone would just go away and leave me in peace.

'What's going on?' Audrey asks.

'Nothing, Auds, go back inside,' Grace says.

'But I heard shouting.'

'It's fine. We'll be with you in a minute.'

'But Mia's lying on the grass. What's wrong with her?'

'Nothing. She's getting up any minute now. Right, Mia?'

'Nope!' I say. 'I'm sleeping out here tonight. Camping! Night night.' I curl up in a little ball and pretend to snore again.

'Oh, for goodness sake,' Grace says.

The next thing I know, she's looming over me. I can see right up her skirt, her massive pregnancy knickers.

'Hi! My name's Grace and I'm the most perfect person in the entire world!' I say in a silly voice, dissolving into more giggles.

'Get up,' she orders. 'I'm putting you to bed.'

'You'll have to catch me first,' I say. I start to crawl away on my hands and knees.

'Oh my God, can you not see yourself right now?' she says. 'You're a total disgrace, Mia.'

I don't answer. I just continue to crawl round in circles, giggling.

'Right, that's it, I'm going to get Mum and Dad,' Grace says.

What? Noooooooooooo. I clamber to my feet and try to follow her. It's useless though. My limbs have gone all floppy and pathetic and I can barely put one foot in front of the other.

'Mia?' Audrey says as I make it up onto the terrace and stagger past her. 'Mia?'

I ignore her and push open the French doors. The disco lights make me feel dizzy. Everyone's on the dance floor, in messy rows doing the Macarena. But where's Grace?

I spot a flash of lilac dress through the archway into the bar. Bingo. I stumble towards it.

'Mia, come dance with me!' It's Poppy, one of my little cousins.

'I can't, Pops,' I say.

'Please!' she cries, grabbing a handful of my dress with her sticky little hands.

'Later,' I say, shaking her off.

I have something to do. But what? I can't remember. Hang on – yes, I do. Grace. I need to stop Grace. That's it. Stop her from telling on me.

I keep going, trying to ignore my wobbly legs and spinny head.

'Someone's in a hurry.'

It's Cara. She's carrying a tray of empty glasses and completely blocking my path. God, I hate her. She's the reason my friends left. She's the reason everything is a mess.

'Get out of my way,' I slur.

'Now that's not very polite. Don't I at least get a please?'

'As if, you stupid interfering cow. Now move.'

She sets down her tray on the nearest table. 'Make me.'

I grab her by the shoulders with both hands and push her. It's only meant to be a little push, just enough for me to get past and catch up with Grace, but it sends Cara slamming into the chairs behind her, sending them toppling over.

'You crazy bitch,' she says, recovering and striding towards me.

She's only little, short and wiry, but she pushes hard, sending me staggering backwards towards the dance floor.

'Sorry, sorry, sorry,' I say as I collide with the dancers on the front Macarena line.

I get my balance back and rush at Cara, pushing her with every bit of strength I have left. She goes crashing into a table this time, the floral table arrangement on top of it tumbling over, water spilling everywhere.

'Mia! What the hell are you playing at?'

It's Mum's voice. I just can't work out where it's coming from. All I know is that it sounds angry. That everyone is angry with me. I back away from Cara and onto the dance floor, where I try to hide amongst the other dancers. There's loads of them. Mum and Dad will never find me. I just have to keep moving.

'Yay! Mia!' Poppy yells, grabbing hold of both my hands and forcing me to jump up and down with her.

The jumping doesn't feel good though. At all. It's like I'm being shaken up like a can of fizzy pop.

'Stop it, Poppy,' I say, shoving her aside.

I'm in the centre of the dance floor now, surrounded by a vortex of dancers, lights flashing, music pounding in my ears. I *think* I'm standing still but my spinning head makes it feel like the entire world could tip at any second.

The introduction to 'New York, New York' kicks in and the DJ announces it's the last song of the night.

'Aw!' everyone choruses, forming a massive circle, arms round each other, leaving me all alone in the middle.

They're all smiling and laughing as they sing along, kicking their legs in time. Grandad Amos and Grandma Sapphire are beckoning me over, making room for me in the kick-line.

I'm stumbling towards them when my stomach does a weird lurch, like I'm going to be sick or something.

But I can't be. I haven't had that much to drink, not really.

I clasp my hand to my mouth but it's too late. Vomit seeps between my fingers.

I turn. Mum and Dad are inside the circle now, coming towards me.

I remove my hand, wiping it on my dress. Maybe that's it. Maybe no one saw.

Another lurch. Bigger this time.

My vomit hits the dance floor with an angry splatter. There's loads of it. Red then blue then green then yellow under the disco lights.

Then Dad is grabbing me by the elbow, my heels skidding in my sick as he hauls me across the dance floor towards the exit.

32

The atmosphere in the car is arctic. No one has spoken a word since we left the hotel this morning. Mum, Dad and Grace won't even look at me.

I'm stuck in the middle seat, just like old times. I fix my gaze on the magic tree air freshener dangling from the rear-view mirror and concentrate all my energy on trying not to puke, not that there can be much left *to* puke. I spent most of the morning with my head down the toilet, completely missing the buffet breakfast.

'Mia, we'd like to see you in the living room, please,' Dad says as we pull into the driveway.

I nod and follow him and Mum inside, leaving Grace and Audrey to unpack the wedding presents from the boot.

'I'm sorry,' I say, the second Dad closes the door behind us.

Mum whips round to face me. 'Sorry isn't going to cut it

this time, Mia,' she says, her eyes flashing with anger. 'Too little, far too late.'

'You just need to let me explain a bit,' I say, my voice sore from all the puking.

'Explain what?' she shouts, making me flinch. 'You completely ruined our wedding night!'

'I'm sorry,' I repeat, sinking down on the sofa.

Mum and Dad remain standing up, taking it in turns to pace up and down on the rug.

'Not good enough,' Mum roars. 'Not only were you completely drunk, you assaulted a member of staff!'

'Assaulted? It was just a push. And she pushed me first!'

It's not just about the push though. They know that and I know that. The push was just the icing on the cake.

'Enough with the excuses!' Dad booms. 'We don't want to hear them, Mia!'

'I can only imagine what people must be thinking and saying today,' Mum says. 'I've never been so embarrassed in all my life.'

I bite down on my lip so hard I can taste blood in my mouth. 'I'm sorry,' I whisper. 'Truly.'

'Stop saying that,' Mum snaps. 'It's meaningless. You've completely shown us up, Mia, the entire family.'

I start to cry, salty hot tears pouring down my cheeks.

'Stop it,' Mum barks. 'I don't have time for this. Literally. We need to pack.'

Mum and Dad are taking the train to London tonight, staying in a hotel near Heathrow airport before their morning flight to New York City.

'Part of me wonders if we need to cancel,' she adds.

'No!' I yelp, wiping away my tears with the sleeve of my hoodie.

If Mum and Dad cancel their dream honeymoon, they'll never let me forget it.

'Can you blame me?' she cries. 'How can we trust you to behave when you can't even behave at your own parents' wedding!'

'Please don't cancel,' I say. 'Please. I'll do anything you say, I swear.'

'We're not cancelling our honeymoon,' Dad says firmly, glancing at Mum, who just shakes her head and rakes her fingers through her hair. 'But we are going to need some time to think about your punishment. Until then, I think it goes without saying you're grounded until further notice.'

'But what about Newquay? It's only a week away.'

I sit on my hands. Newquay will still happen, won't it? Kimmie and the others can't keep up the silent treatment for ever. Can they?

Mum snorts. 'Not our problem. You should have thought of that before you made a complete sham of our special day.'

'We'll be checking in every day, but until we get back you're only to leave the house if you're under Grace's supervision, understood?' Dad says.

'Grace!' I cry. 'But it's her fault all this happened in the first place.'

'Look,' Mum says, wagging her finger, 'I don't know what's going on between the two of you, but there's absolutely no way you can peg anything that happened last night on your sister, no way at all, so don't you even try it.'

'I'm not trying to peg anything on anyone,' I cry. 'I'm just trying to *explain*!'

'Mia,' Mum yells, slamming her fist down on the mantelpiece. 'How many more times do I need to tell you? We're not interested in your excuses. We'll talk about this properly when we get back, but until then Grace is in charge, no arguments.'

Mum and Dad leave for the airport two hours later. I can't bring myself to say goodbye, huddling on the roof wrapped in my duvet instead as I listen to Grace and Audrey wave them off.

I try calling Kimmie again. Out on the terrace last night I fired off dozens of drunken apologetic messages, but so far I haven't heard a peep out of any of my friends in response. This time, the phone rings three times before going through to voicemail. She's clearly screening me and wants me to know it. I have nothing to add to the previous messages I've left (I've run out of new ways to say sorry) so I hang up. I try Stella again but she doesn't pick up either and neither does Mikey.

It starts to drizzle, forcing me indoors. As I'm climbing through the window, I catch my foot on the sill and end up sprawled on the carpet, trapped in my duvet.

The door opens. An upside-down Audrey peers down at me.

'Are you OK?' she asks.

'Fine,' I mutter, rolling onto my front before struggling to my feet.

'You look like a caterpillar.'

'Thanks.'

She hovers in the doorway.

'Did you want anything in particular?' I ask, shuffling over to my bed. 'It's just that I kind of fancy being alone right now.'

'Oh,' she says, blinking. 'I was just wondering if you wanted to watch TV with me? *Mary Poppins* is on in five minutes.'

Audrey adores *Mary Poppins* and knows every word of the script.

'Can't you watch it with Grace?'

'She's having a nap.'

'Sam?'

'He's gone.'

'Gone where?'

'Home.'

'What? Back to Cambridge?'

'Yes, I think so.'

'Why?'

'Grace wouldn't say.'

'When's he coming back?'

'I don't know.'

'Oh.'

It can't be to do with what happened on the grass last night. Can it? Does Grace honestly think something happened between me and Sam?

'Is that a "no" to *Mary Poppins* then?' Audrey asks.

'Yeah. Sorry. Not in the mood.' I chuck myself on the bed, landing with a thud.

'I think Grace is going to make some pasta in a bit,' Audrey adds hopefully.

'Thanks, but no thanks.'

'But what will you eat?'

'I'll make something.'

'But you can't cook.'

'Yes I can. I can make loads of things.' I cross my fingers under my duvet that there's bread and cheese in so I can make cheese on toast.

'But Grace is probably making enough for all of us.'

'I told you, I'm not interested.'

Another long pause.

'I hate it when you and Grace fight,' Audrey says in a small voice.

I shrug. 'She started it.'

'How? What happened?'

'I don't want to talk about it. Ask Grace. I'm sure she'll be more than happy to fill you in.'

'I already did. She said to ask you.'

'Well, sorry. No can do.'

Audrey continues to hover in the doorway, the long sleeves of her hoodie pulled down over her balled-up fists.

'Isn't your film starting soon?' I say.

'Oh, yeah.' She turns to go, then stops. 'Are you sure you don't want to watch it with me?' she asks. 'It might cheer you up?' She hums a couple of bars of 'A Spoonful of Sugar'.

'Positive. Shut the door behind you, yeah?'

'OK,' she says softly.

'Cheers, Auds.'

33

Distant ringing wakes me up. In my sleepy fug, it takes me several seconds to figure out it isn't part of the dream I was having, and then a few more to work out it's the landline. I hear Grace's door creak open and her footsteps cross the landing and head down the stairs.

I roll onto my front and reach for my mobile. It's already gone ten. I usually love the first weekday of the summer holidays, waking up and knowing I have nothing to do and nowhere to be. Not today, though. I wonder how long my friends are going to stay mad at me for. Another week? Two? A month? The whole summer?

For ever?

I could message someone else, I suppose. Stacey or Kat or Tamsin. I scroll through my contacts and even compose a few messages, but I can't quite bring myself to press send. That's the problem; me, Stella, Mikey and Kimmie come as a team of four and everyone knows it.

It's raining out. I can hear it splattering against the windowpane. Maybe I'll just stay in bed today, hide from the world. I yank the duvet over my head and make a cave. It reminds me of the dens Grace and I used to make when we were little. We'd take every sheet and duvet cover we could find and drape them over the dining-room chairs and table to create a tent. We'd sit under it for hours, and if Mum was in a good mood she'd let us have a little picnic in there, and Grace and I would take it in turns to make up stories, and it would feel like the cosiest, safest place on earth.

'Audrey!' Grace hollers. 'Phone for you!'

I stay where I am as Grace makes her way up the stairs, her voice getting louder as she continues to call Audrey's name. A few seconds later the door bursts open.

I peel back my duvet so my head is poking out. 'Ever heard of knocking?' I ask.

Grace ignores me and walks over to Audrey's bed. 'Auds,' she says. 'Phone for you.'

'God, just let her sleep for once,' I mutter.

Grace glares at me over her shoulder. 'It's hardly the crack of dawn. I've been up since eight.'

'Well, of course *you* have,' I mutter, rolling over so I'm facing the wall.

'Auds,' Grace says. 'It's Lara on the phone. C'mon, Audrey, wakey, wakey.'

There's a gasp, followed by a clunk.

Now what?

I roll over and sit up. The phone Grace was holding is

lying in the middle of the carpet and Audrey's duvet has been pulled back to reveal a row of cushions.

'Oh my God, oh my God,' Grace whispers, grabbing at the cushions and tossing them aside as if she's expecting to find a pocket-sized Audrey hiding beneath them. As she's doing this, a piece of paper flutters through the air. I jump out of bed and scoop it up just before it hits the floor. It's folded in half, our names printed on the front in Audrey's familiar round, fat handwriting.

I bend down to pick up the phone. 'Lara?' I say. 'We're going to have to call you back.'

Grace snatches the note out of my hand. I snatch it back.

'Just open it, for God's sake,' she says.

'Fine,' I snap, unfolding the note.

We read it in silence.

Dear Grace and Mia,

I'm not sure how long it will take for you to realize I'm gone, since half the time you don't seem to notice me anyway. I'm sorry if you're worried or anything like that but I'm just so sick of being stuck in the middle of your arguments all the time. No one tells me what's going on. I don't know, maybe with me out of the way you'll sort things out finally.

Love,
Audrey x

'Shit,' Grace says, sinking down onto Audrey's bed.

288

I haven't heard her swear in ages. It sounds weird, like she's speaking lines from a play.

'Didn't you see her leave?' she asks, looking up at me. I'm still in the centre of the room, the phone dangling from my right hand.

'No.'

'But you share a bedroom with her!'

'Do you think I don't know that? What about you? You're the one that's been up for hours.'

'She must have left before I got up. I would have heard her otherwise.'

Which means wherever Audrey's gone she's got at least a two-and-a-half-hour lead on us.

'Lara's been trying to get hold of her since before nine. That's why she ended up trying the landline,' Grace says. 'She couldn't get through on Audrey's mobile.'

I toss the landline phone on my bed, grab my mobile off my bedside table and call Audrey's number.

'Voicemail,' I report. 'Should I leave a message?'

Grace heaves herself up off the bed and plucks the phone from my hands.

'Oi!' I cry.

'Audrey,' she says into the phone, turning her back on me. 'It's Grace.'

'And Mia!' I shout. 'I'm here too! In fact, it's my bloody phone we're calling you on!'

Grace lowers the phone to her chest. 'For God's sake, Mia, will you shut up for one minute!' She returns it to her ear. 'Audrey, we found your note and we're worried about you. We need to know where you are so we can come get you and bring you home. Ring me as soon as you get this message, OK?' She hangs up.

'Now what?' I ask. 'We sit and wait for her to ring us back with her location? Because that sounds like a foolproof plan.'

'She can't have gone far,' Grace says, pacing up and down on the rug. 'This is Audrey we're talking about. She never goes anywhere by herself. She'll probably be back by teatime.'

Although she sounds decisive, I know Grace well enough to hear the doubt in her voice. I go over to the window and shove aside the curtains, my eyes immediately drawn to the bottom of the garden.

'Don't count on it,' I say.

'What do you mean?'

'Come look.'

Grace joins me at the window. 'What am I supposed to be looking at?' she asks.

I jab the glass with my finger. 'Beyoncé's hutch,' I say.

Grace's eyes bulge. The hutch door is hanging wide open.

'She's taken Beyoncé with her,' I say.

Translation: Audrey means business.

'How did she seem last night?' Grace asks.

We're slumped on the floor, our backs against my bed frame. We've called everyone we can think of and not one of them has seen or heard from Audrey.

'I don't know. Normal, I guess.'

'Did she say anything?'

'No. She just put her pyjamas on and turned out the light.'

'But she must have left some sort of clue as to where she's gone,' Grace says. 'She can't just vanish into thin air. Are you sure you have no idea?

'I told you, no.'

'But you're her sister!'

'So are you!'

'Well, you share a room with her!'

'Exactly. A room, not a brain.'

Grace checks the time on her phone. 'Mum and Dad don't land for another five and a half hours,' she says. 'We need to find her before then.'

'Oh, I see, so *that's* what you're worried about. Audrey going missing on your watch.'

'Of course not,' Grace snaps. 'How could you say something like that?'

'Sorry,' I mutter, only half meaning it.

We sit in silence for a few minutes.

I take out my phone and google 'popular destinations for teenage runaways'. Loads of stuff comes up about illegal raves and festivals and drugs. I try – and fail – to imagine Audrey at a rave. She doesn't even like school discos very much.

I let my eyes drift around the room. Something doesn't look right. Something *else* is missing, something we haven't noticed yet. But what?

My gaze keeps snagging on the noticeboard that hangs

over Audrey's bed. It's covered with cinema tickets and clippings from magazines and old birthday cards. Something about it doesn't look right, though. There's a big gap in the centre.

A postcard-sized gap.

That's when I realize what's missing. A postcard with 'Greetings from Windermere' on the front.

I leap up. 'I think I know where she is,' I say.

'Where?' Grace cries.

'Frankie's of course. She's gone to the Lake District.'

34

An hour later we're sitting in a massive traffic jam on the motorway going absolutely nowhere.

Next to me, Grace shifts in her seat, her bump pressing up against the steering wheel. Now I get why heavily pregnant women are advised not to drive if they can help it. She's wearing her pregnancy jeans, which look like normal jeans apart from round the waistband where there's a stretchy band of Lycra where the zip and button would normally go.

We were in such a hurry to leave I didn't have time to get dressed properly. Over the top of my pyjamas bottoms and my 'It's All About Mia' T-shirt, I'm wearing my bright yellow raincoat, my bare feet sweating in a pair of spotty wellies I think might be Mum's.

I try Audrey's mobile for about the seven-hundredth time. 'Voicemail again,' I report, hanging up.

'I at least hope she's on a nice warm train or bus,' Grace

says as rain pelts the car from what seems like every possible direction.

'Me too,' I murmur.

The bad weather is making the radio crackle and we don't have the right lead to plug in either of our phones, forcing us to sit in silence. Now we're pretty sure we know where Audrey is headed, we have absolutely nothing to say to each other.

The car is boiling, the windows all steamed up. I fiddle with the various knobs on the dashboard but none of them seem to do what I want them to.

'Which one of these is the air con?' I ask.

'It's broken, remember?' Grace says. 'You'll have to open a window.'

'But it's pissing it down.'

She shrugs.

I sigh, pull up the hood of my jacket and wind down the window. Rain spatters my face and pyjama bottoms.

'Can you see what's going on?' Grace asks after a bit.

I take off my seatbelt and stick my head right out. It's bumper-to-bumper and grey gloom as far as the eye can see. I take out my phone and google 'traffic jam M1'.

'There's been a massive accident at the next junction,' I say. 'They're clearing it but it sounds like it's going to take a while.'

Grace bites down hard on her lip.

'Why? What's wrong?' I ask.

'It's just that I really need the loo.'

'You always need the loo.'

'Mia, in case it hadn't escaped your attention, I'm pregnant.'

I gasp. 'No! Really? You *never* talk about it.'

Grace glares at me. 'I have a baby pressing down on my bladder, Mia, a *baby*, and until you know what that feels like you have absolutely no right to make fun of me.'

I roll my eyes towards the roof of the car. 'Go take a pee, then. I'm not stopping you.'

'Where exactly? We're miles away from the nearest service station.'

'Just go at the side of the road.'

'Are you serious?'

'That bloke just did,' I say, pointing to a man zipping up his fly and jogging back towards his lorry.

'I am not going to the loo on the side of the M1.'

'Only trying to help.'

We sit in silence for a bit. By now my pyjama bottoms are soaked through and sticking to my thighs.

'Maybe we should play a game or something,' Grace suggests. 'To help keep my mind off it.' A pause. 'Fine,' she says, noticing my unimpressed expression. 'No car games.'

There's another long pause. I wind my window up half-way, rest my head against the glass and close my eyes.

'I didn't tell on you, Mia,' Grace says.

'Huh?' I say, twisting my head to look at her.

'At the wedding. You know, when we were out on the grass and I said I was going to fetch Mum and Dad. I didn't mean it.'

'Oh.'

'I said it to scare you mainly,' she says. 'I hoped the idea of them finding you like that would sober you up a bit.'

I shrug and return to looking out the window.

'By the time I'd calmed down a bit they'd already found you on the dance floor, you know . . .'

'Puking my guts up?'

'Yes.'

'Right.'

My damp pyjama bottoms are starting to itch.

'You called me a disgrace,' I say.

She winces slightly. 'I know. I was angry. It was Mum and Dad's special day and there you were, absolutely hammered.'

I close my eyes again. Like I need reminding.

'It's all about Mia . . .' she says.

'What?' I open my eyes. Grace is staring at the words on my T-shirt. I fold my arms round my chest.

'It certainly was the other night,' she says.

'That's the thing, though,' I say. 'People only seem to notice if I do something bad.'

She raises an eyebrow but doesn't say anything.

'Look, while we're on the subject of the other night, nothing ever went on between me and Sam, OK?' I say. 'We're just mates.'

'I know,' she says, sighing.

'I mean, me and Sam? As if.'

'There's no need to be rude, that's the father of my child you're talking about.'

'Keep your knickers on, I didn't mean it like that. I just

can't believe you thought I'd actually go after him. It'd be like snogging my brother or something.'

'I don't know. After all that stuff came out about you and Paul and Aaron, I saw you rolling around on the grass and jumped to conclusions.'

'We were hardly rolling around,' I mutter. 'Not like that anyway.'

'Look, if I'm being perfectly honest, I don't know what I thought, Mia. I feel like I just don't know you any more. It's like you're a stranger sometimes.'

'Well, same with you,' I hit back. 'It's like having a robot for a sister.'

Silence.

'Why did he go home?' I ask finally.

'Sam? He said he needed "a break". I can't say I blame him. It wasn't exactly a relaxing weekend.'

'When's he coming back?'

'I don't know. In a few days maybe.'

There's a grumbly roll of thunder, followed a few seconds later by a dim flash of lightning.

'I still don't quite understand what happened the other weekend,' she says. 'With Paul and Aaron. Why you lied.'

'There's no point even talking about it,' I say. 'You've clearly already made up your mind about what you think went on, so I'd just be wasting my breath.'

She frowns. 'No, I haven't.'

'Yeah, you have. You think I'm a slut and a liar, same as Kimmie and everyone.'

'No, I don't. I would never call you either of those things.'

297

'Maybe not in so many words.'

You're a total disgrace, Mia.

'Please, just tell me what happened. I want to under-stand.'

The rain is getting ridiculous now, coming down in heavy sheets. Reluctantly, I wind up the window all the way and peel off my raincoat, lying it on the back seat next to Grace's baby book.

'What did you mean when Stella asked you if you'd slept with Aaron and you said you didn't know?' Grace asks.

I shrug and fiddle with the drawstring on my hood, threading it through my fingers.

'Was it your first time?'

I don't answer her.

'Oh, Mia. Why didn't you just say so?'

'How could I? They all thought I did it ages ago. With Jordan.'

I didn't even have to lie about doing it with him. Not really. Everyone assumed we were doing it from the start. I just didn't bother correcting them. Jordan said he didn't mind that I wanted to wait. He even said it was 'classy'. At least, he did at first.

'It's OK to be a virgin, you know that, don't you, Mia?' Grace says.

'Of course I do,' I snap.

I don't even know if I am one any more, whether what happened in Aaron's bedroom actually counts as sex or not. So far Google hasn't given me a firm answer either way.

'And Paul?' she asks.

'I told you, nothing happened. Nothing like that.'

She nods. 'I'm sorry I got you into trouble with your friends,' she says. 'But I had to say something, don't you see? Paul is more than twice your age. Imagine if you were in my position and it was Audrey you'd just overheard having that conversation.'

'It wouldn't be the same. Audrey's thirteen.'

'She's still your little sister though, and she'll never stop being your little sister, no matter what age she is. Just like you'll never stop being mine.'

There's a pause. I glance at the satnav. We'll be lucky to reach Frankie's place before dark the way we're going.

'Have you heard from Kimmie or anyone?' Grace asks, rubbing her lower back.

'Hey, why don't you push your seat back?' I suggest. 'We're not going anywhere for a while.'

She nods, unclipping her belt and adjusting her seat, leaning it right back. I do the same so we're both reclining as far as we can go, almost horizontal.

'So, have you?' she asks, resting her hands neatly on her bump. 'Heard from any of them?'

'Like you actually care.'

'Of course I care. They're your best friends.'

'Not any more. You saw the way they looked at me the other night. They hate me.'

'It'll blow over.'

I shake my head. I've never seen them that angry before, especially Kimmie. And Kimmie just doesn't get angry normally. It's not in her DNA.

'Why did you go home with that Aaron boy?' Grace asks. 'If it's true what you said about not even liking him that much.'

'It's none of your business.'

'Please, Mia. Just talk to me. You used to all the time.'

'I know. That was before.'

'Before what?'

Before everyone realized how amazing you are and started comparing us all the time. Before I worked out we were different. There's a weird lump in my throat. I swallow hard but it doesn't go away.

'I don't know, it's just hard being your sister sometimes,' I say eventually. My voice sounds weird, sort of quivery.

'How do you mean?'

'Grace, you got the best GCSE and A-level results in Queen Mary's history. You were the star of the netball team, the best singer in the choir. You're going to one of the best universities in the entire world. God, everyone worships the ground you walk on,' I say, the words pouring messily out of my mouth. 'Do you have any idea what it's like to try and live up to that?' I add.

She doesn't say anything.

'Exactly. And to make matters worse, Mum and Dad prove it's not a fluke by then having Audrey. And I'm just left in the middle, looking like a complete disaster whatever I do.' I realize I'm out of breath and that my heart is thumping.

'That's not true.'

'How would you know? Your life is perfect.'

300

Her face softens. 'Is that what you think, Mia? That my life is perfect?'

'Of course,' I say.

'Don't get me wrong, I'm happy, but my life is far from perfect, Mia, believe me. It's tiring and frustrating and stressful sometimes.'

'Well, it's not from where I'm standing,' I say, my voice cracking.

'It's not like everything gets handed to me on a plate, Mia. I worked my arse off for those grades. And everything else.'

I bite my lip, remembering all those times I got up to go to the loo in the middle of the night and saw a strip of light under Grace's door as she revised into the early hours of the morning.

'You were clever to start with, though,' I say.

It's a well-known family fact that Grace could write her full name at the age of two, that she's always been naturally bright.

'I know that,' she says. 'It doesn't mean I don't have to put the work in, though. I don't just turn up to the exam and magically know all the answers.'

'So, I'm lazy, is that it?'

'That's not what I said. I just think maybe you haven't worked out what your thing is yet.'

Not this again. Why can't people accept that maybe not everyone has a thing?

'I meant what I said just now,' she continues. 'About my life not being perfect.'

301

'Then why don't you show it once in a while?' I ask.

'It's not that easy. I have all these expectations on me.'

'Boo hoo.'

She glares at me. 'I'm trying to be honest with you, Mia.'

'Sorry,' I mutter, peeling my damp pyjama bottoms away from my legs and trying to squeeze out some of the moisture.

'When you have a reputation for never making mistakes, it becomes very hard to know how to behave when you do.'

I look across at her. 'Are you talking about the baby?'

She looks guilty, placing her palms on the bump as if covering the baby's ears.

'But I thought you had it all figured out from the beginning,' I say. 'That's what you told Mum and Dad.'

She hesitates. 'We may have given them a slightly edited version of events. Put very simply, I went to pieces. After doing the test I cried for about three hours straight. I felt like my life was over. I knew I wanted kids someday, but I imagined having them in my late twenties at the very earliest, not now. I was just so angry. We'd been careful, we didn't deserve to get caught out.'

'Did you think about getting rid of it?'

'Yes,' she says, not even missing a beat; *not* what I was expecting. 'We talked about it a lot.'

'So why didn't you?'

Another guilty glance down at her bump. 'One night I woke up with blood on my knickers and I completely freaked out. The idea I might lose the baby was horrible. We went to the doctor and she checked me out and reassured me everything was OK and that a bit of spotting was normal, and as we left the hospital, we both just knew; we definitely wanted to keep it.' She sighs again. 'Look, I know we turned up in Rushton acting all calm and collected, but that's because we kind of were by that point. We'd done all our crying and freaking out and arguing back in Greece. Plus, I guess I wanted to prove I had everything under control. I didn't want Mum and Dad to worry.'

'Typical Grace,' I say, drawing her name with my finger in the steamed-up window. 'Can't stand to come across as a work in progress.'

'Something like that,' she says quietly.

There's a pause.

'God, I need a wee,' she says.

I offer her an empty Coke bottle from the footwell.

'Very funny,' she says.

'Beggars can't be choosers, Grace.'

'It's because we stopped talking,' she says. 'I need you to keep going, distract me from my weak pregnant lady bladder.'

'Well, what do you want me to talk about?'

'Tell me about what happened with Aaron.'

'Grace—' I begin.

'Please,' she says. 'No judgement, no interruptions, I swear. I just want to listen.' She glances at me. 'I promise not to breathe a word to anyone,' she adds. Then she crosses her heart, across her chest the way we used to when we were little anytime we exchanged secrets, big or small.

'I dunno, it's kind of a long story. It's not just about that night.'

303

She raises her eyebrows at the satnav display. 'I think we've got time.'

I hesitate, unsure where to start, before taking a deep breath. 'Thinking about it, I suppose it all kind of started to go wrong the morning I found out you were coming home . . .' I say slowly.

I expect Grace to butt in or defend herself but she doesn't. She just listens. And when I'm finished she holds onto me tight until the cars behind start beeping at us to get moving.

35

'Better?' I ask Grace as she emerges from the service station toilets twenty minutes later.

'Blissful,' she confirms.

'Have you got any cash so I can get a bag of crisps or something?' I ask. 'I'm starving.' Apart from half a protein bar I found under the passenger seat, I haven't eaten a thing today.

'We should eat something proper,' Grace says. 'We've still got a long drive ahead of us.'

Our choices are limited to McDonald's or the 'Fresh Choice' café, which looks anything but.

'McDonald's it is, then,' Grace says, heading towards the queue.

'But you hate McDonald's,' I say. 'You think it's the devil's food.'

'It'll be quick at least,' Grace says. 'And besides,' she adds sheepishly, 'Bean's kind of been craving Chicken McNuggets lately.'

*

'This is so weird,' I say ten minutes later.

Grace is sitting opposite me alternating dunks of her chicken nuggets into a packet of barbecue sauce, with noisy slurps of her chocolate milkshake.

'It's like you've been body-snatched or something,' I add.

'I told you, it's Bean.'

'Whatever. Everyone knows cravings are just an excuse for pregnant women to stuff their faces with all their favourite foods.'

'Not true,' Grace says. 'Just look at Mum; when she was pregnant with you she licked bricks.'

'What?'

'I'm serious. It's really common apparently.'

'That's so gross.'

'Pregnancy kind of is,' Grace says, shrugging.

'Mum and Dad are going to be landing soon,' I say, glancing at my phone.

'I know. They said they'd try to ring us once they're through passport control.'

'What are we going to say?'

'I don't know yet. It depends on whether we've reached Audrey or not by then.'

I rub my chest with my fist. I've eaten my cheeseburger too quickly and need to burp.

'Did you have any idea?' Grace asks, taking Audrey's note out of her pocket and smoothing it out on the sticky table. 'That Audrey felt this way?'

The sight of it makes my stomach flip-flop with worry.

'Not really,' I admit. 'I mean, I knew it bothered her when we argued, but not enough for her to do this.'

'Same here.' Grace wipes her salty fingers on a napkin.

'Are we bad big sisters?' I ask.

She considers this for a few seconds. 'I just think life maybe got in the way for a bit. The only thing we can do now is bring her back and do our best to make it up to her.'

I nod. 'I just hope she's OK, Grace,' I whisper.

'Me too, Mia,' she whispers back, reaching for my hand. 'Me too.'

We know we're getting close when the terrain around us begins to change. After miles and miles of just motorway with fields on either side, I can see actual mountains now, their jagged tops dark and menacing against the pinky orange sky. We're getting closer.

My phone beeps. 'I'm going to run out of battery any minute,' I say.

'Use mine,' Grace replies.

I try Audrey once more and leave her a final voicemail letting her know we're nearly there.

It's almost dark when we pass the sign welcoming us to Windermere. Grace steers the car through the winding streets, through the town centre as featured on the postcard, and out the other side again, the gaps between the houses getting bigger and bigger.

'Frankie wasn't kidding when he said he was living in the middle of nowhere,' I say.

We haven't seen another house or human being for at

least three miles now, the road getting increasingly narrow and windy as the car chugs uphill.

Finally the smooth voice of the satnav informs us we've reached our destination as we drive up to a large stone cottage with lots of tiny windows. My legs feel stiff and slightly numb after so many hours cooped up in the car. I glance at Grace. She's peering up at the house, a worried expression on her face.

'Is this definitely it?' I ask.

'Yes, I think so,' she says. 'Number fifty-five, look.' She points at the brass number on the rickety gate.

'Do you think we maybe got here first?' I wonder aloud.

'I don't know about that,' Grace says. 'Auds had a pretty good head start on us. And all the trains up here were running OK – I checked on my phone when we were at the service station.'

We approach the front door cautiously. The doorbell is disconnected, hanging off the wall, stray wires sticking out in all directions. Grace uses the knocker instead, thumping it against the door.

Silence.

I push in front of her and have a go.

Again, nothing.

I drop to my knees and stick my fingers through the letterbox, forcing it open so I can peer in. The hallway is pitch black and smells of fresh paint and wood shavings.

'Audrey?' I call. 'Are you in there? It's Mia. Let us in.'

Grace groans as she crouches down to join me at the letterbox, her body creaking with effort. 'Auds,' she calls, her McDonald's breath warm on my cheek. 'It's Grace. Open the door, sweetheart.'

For a few beats, apart from the gentle fizz of the never-ending drizzle, there's absolute quiet. With every second that passes, my heart sinks further and further, from my stomach to my knees, to my feet. I've got it wrong, haven't I? Audrey isn't here after all. She's on the other side of the country, wet and lonely and scared.

Then we hear it. A loud creak on the stairs. Grace's fingers seek out mine. She squeezes. I squeeze back. Together we watch as a fat torch beam bounces on the stairs, a few seconds later illuminating a familiar pair of battered pale-pink Converse.

I help Grace stand up just in time for the door to ease open a few centimetres, Audrey's brown eyes peering over the top of a chunky safety chain.

My body floods with love and relief.

'You found me,' Audrey whispers, her voice wobbling all over the place.

'Of course we did, you dumb-arse,' I say. 'You're our little sister.'

She starts crying properly then, snot bubbles and everything.

'Now, are you going to open the door or what?' I ask.

The second the door is fully open, Grace and I lunge at Audrey, sandwiching her between us. We're all crying now, hot, messy, happy tears.

'Are you sure you're OK?' Grace asks when we finally separate, gripping Audrey by the shoulders and looking her up and down as if inspecting her for injuries.

Audrey wipes her eyes and nods. 'Positive.'

'Why didn't you ring us back? Didn't you get our messages?' Grace asks, rifling in her bag for a tissue. 'We've been worried sick.'

'There's no mobile reception here. I walked up the lane for a bit but it didn't make any difference and it was starting to get dark so I thought I'd better come back to the cottage, then try again in the morning.'

'Is Frankie not here?' Grace asks, looking over Audrey's shoulder.

'No. He's been at his niece's wedding in Cornwall, remember?'

'Wait, he doesn't know you're here?'

Audrey shakes her head and looks guilty.

'How did you get in then?' I ask.

'I found a key under a plant pot.'

'You broke in?' Grace cries.

'It's not breaking in if you use a key. Is it?' Audrey asks, looking a bit scared suddenly.

'It is if you don't have permission,' Grace says.

'Frankie wouldn't mind. He said I could come visit him in the holidays. I'm just a bit early, that's all.'

I can't help but grin.

'I haven't touched anything!' she adds.

'That's not really the point,' Grace says, folding her arms across her chest.

'Look, never mind that. Can we come in?' I ask. 'My hair's getting well frizzy.'

Audrey nods and leads us inside.

310

We stick our heads into each of the downstairs rooms in turn. All the furniture is draped with white sheets and the shelves and the windowsills are bare. The smell of paint tickles my nostrils.

'Frankie's been staying with his sister while they do the work,' Audrey explains. 'That's how I knew it would be empty.'

I try flipping a couple of the light switches but nothing appears to be working.

'The electricity isn't on,' Audrey confirms. 'Or the water.'

Upstairs, we discover Audrey has set up camp in the corner of the smallest bedroom at the very back of the house. Her SpongeBob SquarePants sleeping bag is already unfurled on the bare mattress, her belongings lined up neatly against the skirting board, a couple of fat church candles providing just enough light for us to see each other's features properly.

Beyoncé is nestled on Audrey's travel pillow nibbling a lettuce leaf.

'I can't believe you ran away with your guinea pig,' I say, taking off my raincoat and wellies.

'What was I meant to do?' Audrey asks, scooping Beyoncé up in her arms. 'I couldn't trust you to feed her. You hate her.'

'Hate is a strong word, Audrey. I'm not keen on the nasty little ball of fluff, that's true, but I wouldn't purposefully starve her. I'm not a monster. Oooh, is that wedding cake?'

'Yes, want some?' she asks, holding up a plastic container stuffed full of leftovers.

I never got any at the wedding (for obvious reasons) so I help myself to a slice of each flavour. We sit on the bed and munch in silence for a bit, listening to the rain patter against the windowpanes. After about a minute Grace takes out Audrey's note and sets it down in front of her.

Audrey chews on her fingernail.

'Is this really how you feel, Auds?' Grace asks, her voice gentle.

'Sometimes.'

'Why didn't you talk to us about it?'

'It's not that easy,' Audrey says, her voice going all wobbly again. 'Whenever I try to keep the peace, you always tell me it's between the two of you, like that means I'm automatically not going to worry about it. But I do! I worry all the time. I'm just so tired of feeling like I'm stuck between you all the time and no one noticing I'm even there.'

I stare at her. Audrey feels stuck in the middle? But that's *my* place.

'It's like you don't even realize I have eyes and ears sometimes,' she continues. 'You two are so loud and confident, I just fade into the background half the time.'

'You?' I splutter. 'But you're like school royalty. Everyone at Queen Mary's worships the ground you walk on.'

'Only when I'm in the water. I mean, it's nice that people are supportive and stuff, but sometimes I worry what it would be like if the swimming was taken away from me and I was just plain old Audrey.'

'But why would it?' I ask.

'I don't know, I'm just saying "what if". I know I'm only

popular a bit because people think I might win an Olympic medal some day and become some kind of celebrity.'

'Do you want to stop swimming?' Grace asks gently. 'Is that what this is about?'

'No!' Audrey yelps. 'I *love* swimming. I just don't want it to be my whole identity.'

I continue to stare at her. All this time I've been worrying about being pigeonholed as the party girl with big hair, oblivious to the fact Audrey has been dealing with the same kind of insecurities.

'Mum and Dad's lives revolve around you,' I say. 'How can you feel left out when you're at the centre of everything they do? I mean, they planned their entire wedding and honeymoon around your training schedule.'

'I know. And that's part of the problem,' she says. 'Ever since things got really serious, all Mum and Dad seem to talk to me about is swimming stuff. It's all schedules and meal plans and working out who's taking me to the pool and when. I don't know, sometimes I worry if I suddenly stopped swimming, I'd stop existing altogether.'

A brand-new tear, big and fat, escapes from her right eye and rolls determinedly down her cheek.

'Oh, come here, you wally,' I say, kneeling in a slice of cake as I crawl across the mattress to hug her. Grace waits a second before putting her arms around us both, resting her chin on my shoulder. She smells of chicken nuggets and the oil she rubs on her belly to prevent stretch marks.

'It'll be OK, Auds,' Grace says as we separate and continue to eat our cake. 'When Mum and Dad get back from

New York we'll all sit down and have a proper talk. You shouldn't have to bottle this stuff up, OK?'

Audrey nods. 'I really didn't mean to scare you,' she says.

'That's OK, Nemo,' I reply.

'Really?'

'Really,' Grace clarifies. She checks the time on her phone. 'It's way too late to drive back tonight,' she says. 'Let's spend the night here and head back in the morning. In the meantime we should probably drive somewhere where we can get some signal so we can get in touch with Mum and Dad. If they try to get hold of us and can't, they'll be frantic.'

We drive back into town. Mum and Dad must still be at the airport because Grace's call goes straight through to voicemail. We leave a long message explaining we're all getting an early night, in the hope they won't try to contact us again until tomorrow morning. On our way back, we stop at a late-night supermarket, where we purchase bottles of water, a trio of unappetizing sandwiches and a toothbrush each for me and Grace. By the time we've got back to Frankie's and have eaten our rubbish sandwiches, we're all exhausted, flopping onto the mattress in a heap and falling asleep within seconds of each other, our limbs tangled up in a messy heap, sisters reunited.

36

A hand on my shoulder jerks me awake. It takes a couple of seconds for my brain to catch up and remember where I am. I guess the candles must have burnt out, because despite the lack of curtains hanging at the windows, the room is as black as ink. It's started to rain again, a steady pitter-patter against the rickety old glass.

'What is it?' I croak. My left arm is totally dead. I pick it up with my right and whack it against the mattress.

'They've broken,' Grace says. Her voice sounds weird, panicky.

'What have?' I ask, the feeling in my arm slowly returning.

'My waters,' she says, her voice continuing to quiver. 'I think the baby's coming.'

I sit up. 'You're joking, right?'

'I don't think so,' Grace says. 'The mattress is wet through. Feel.'

She grabs for my hand. I shake her off. As if I want to *feel*. 'Look, are you sure you haven't just peed yourself?' I ask. 'I know what you're like these days.'

'Yes, I'm sure,' she growls, spit hitting my cheek.

'God, I was only asking, there's no need to bite my head off. It doesn't necessarily mean the baby's coming though, does it? Your waters can break, like, days before you actually give birth.'

'How do you know that?'

I hesitate, not wanting Grace to know I've been looking at her stupid pregnancy book. '*One Born Every Minute*,' I bluff.

'No,' Grace says. 'It feels really, really weird. And I've been awake with stomach pains literally all night. Bean's coming, I'm certain, Mia.' She lets out a low almost animalistic moan, her left hand gripping my wrist so hard I yelp out in pain.

'OK, OK, I believe you,' I say, prising off her fingers one by one. I reach for my phone to check the time before remembering it ran out of battery ages ago. 'Where'd you leave your phone?' I ask, clambering out of bed, my eyes slowly adjusting to the dark.

'In my bag,' Grace says. 'You'll need to turn it on, though.'

I walk round the edge of the bed, feeling for Grace's bag on the floor. Her phone seems to take for ever to turn on. Behind me, she continues to groan. Finally the phone lights up. It's 3.33 a.m.

'When's the due date again?' I ask over my shoulder.

'The twelfth of September.'

Of course. I remember Grace being really smug about the fact the baby will probably be the oldest in its year at school.

'It's too early,' she says, her voice breaking. 'It's too early, Mia.'

'No, it's not,' I say firmly. 'I was early, remember, and I was fine.'

Grace lets out another growl. Audrey, curled up at the end of the mattress like a cat, doesn't even stir.

'Oh God,' Grace cries. 'It hurts, Mia! It really hurts!'

'OK, OK, I get it. What should we do? Ring an ambulance?'

'How?' she wails. 'There's no signal, remember?'

Shit, she's right.

'Auds?' I say. 'Audrey, wake up.'

The body at the end of bed squirms. 'What's wrong?' a scratchy voice asks.

Grace answers by letting out a long moan.

'We think the baby might be coming,' I say.

Saying the words out loud unblocks a fresh wave of panic. Because this is actually happening. We're all alone, miles away from home and Grace is in real-life labour.

'What?' Audrey cries, sitting bolt upright. 'Seriously?'

'Yes.'

I swallow.

Now what?

Help, that's it. We need help.

'Now, listen to me, Audrey,' I say. 'When you tried to get some phone signal earlier, how far did you go?'

'Oh my God, I can't believe the baby's coming! This is so exciting!' she says, bouncing up and down.

Grace yowls in disagreement.

'Audrey, focus,' I say. 'How far did you go?'

'Um, er, let's see, I walked for about fifteen minutes one way and another fifteen the other.'

Not the answer I was after. There's no way I can send Audrey out in the pitch black, not to mention the fact it's still absolutely chucking it down outside.

Think, Mia, think.

'How far away was the nearest house?' I ask Grace. 'Do you remember from the drive up here?'

She responds by grabbing a handful of my T-shirt and wailing.

'Light,' I say. 'We need some light.'

Audrey leaps off the bed and relights the candles.

I thought the light might be comforting, but somehow everything was actually a whole lot less scary in the dark. The flickering light reveals the sweat pouring down Grace's face and the terror in her darting eyes. I can make out the wet patch on the mattress. It smells faintly of Mum's baking, which is just plain weird. According to Grace's book, some women experience 'a trickle', others 'a gush'. Grace is clearly in the 'gush' category.

Wait a second. The book. Of course.

'Audrey,' I say. 'Find the keys and go down to the car. On the back seat there's a book. Bring it up here.'

She springs into action, pulling on her hoodie and Converse and grabbing the torch.

'Hurry, Audrey,' I say.

She stands up, her laces still undone, and clatters down the stairs and out the front door.

I turn back to Grace. 'Here, drink this,' I say, thrusting a bottle of water in her face and holding it to her lips. Most of it ends up dribbling down her chin.

'Mia!' she yells. 'Be careful. It's going all over me.'

'I'm bloody trying!' I yell back. 'You keep moving about.'

'I don't have my bag,' Grace says, looking frantically about the room.

'It's right here,' I say, pointing at her handbag.

'Not that one, my hospital bag.'

'Well, what was in it?' I ask.

'Everything!' she bellows.

'There's no need to shout at me!'

Audrey bursts back into the room with the book.

'Keep drinking,' I instruct Grace, shoving the bottle into her trembling fingers.

I snatch the book from Audrey's hands and flick through its pages until I find the chapter I'm looking for – 'The Labour'.

'Torch!' I bark.

Audrey slips the torch into my hand. I shine it on the page, my eyes skimming the words.

'OK, contractions,' I say. 'How far apart are they?'

'How am I supposed to know?' Grace cries. 'I haven't been counting. I just know it hurts. A lot.' As if to demonstrate, she lets out a howl of pain that sounds like she's being murdered.

'OK, I think that was probably one,' I say. 'Audrey, start counting.'

'What?'

'Counting. You know, one, two, three . . .'

'Oh! OK.' She starts to count.

'Sam,' Grace says. 'I want Sam.'

'I know you do. But he's in Cambridge and we have absolutely no way of contacting him right now so you're stuck with us for the time being, OK?'

She starts to cry. So presumably not OK, then. I try to block her out and keep reading.

Oh God. Oh no.

'What is it?' Grace asks between her tears. 'What does it say?'

'You need to check if part of the baby is showing,' I say.

Grace is still in her stripy top from yesterday and a massive pair of maternity knickers. 'In that case, you're going to have to help me take my pants off,' she says.

'What? You want *me* to look?'

'Well, *I'm* hardly going to be able to, am I?' she says, gasping with pain.

For the next few seconds communication is impossible because Grace is screaming so loudly.

'How long was that?' I ask Audrey.

'How long was what?'

'The contraction?'

'Oh! I don't know,' she admits. 'I got distracted by all the noise and forgot where I was.'

'Audrey!'

'Sorry,' she says, her lower lip wobbling.

Which is all I need. Both of them in tears.

'Shit, sorry, I didn't mean to shout. Where were you roughly?'

'I don't know. Maybe about sixty?'

'OK. Fine, we'll go with that.'

'Go see if you can find some towels,' I say, mainly because that's what they always seem to request in old-fashioned films – towels and hot water.

Audrey nods and races out of the room again, taking the torch with her.

Removing Grace's knickers is harder than I thought it would be. She's too busy groaning to listen to my instructions, making it tricky for me to manoeuvre them over her bent legs.

At first I think she's shat her pants because there's brown sticky stuff all over her knickers. Gross. The second I've got them over her feet, I fling them as far away as possible.

'Right,' I say, steeling myself for the actual looking-at-my-sister's-vagina bit.

'Oh my God!' Grace cries, her eyes widening.

'What?'

'Fire!'

I whip round. Over by the window, Grace's pants are aflame.

'Shit!' I cry, racing over to them. The stupid things must have landed on one of the candles.

I stamp up and down on them, dousing them in water for good measure, totally soaking the bottom of my pyjama bottoms in the process.

'What am I supposed to wear now?' Grace asks as I poke at her fried knickers with my foot.

'Trust me,' I say. 'You did *not* want to put those back on.'

'How do you know that?'

'Because they were covered in brown goo!'

'That's. The. Mucus. Plug,' Grace gasps in ragged bursts.

'The mucus what?' I guess I haven't got to that bit in the chapter yet.

'Mucus plug! It clogs up the cervix to keep fluid from escaping.'

I clasp a hand to my mouth. 'Oh my God, you've basically just described vagina snot.'

'Mia!'

'Well, that's what it sounds like!'

'Shut up about the mucus plug and look between my legs!'

'Stop yelling at me!'

'Mia!'

I peer between her legs, terrified I'm going to see a baby's head hanging out or something. Luckily I see nothing of the sort, just Grace's vagina and absolutely no baby.

'Well?' she demands.

'Nothing yet.'

She flops her head back on Audrey's travel pillow. 'I want Sam,' she says again.

Audrey returns with a bundle of towels in her arms, her eyes bulging when she spots that Grace is half-naked.

'Where are your pants?' she asks, frowning.

'Don't ask,' I reply.

We arrange towels on the bed and sit on either side of Grace, holding one hand each. We take long deep breaths and try to encourage Grace to join in with them, mainly because that's what I've seen on television and I've run out of ideas as to what else we can do. I still feel quite daft though, like a children's TV presenter, as I chant 'in and out'. At some point Audrey takes my other hand, so we're sort of sitting in a little circle, like we're conducting a séance. We continue to time the contractions, each one bringing a fresh wave of bloodcurdling screams. Now that I've seen her vagina once and know what to expect, I keep peeking between Grace's legs every few minutes just in case, every time stupidly relieved the baby appears to staying put, at least for now.

Even though the book is full of assurances that it's perfectly normal, I wasn't prepared for how much blood and other weird sticky stuff there'd be. It's everywhere, on the towels, on the wall, on Grace, on my clothes and hands and arms and cheeks.

Sweat is pouring down Grace's face, the heat radiating off her like she's a human hot-water bottle.

'You're absolutely boiling,' I say, tugging at her top. 'Maybe we should take this off.'

We have a go at pulling it over her head but she's too exhausted even to lift her arms.

'Hang on!' Audrey says. She jumps off the bed and rummages in her backpack.

'What's that?' I ask.

'Dad's Swiss Army Knife.'

'Get you, professional runaway,' I say.

Carefully we cut through Grace's top until it falls away from her blazing hot skin. Before she got pregnant, Grace was always a bit prudish about nudity, favouring one-pieces over bikinis and always wearing a bra, even when she was just chilling around the house, so it's all a bit odd and *very* unGrace-like to see her totally naked, splayed out on the bed, gigantic belly, legs akimbo, wailing like a banshee.

That's when things go up a gear, Grace's yells taking on a new intensity.

'I think I want to push,' she cries.

'But you can't!' I tell her. 'If you push, the baby might come out.'

I can't deliver a baby, I just can't. Under absolutely no circumstances.

'I want to push,' Grace insists, clambering onto her hands and knees, her bare bottom in the air.

'But you can't,' I say. 'Tell her, Audrey.'

Audrey just gapes at me. 'I'm scared,' she mouths.

I pretend not to understand her. Because if I do I'll have to acknowledge that I'm scared too, and if I do that, I'm not sure I can take it back.

'You just need to hold on a bit longer,' I say to Grace.

Just until it gets light enough for me to send Audrey to get help. Professional help.

'I can't, Mia,' Grace screams, almost deafening me. 'It's coming!'

I throw a look at Audrey. Her eyes are wide with fear.

'Should I go?' she asks, looking out the window.

The sky is slightly less black than it was earlier but it's still basically dark out. At least it's stopped raining so hard.

Grace lets out another scream.

'OK,' I say. 'But stick to the main road. And if you need to knock on someone's door to use their phone, don't go inside, but insist they bring the phone to you, OK?'

'OK,' Audrey says.

'And Sam!' Grace yells. 'Ring Sam.'

'I will,' Audrey promises, grabbing the torch and her mobile.

'Be careful,' I yell after her.

The door slams shut behind her, leaving Grace and me alone.

I grab the book, my eyes struggling to focus on the relevant page. Not that it's all that much help right now seeing as it assumes we'll be tucked up in a nice, safe hospital full of medical equipment and people who know what they're doing at this point. There's certainly no handy how-to guide for amateur midwives at the back for me to refer to.

Grace lets out another scream, almost dislocating my wrist as her body twists and writhes.

'Fuck!' I cry, peeling her fingers away. 'That really hurt!'

She doesn't even reply, just growls in my face like a wild animal, spit flying everywhere.

Hurry, Audrey, hurry.

The growling goes on for another twenty minutes, intermingled with the odd swear word and episode of screaming, the contractions now so close together I've given up counting.

I have another look at her bottom end. This time it looks different. I can see something.

'Oh my God, Grace,' I say. 'I think I can see the top of its head!'

Grace doesn't answer, just continues to wail.

I grab a clean towel. 'I think it's time,' I say.

She nods, gripping onto the headboard and gritting her teeth.

I get into position. Is this really happening to me? I haven't got time to decide.

'Push, Grace,' I say. 'Push like you've never pushed before.'

She lets out a roar and all of a sudden the entire head is poking out of her vagina. It's without doubt the weirdest, grossest thing I've ever seen in my entire life. I put my hands out ready.

'Yes!' I cry. 'Just like that! Another one just like that, Gracie!'

She pushes again, and again, the shoulders suddenly visible, then the torso, until suddenly the entire baby slithers out like an eel and I almost drop it.

And there it is. An actual baby, tiny and warm and writhing in my arms, umbilical cord still attached. It's covered in blood and goo and looks like a horrible little alien with hair, but I don't care, it's out and it's alive. There's a moment of horrible silence before it lets out a mewing cry, a bit like the noise next-door-but-one's cat makes when it's hungry.

Grace collapses on her side before rolling onto her back. 'Is it OK?' she says. 'Please tell me it's OK.'

'It's crying,' I say.

And crying is good. Because crying means it's breathing. And breathing is most definitely good.

'What is it?' she gasps.

'Um, a baby.'

'No! Boy or girl?'

'Oh. Hang on.'

I peek under the towel I've wrapped it in. 'It's a boy, Grace,' I say, placing him in her arms. 'A really fucking beautiful baby boy.'

I can hear sirens in the distance. Then my legs sort of give way and I sink down on the floor, my bum hitting the floorboards with a thump.

That's when I start to cry.

37

'Is he OK?' Sam asks.

I peer into the hastily purchased car seat next to me. Elijah William Brendan Castle is fast asleep beneath a fleecy blanket, his tiny hands balled up into fists on either side of his crusty little face.

'For about the thousandth time, he's fine,' I reply.

Sam grins sheepishly. 'Sorry,' he says.

Even though he was on the small side at five pounds exactly, on our arrival at the hospital the midwife declared Elijah perfectly healthy, and after a day and night of observation, he and Grace were allowed to leave after breakfast this morning.

The five of us are squeezed into Sam's car. We've left Mum and Dad's parked at Frankie's, to be retrieved at a later date. Frankie was very nice about everything when we finally managed to get hold of him on the phone, even refusing Sam's offer to buy him a brand-new mattress and set of towels, despite the fact they're totally ruined.

We've been on the road for three hours now, sticking to the slow lane at Grace's insistence. Having reportedly spent most of last night sitting on the edge of her hospital bed gazing at Elijah, she's finally surrendered to sleep, snoring away in the front passenger seat. Audrey is asleep too, dribbling on my shoulder.

'Are you not tired?' Sam asks.

'I'm OK.'

I managed to grab a few snatches of sleep last night, but I had crazy dreams about Grace being in labour and kept waking up, sweaty and confused.

Everything after the ambulance arrived is a bit of a blur. I know the paramedics must have delivered the placenta and cut the umbilical cord, but I don't remember any of it. All I remember is the crazy relief I felt as they swooped in in their green uniforms, armed with medical equipment. In the ambulance, Grace held my hand and didn't let go until we arrived at the hospital in Kendal.

I take another glance at Elijah. I keep trying and failing to equate the baby in the car seat next to me, all clean and dressed and sweet-smelling, with the sticky, bloody thing that slithered into my hands not even forty-eight hours ago.

'Is there a John Lewis bag back there?' Sam asks.

I spot one squished at Audrey's feet.

'Yeah,' I reply. 'Why?'

'Take a look inside it,' he says.

I reach for it, frowning as Sam watches me in the

rear-view mirror. I empty the contents on my lap. The cuddly lizard from John Lewis tumbles out.

'When did you get this?' I ask.

'That day we went to Waterside. I ran back to get it while you were in the loo.'

I look down at the lizard. Its eyes have been stitched on wonkily.

'Anyway, it's yours,' Sam says.

'Mine? Why?'

'Consider it a totally insubstantial thank you gift.'

I shake my head and can't help but smile.

There's a pause.

'Sam, would you be offended if I regifted it?' I ask.

He grins. 'Course not.'

'Thanks.' I nestle the lizard next to Elijah in the car seat. It's almost as big as he is.

'His first cuddly toy,' Sam says.

Another pause.

'He looks like you, you know.'

'Huh?' I say, meeting his gaze again in the rear-view mirror.

'Elijah. He looks like you.'

'Oh, it's the 'fro,' I say.

Just like me when I was a baby, Elijah has a ball of black fuzz that sits on the very top of his head like the bobble on a hat.

'No,' Sam says. 'It's more than that. The look in his eyes. Pure Mia.'

As if on cue, Elijah opens his eyes, blinking a few times before fixing his gaze on me, and sort of frowning.

'Yeah,' Sam says. 'Determined.'

'Ha. Good luck with that.'

He laughs.

I give Elijah my right index finger. He hesitates before letting his impossibly tiny digits curl round it, gripping on tight.

If I listen really hard I can hear 'Shake It Off' playing on the radio, the volume turned right down. I haven't heard it since the night of the wedding.

'I'm sorry, by the way,' I say.

Sam frowns at me through the rear-view mirror. 'What for?'

'About what happened at the wedding. You know, outside, on the grass. I was drunk and feeling sad and I acted like an idiot.'

'Don't worry about it. We've all been there.'

'Grace hasn't,' I point out.

'Oh, I don't know about that. When you get the chance, ask her about the night she discovered ouzo.'

I raise an eyebrow.

'Trust me,' Sam says. 'She has her moments.'

There's a pause.

'Are you still sad?' he asks.

'Huh?'

'You said you were sad and that's why you acted the way you did.'

I shrug. The last two days have been so consumed by Grace and Audrey and Elijah that it's been easy to ignore the mess with my friends, the fact they still clearly hate me.

'I'll be OK,' I say.

I'm not sure I really believe this, though. Every time I imagine my life without my friends in it, it feels like the complete opposite of OK.

'Is there anything I can do to help?' Sam asks.

I sigh and shake my head. 'Thanks, but I have a feeling this is something I have to sort out on my own.'

When I step into the hall two hours later, the house seems different somehow, like someone's come in and moved all the furniture a fraction in our absence. It feels like we've been away for longer than two nights, weeks not days. It's not just the house that feels different, though. *I* feel different too, in ways I can't quite explain.

I stoop to pick up the post off the doormat. There are a few bills for Mum and Dad, a pizza delivery menu, a couple of taxi cards, and a squishy package addressed to me, which must have only just fitted through the letterbox.

'Coming through,' Sam whispers.

I step aside so he can get past with the car seat. Grace and Audrey follow, a slightly bewildered Beyoncé in Audrey's arms.

'I'll put the kettle on,' Grace says, padding towards the kitchen.

I head upstairs. Audrey's pillows and duvet are still on the floor. I pick them up and roughly make her bed. Then I sit down and squeeze the package, confused as to what might be inside.

I rip it open and reach inside. It's the T-shirts I designed for Newquay.

I unfold one and hold it up against my torso.

It's All About Kimmie.

I still haven't heard from her, from any of them. It's the longest we've gone without speaking. I keep checking the Newquay WhatsApp group just in case I've missed a notification for some reason but no one has posted a thing since the Friday before the wedding.

Our flight to Newquay is due to leave first thing this coming Monday morning. Stu was supposed to be driving us to the airport in return for a new Xbox game. I wonder if they're planning to go without me? The thought of my empty seat on the plane makes my heart ache. I keep imagining all the stuff I'd planned – the surfing lessons and the nightclubs and the BBQs on the beach, only with me missing. It just doesn't feel right. We come as a four, not a three. Mia and Stella and Mikey and Kimmie. I just don't know how to put it right again.

The rest of the week passes in a blur of dirty nappies and not enough sleep, cheese on toast and endless rounds of tea, and epic phone calls to Mum and Dad. It takes every ounce of persuasive power the four of us possess to convince them not to get on the next flight home and to complete their honeymoon as planned. They've been on the phone almost constantly though, and we've narrated the story of Elijah's birth at least ten times. It still doesn't quite feel real though, no matter how many times I describe it. It's almost like it happened to someone else and I'm just pretending I was there, making it up as I go along.

*

It's Saturday morning. I'm sitting out on the patio when Grace emerges from the kitchen, cradling a cup of tea.

'Mind if I join you?' she asks.

'Go for it,' I reply.

She sits down and puts her feet up on the table next to mine. She looks exhausted but happy, the dark circles under her eyes offset by an almost permanent smile of wonder. 'They nice?' she asks, nodding at the fancy box of macaroons balanced on my thighs. They were a gift from Sam's mum who came to visit yesterday (hands-down the poshest woman I've ever met).

'They're insane,' I admit, offering up the box. 'Can't stop eating them.'

Grace chooses a pistachio one and takes a delicate bite.

'Back to normal tea, then?' I ask, leaning across to peer into her mug.

'Yes,' she says.

'Thank God. That raspberry stuff was evil.'

'Oh, it wasn't that bad. In fact, it was quite nice once I got used to it.'

'What was it meant to do again?' I ask. 'Facilitate an easy birth or something?'

There's a beat before we both burst out laughing.

'You should ask for your money back,' I say.

'Don't,' Grace gasps, clutching her stomach. 'My tummy muscles can't take it.'

By the time we've calmed down Grace's tea is stone cold.

I set the box of macaroons on the table and sit back in my

chair, my arms dangling over the sides. Grace reaches across and grabs my hand, taking me by surprise. Her fingers are soft and warm.

I glance over at her. She's looking at me intently, her eyes wide and unblinking.

'I couldn't have done it without you, you do know that, don't you?' she says.

'Yeah, you could have,' I say, letting our joined hands swing back and forth. 'You're "Amazing Grace" – you can do anything.'

She winces ever so slightly at the nickname. 'I mean it, Mia. You were . . .' She pauses as if searching for the right word. 'Miraculous,' she says eventually.

I raise an eyebrow. Miraculous. Now, there's a new one.

'Miraculous Mia,' she says.

For once I don't argue. I just shake my head and smile and let my head drop back so I'm looking up at the brilliant blue sky. Grace does the same, so we're matching.

We're sitting like that, our fingers still entwined, when we hear Audrey yelling our names from indoors. Frowning at each other, we stand up and head inside, as surprised as each other to discover Mum and Dad struggling through the front door with their suitcases, a day early.

Half an hour later we're all in the living room, Mum and Dad installed on the sofa. Elijah is tucked in the crook of Mum's arm, and she and Dad are gazing down at him with complete heart eyes. It turns out they managed to get on an earlier flight and wanted to surprise us.

335

'We would have tidied if we'd known,' Grace says, gesturing at the messy living room.

'Don't be daft,' Dad says, not taking his eyes off Elijah.

They ask for yet another account of the labour; Grace, Audrey and I taking it in turns to narrate while Mum and Dad listen open-mouthed, despite the fact they've heard it all before. After about a billion questions they distribute New York-themed gifts – fridge magnets and snow globes and jumbo packs of Reese's Pieces and 'I love NYC' T-shirts (plus a babygro version for Elijah).

I'm in the kitchen making a round of tea when Mum comes in. She looks tanned but exhausted. I don't think she slept on the flight, which means she's been awake for at least twenty-four hours now.

'Need some help?' she asks, yawning.

'No, I got it,' I say, counting out mugs from the cupboard and lining them up on the draining board.

She sits down on a stool and watches as I reach for the tea bags. 'You're different,' she says.

I raise an eyebrow. 'Different how?'

'I'm not sure, just different. More grownup.'

'It's only been a week since you last saw me,' I point out.

'A pretty extraordinary week though, wouldn't you say?'

'That's one way of putting it, I suppose.'

There's a pause as I drop tea bags into the row of assembled mugs.

'What you did for your sister was so special and amazing, Mia.'

I bite my lip. 'Special' and 'amazing' are adjectives

usually reserved for Grace. Then Mum's face changes.

'Although it doesn't erase what happened last weekend –'

I chew my thumbnail and look at my feet, embarrassed at the reminder.

'– I don't think it's going to do either of us any good to dwell on it.' Mum continues. 'So here's what I propose. Starting today we turn over a fresh page, and going forward you're fully responsible for what you write on it, OK?'

I nod.

'Because I believe that page could be filled with wonderful things, Mia, incredible things. But it's up to you, you're the only one who can change the narrative.'

I nod again and try to let her words sink in.

I'm getting a second chance. A proper one.

I raise my head. 'Thank you, Mum,' I whisper.

There's a long pause where Mum just looks at me, her head tilted to one side. 'I'm so bloody proud of you, Mia,' she says eventually, her eyes glistening with the beginnings of what look like tears.

This makes me go red for some weird reason, which is totally not like me.

'We both are,' Mum continues. 'Me and your dad. Grace said you were just incredible during the labour.'

'It wasn't like I had much of a choice,' I say. 'I was hardly going to file my nails and leave her to it, was I?'

'Stop playing it down.'

I shrug, mainly because I don't know what else to do.

'I mean it. You really stepped up, Mia. Not many

sixteen-year-olds can claim to have safely delivered a baby into the world.'

'Nearly seventeen,' I say, reaching for the kettle.

I'm still having trouble with the word 'delivered'. Surely it was Grace who delivered the baby? I was just the one there to catch it.

Mum smiles. 'Sixteen *or* seventeen, no one's ever going to be able to take that away from you.'

'I'm not planning on a career in midwifery any time soon if that's what you're getting at,' I say.

'Why not? You'd be brilliant.'

I put down the kettle. 'Mum, you're not serious.'

She holds up her hands. 'Just a suggestion.'

'No bloody way. I saw things the other night I never *ever* want to see again.'

She laughs. 'Fair enough.'

There's another pause. I open the fridge and reach for the milk I bought earlier.

'I also wanted to apologize,' Mum adds.

'Apologize?' I say, unscrewing the lid. 'What for?'

She takes a deep breath and makes me put down the milk, holding both my hands in hers. 'I'm not sure your dad and I have always been very fair on you, Mia, especially over the last few months. We try our best to treat you girls equally but I don't know if we've always succeeded in doing that. I just wanted you to know that we're sorry and that we're trying. I never ever want you to think we're not proud of you, Mia, because we are, OK? More than you'll ever know probably.'

I squirm. I'm so unused to praise from Mum I have absolutely no idea how to take it.

'I guess what I'm trying to say is that success or achievement isn't always about getting straight As or winning medals, and I'm sorry if your dad and I haven't always made that clear.' She smiles and leans against the counter. 'You know what I said to your dad earlier?'

I shake my head.

'I said, it wouldn't surprise me if Mia took over the world one day.'

I pull a face.

'I mean it,' she says. 'And so does that RS teacher of yours.'

I frown and look up. 'Miss Linden? Wait, when did you talk to Miss Linden?'

'I didn't. She says so in your school report.'

I swallow. As far as I was aware it was still under my mattress, where I shoved it.

'I found it while I was changing your bed sheets,' Mum explains.

'Oh.' I pause. 'Did she really say that?' I can't resist asking. 'About me taking over the world?'

'She sure did. She thinks you're a proper force to be reckoned with. She really wants you to join the school Feminist Society too, thinks you'd make an excellent chair.'

'The chair? Me?'

'Yep, she thinks you'd be wonderful at the job.' Mum's face changes. 'Hang on a second – haven't you read it? I put it back.'

I shake my head.

'Why not?'

'I dunno,' I say, fishing the tea bags out of the hot water with a spoon, catapulting them into the sink one by one.

'Oh, Mia,' Mum says. 'Come here.' She holds out her arms. I put down the spoon on the counter and let her hug me. 'I love you,' she says. 'So much.'

'I love you too, Mum.'

We break apart, our faces identically tear-stained. Mum starts to laugh, wiping her tears on her sleeve before reaching to smudge mine away with her thumbs. Gently she pushes a loose curl behind my ear, pausing to tweak the lobe, the way she used to when I was little to signal she'd finished combing my hair.

'You must be getting excited about Newquay,' she says, resting both hands on my shoulders.

'I thought I was grounded until further notice.'

She lets her arms fall to her sides. 'About that. Your dad and I had a chat on the plane and we both agreed that we want you to go. Providing you take it steady with the drink and check in with us every day. New page and all that.'

I fiddle with the hem of my T-shirt.

Mum tilts her head to the left. 'What's wrong? I thought you'd be happy.'

'I'm not going.'

'What?'

'We kind of had a falling-out at the wedding. No one's talking to me.'

'Why not?'

'It's a long story. It's all my fault, though.'

'Oh, Mia, I'm sorry. I know how hard you worked to pay for it. Maybe they'll come round at the last minute?'

'I doubt it.' It's been a week. If they were going to forgive me, surely they would have by now.

'Have you tried talking to them?'

'I've called and messaged about a hundred times.'

'But have you tried talking to them face-to-face?'

'They're not gonna speak to me if they're not even returning any of my calls or messages. Anyway, I wouldn't know what to say. You know what I'm like, I'll only come out with the wrong thing and make it even worse.'

'Maybe try writing down how you feel then. That way you can say exactly what you want.'

'I'm not good at this stuff, Mum.'

'That Miss Linden of yours begs to differ,' she says. 'Look, at least give it a try. You never know, getting everything off your chest might just be the key.'

Later that evening, I sneak upstairs. Before I do anything else, I reach under my mattress and pull out my school report. I sit down on the floor and flip to the last page. Squished beneath the table of numbers and grades, Miss Linden has added a handwritten message:

Mia is a bright, inquisitive and charismatic young woman, bursting with energy and ideas. She brings the classroom to life and I'm proud to teach her. My only fear is that she doesn't realize just how much potential she has. I truly believe the world will be hers for the taking if she just puts her mind to it.

P.S. The Feminist Society is on the lookout for a new chair and I suspect Mia's personality and magnetism would make her the perfect candidate. Something to consider over the holidays perhaps?

I read it twice, then hug it to my chest for a few seconds as I process her words.

I exhale, set it aside and stand up.

Time to try and be the Mia in the report; the one Mum and Miss Linden claim to see.

Time to face up to things and say sorry. Properly.

I head over to the desk. I find some paper in one of the drawers, pick up a pen and start to write. It's not as simple as just starting at the beginning though, and it takes me ages to figure out what I want to say, balled-up pieces of paper soon littering the carpet like snowballs. In the end I figure out my only option is to tell my friends absolutely everything, in all its ugly messed-up glory.

No more lies, no more excuses, just the truth.

38

Dear Stella, Mikey and Kimmie,

I thought about writing you guys individual letters until I realized:

a) That would take bloody ages,

and

b) It would basically be all the same stuff anyway.

So here I am, writing to all three of you at once. I hope that's cool.

I suppose I should start by saying sorry. I know I've said it loads on texts and voicemails and stuff but that doesn't mean I don't mean it when I say it again now. The opposite. I mean it loads.

Kimmie, I'm so sorry about what happened with Aaron. I was in a bad place that night. That's not an excuse by the way, I just want to try to explain a bit why I did what I did.

I'd had a really shit couple of days. I didn't let on how crap I felt after that supply teacher ripped into me. And I lied about what Ms Parish said afterwards. I did get into trouble. I don't know why I didn't tell you. I suppose I felt embarrassed and I was worried that if I let on I was embarrassed, you'd be embarrassed for me. Then we went back to Stella's and I saw the uni prospectuses under your bed, Stells. And it really hurt. I know it shouldn't. I mean, if you want to go to uni, you should go, of course you should. I just felt really stupid because I didn't know about it and I'd been banging on about flats and stuff. But instead of talking to you about it, I just got really annoyed and sort of shut down. I'm sorry.

When I said nothing happened with Paul after all, I was sort of lying. Something did happen, just not the thing I told you originally. I tried to kiss him the night I babysat and he totally freaked out at me. That's kind of why I ended up down the park with Aaron. I didn't go there looking for him or anything. I just needed to get out of the house and I was walking past and there he was with his mates, and they were having a laugh and drinking beer and it looked like fun, and when he started paying me attention, it felt nice. I'm not going to pretend I was really drunk or anything because I wasn't. I'd had a few beers but I knew what I was doing and I knew that it was wrong and I did it anyway. I'm not proud of it, not one bit, and if I could go back and undo it all, I would. I was just feeling really shit about myself and I stupidly thought going home with him would make me feel better.

I'm so sorry, Kimmie, please believe me when I say it. I was stupid and selfish and I don't blame you for going silent on me. For what it's worth, we didn't actually do it. Not properly. I've never done it with anyone properly, not even Jordan. I'm sorry I lied about that too. It's just that you all assumed we were doing it right from the beginning and I didn't know how to tell you that we weren't. It sounds stupid written down like this, but I was worried you wouldn't like me as much if you knew the truth or that you'd think I was lame. I don't know if any of this makes sense or not, or if it even makes a difference. I hope it does, at least a bit. I never set out to hurt anyone but I get that I have and I'll do anything I can to put it right.

It all goes back further than that though, if I'm really honest with myself (and you). I know I act like I'm all confident and stuff, and most of the time I am, but sometimes I'm putting on a bit of a show, pretending I've got it sorted when deep down I don't have a clue. Having sisters as amazing as Grace and Audrey makes it hard to feel special or stand out. I try not to let all their achievements get to me but it's hard not to compare myself to them. I guess what I'm trying to say is, it's not always easy being a Campbell-Richardson. I'm working on it, though. I'm working on everything.

I dunno what you guys are planning to do about Newquay. I've been looking forward to it all year and the idea of the four of us not going together makes me feel really, really sad. You probably still totally hate me and wouldn't touch me with a bargepole, never mind share a caravan with me, but on the off chance you can forgive me, I'm going to be at the airport tomorrow. You can tell me to bugger off if you want to but that's where I'll be.

Finally, I ordered these T-shirts ages ago. I've had this fantasy about us wearing them on the plane. Just so you know, I'll be wearing mine tomorrow.

Yours hopefully,

Mia xxx

39

The following morning, I set off for the farmers' market forty-five minutes earlier than usual, a tote bag looped over my shoulder.

I head to Stella's first. Stu answers the door in his underpants and a faded Nirvana T-shirt that smells like dead people.

'Is Stella in?' I ask.

'She's still in bed,' Stu replies coldly.

'Oh.'

I wait for him to tell me to go on up, like he would ordinarily, but he doesn't.

'Well, can you give her this?' I ask, fishing Stella's T-shirt out of the bag. 'And this.'

I hand him an envelope with Stella's name on it. Inside is a photocopy of the letter. I'm giving the original to Kimmie.

At Mikey's, The Accident answers the door, his face covered with baked bean juice.

'Mikey's at Stella's,' Mikey's mum calls from the kitchen.

'Oh.'

'Well, can you give him this when he gets back, please?' I ask, handing her his T-shirt and envelope over the top of The Accident's head.

At Kimmie's, Sophie answers the door. The second she sees me, her eyes narrow into a glare. I'm guessing Kimmie has filled her in.

'She doesn't want to see you,' Sophie says, her arms folded across her chest like a nightclub bouncer. I half expect her to follow up with 'your name's not on the list, you're not coming in'.

'Fair enough,' I say, subtly trying to peek over her shoulder. 'Could you make sure she gets these at least?'

Sophie hesitates before taking the T-shirt and envelope, peering at them suspiciously.

'Oh, and could you tell her that Grace had her baby?' I add. 'A little boy. Elijah. And let her know if she wants to come over and meet him at some point, she totally can.'

'I'll tell her,' Sophie says before shutting the door in my face.

I take a deep breath and walk back down the driveway, wondering if Kimmie is watching from her bedroom window, but too afraid to look.

I've done all I can. Now I just have to wait and see if it's enough.

Epilogue

'Should we wait?' Grace asks as she pulls up outside the terminal.

It's painfully early, the sun only just up.

'I don't know,' I say, looking up at the signs. 'I'm not sure you can. This is drop-off only.'

'But what if they're not there?' she asks.

'Or if they totally blank you?' Audrey pipes up from the back seat.

'I don't know,' I admit. 'I reckon I'm just going to have to chance it.'

I climb out of the car and retrieve my luggage from the boot. Grace and Audrey get out too, waiting on the pavement as I heave my rucksack on my shoulders and check I've got everything.

'Your T-shirt looks really cool,' Audrey says.

I look down at my brand-new 'It's All About Mia' T-shirt.

'Cheers, Auds,' I say. 'They came out good, didn't they?'

'Really good.'

'Maybe I'll make you one one day.'

'Yes please.'

I turn to Grace. 'Thanks again for driving me.'

'No worries. Now, are you sure you don't want us to wait? I could maybe park up somewhere else.'

'Don't be silly, you need to get back for Elijah's next feed. Worst comes to worst, I can get the bus back. It's only 40 minutes back to Rushton.'

'OK. Well, fingers crossed, I guess.'

'Yeah.'

She holds out her arms. I'm still getting used to seeing her without her massive baby bump. It's weird, but I almost miss her funny waddle and her freaky pregnancy jeans and the smell of her disgusting red raspberry leaf tea. As she hugs me, I realize she smells of Elijah now, of milk and olive oil and freshly washed cotton. I turn to Audrey, hugging her just as tightly.

'I should have recorded a clip of me snoring for you to play while I'm gone,' I say as we separate.

'You so should have!'

'Maybe next time, you little weirdo.'

She grins.

'I'd better go,' I say, checking the time on my phone. 'I've got to check in and all that.'

'Like I said, fingers crossed,' Grace says.

'Fingers crossed,' I repeat, taking a deep breath and heading towards the door marked 'Departures'.

The airport is busy, crammed with stressed-out parents and kids riding Trunkis and groups of friends chattering excitedly. I look for Stella, Mikey and Kimmie. Maybe they've gone through to the gate already.

'Is it possible to see if my friends have checked in if I give you their names?' I ask at the check-in desk.

'I'm afraid not,' the woman behind the counter says, handing me my boarding pass.

'OK, thanks,' I murmur.

I go through security, then duty-free, weaving in and out of the displays of perfume and bottles of whisky and giant Toblerone bars, on constant alert for Mikey's hyena laugh and Kimmie's impossibly shiny hair and Stella's embroidered denim jacket, my heartbeat quickening every time I see anyone even vaguely fitting their descriptions. It feels like everyone here is in a group, that I'm the only person in this entire airport who's alone.

I'm one of the first people to arrive at the gate.

The seats around me begin to fill up with families and loved-up couples and groups of friends, multiple versions of Stella, Mikey and Kimmie, but none of them the right ones. None of them mine.

There's a stewardess now, checking the lists – it won't be long now before we can start boarding. I'm unsure what do, whether I should board the plane alone or not, but resigned to the fact my friends aren't coming.

That's when I hear a familiar voice yell the immortal words, 'Hold that plane!'

Mikey.

Seconds later, he, Stella and Kimmie career round the corner, all three of them red-faced and out of breath.

All three of them wearing their T-shirts.

All three of them looking at me.

I abandon my hand luggage and leap up. We collide in the middle of the lounge, bashing heads and knees and elbows. I don't realize I'm crying until we separate from our messy hug and I see the damp patch on Mikey's shoulder.

'I thought you weren't coming.'

'Of course we were coming,' Mikey says indignantly. 'As if I saved up all my pocket money to stay at home.'

'Stu's car broke down about a mile away,' Stella explains, her chest heaving up and down. 'We had to walk down the hard shoulder with all our luggage. Nightmare.'

'We only just made check-in,' Kimmie adds, out of breath.

Her T-shirt is a bit baggy on her. 'I knew I should have gone for an extra-small,' I say.

'No, I like it like this,' she replies. Just like Kimmie.

'I'm so sorry,' I tell her. 'More sorry than I've ever been in my life.'

'I know,' she says simply. 'I know you are, Mia. Apology accepted.'

I start crying again.

Mikey plants himself in front of me. 'Who or what are you, and what have you done with our friend Mia?' he asks.

'Oh, piss off,' I say.

'That's more like it!' he crows.

We start laughing then. All four of us at once. Me and my best friends.

And it's the best sound in the entire world.

Acknowledgements

I would like to thank the following people for helping me conquer that 'difficult' second book.

The dream team: my wondrous editor, Bella Pearson, and my magical agent, Catherine Clarke. Your patience, encouragement and vision kept me afloat when I was convinced drowning was inevitable! To say you're both a pleasure to work with is an almighty understatement. Thank you, thank you, thank you for not letting me give up on Mia.

Everyone at David Fickling Books. Your energy and commitment astonish me every single day. Special thanks to Carolyn McGlone for being not only being incredible at her job but also bloody lovely company on our various jaunts across the UK (long live our couples railcard!), Phil Earle for continuing to spread the word with such genuine and infectious passion, Rosie Fickling for her most excellent editorial notes and David Fickling for almost unnatural levels of enthusiasm and joy. As I've said countless times before, I'm so happy and proud to be a DFB author.

David Levithan for overwhelming kindness and generosity.

Alice Todd for another proper stunner of a cover, and Alison Gadsby for so much hard work on the design and layout. I can't wait to hold a copy in my hands!

Lisa Rundle for taking the time to share her experiences of life as the mother of a budding young swimmer – your insight was invaluable.

My Monday-night writing-group buddies (Paul, James, Fiona, Chris, Maria and Sara-Mae), thank you for your thoughtful and always helpful feedback. Here's to the next four years!

It's no secret the UK YA community is made up of outstanding individuals, many of whom have become genuine mates. Thank you to everyone who has shared experiences, offered advice or been kind or supportive in any shape or form. In particular, Jenny Downham for countless wise words, Lucy Ivison and Non Pratt for being motivational, inspirational and hilarious in equal measure, and Jess Vallance for a bit of everything.

Second books are notoriously hard. Massive thanks to all my friends and family for their support/indulgence. Particular thanks to Gregory Ashton for being the ultimate brainstorming partner, Matt Phillips for his continued kindness and cheerleading, Katherine Jackson for the Wednesday-morning chats, Nikki Dibley for reading some early chapters and making the right noises, Hayley Rudd for being the housemate from heaven, and Jake and Isla Elliott, my little rays of sunshine.

Finally, Mum and Dad, for being, well, Mum and Dad. Mum recently expressed concern that people might read my books and assume the characters are based on them. Therefore I'd like to take this opportunity to state that my parents do not roll around on the living-room carpet snogging like Mia's do (at least they don't in front of me).

The Campbell-Richardson Ultimate Wedding Playlist

1. Back for Good – Take That

2. I Wanna Dance With Somebody – Whitney Houston

3. A Little Respect – Erasure

4. Sex On Fire – Kings of Leon

5. Single Ladies (Put A Ring On It) – Beyoncé

6. Got My Mind Set on You – George Harrison

7. Walking On Sunshine – Katrina and the Waves

8. We Are Family – Sister Sledge

9. You Make My Dreams Come True – Hall & Oates

10. Higher and Higher (Your Love Keeps Lifting Me) – Jackie Wilson

11. You and Me Song – The Wannadies

12. Shake It Off – Taylor Swift

About the author

Lisa Williamson was born and grew up in Nottingham. Following a degree in drama, she worked as an actor for over a decade before writing her debut novel, *The Art of Being Normal*.

Lisa loves writing about characters who are different from her and Mia Campbell-Richardson definitely fits the bill. She's everything Lisa wasn't at 16 – loud, daring and uber confident. With no idea what's she's doing or where she's heading, she's the sort of girl who doesn't usually get to be at the centre of the story. This is exactly why Lisa wanted to take the time to get to know her and figure out what's really going on behind the big hair and fiery attitude.

When she's not writing, Lisa likes long walks, long talks, dessert of all kinds, good books and bad TV. She lives in East London.